# Marrying the Master

## A Club Volare Novel

### Chloe Cox

# DEDICATION

To anyone who ever gave me a book, even if it was just to get me to be quiet.

# CONTENTS

# *Just a Quick Note...*

Dear Reader,

No lie, I have been waiting to write Roman and Lola's story since I first conceived of Club Volare. I'm actually a little speechless now that I've gone and done it.

I don't know how many of you have experienced this in your own lives, but sometimes the most obvious love is the one that's right there in front of you. Usually when that happens I kind of feel like nature just has to take its course—even if the two lovebirds have managed to build up some momentum, by that time I definitely don't want to be in front of it!

Anyway. Force of nature or no, I find that the loves that are most important to us are the ones that are hardest to confess in real life. Which is a shame, really—those are the people who deserve it the most, right? Anyway, writing about Roman and Lola helped me find a way to tell someone that I loved them. I hope it at least brings you some happiness, if not, you know…more. :)

Chloe

*Those who fly...*

# *prologue*

Lola Theroux opened the first door she could find, ducked blindly inside, and quietly shut that door behind her. Only then did she breathe.

Only then did she look around.

She was pretty sure she'd just stepped into a broom closet. Didn't matter. She'd just needed to escape before *he* saw her, and, well, a broom closet would just have to do.

In just a few moments, she'd be taking the last irrevocable step. She'd thought of little else in the past few days, but seeing him standing there, waiting for her, brought it all home like a slap to the face.

Well, no. If she were being totally, completely honest, a slap to the *face* was not what she thought about when she looked at him, and that's what made it so difficult to think straight. Instead she thought about the previous night, about how he had actually *spanked* her, and a warm flush began to spread across her skin. She thought about all the nights ahead of her, and the warmth started to pool between her legs. And then she thought that maybe she'd already taken those last steps. Maybe she was already lost. Maybe last night…

She shuddered, her eyes closed even in the dark, thinking of his hands on her. Thinking of the heat of them, thinking of the rough tread of his calloused fingers, thinking of the way they'd raked across her skin. The way they'd lulled her into a sort of trance, then ripped her out of it, hot and hard and urgent, stoking her own desire until she'd lost all control.

She *had* lost all control. She'd done something she'd both dreamed about and dreaded. And it might — would — change everything.

And now she'd come here, to the City Clerk's Office, silent and awkward and with her mind reeling, somehow still feeling the aftershocks of last night's orgasms, to follow through on a promise. A promise that was the only way to save Club Volare in the aftermath of the exposé that had run in *Sizzle*, the tabloid story that had set the city on fire. The story had gotten the attention of all of New York — including the worst sort of government official: the morally outraged kind.

Lola hadn't thought it would matter at first. Volare scrupulously obeyed all local and federal regulations. They paid their taxes. They ran the safest place in New York, and would never settle for less.

But she hadn't counted on the determination of an angry little man from the state senate, which was why Lola was at the City Clerk's office. Club Volare needed to be in compliance with a ridiculously antiquated law from the seventeenth freaking century—something about unmarried couples running public houses, which came right after a law about witch burning that the city had had the good sense to repeal—or they would not only lose their liquor and cigar licenses, but be subject to ridiculous penalties and charges. Not only that, but Senator Prude was rumored to be getting the health department involved. Just because Senator Harold Jeels had issues with sex, and had found a loophole, *and* none of the other politicians felt they could stick their necks out for a sex club, Volare would be closed. And the owner…

Roman Casta.

Lola owed him so much. He'd been an instrumental part of her life even before she'd come to work for him running Volare. And she admitted that she did love him—in a limited way. Lola had worked incredibly hard to get over Roman as soon as it became clear he would never look at her romantically all those years ago, but she could admit to platonic love, at least. And she loved Volare. So that was why she was here at the clerk's office. To be precise, that was why she was hiding in a broom closet at the clerk's office.

A broom closet. Really. It had looked just like a bathroom from the outside. *Well, I suppose a closet isn't totally inappropriate*, she thought.

3

After all, she would be entering a different sort of closet in a minute. She was already halfway in. After this, there'd be no going back. She'd have to commit to the charade, and hope it didn't break her.

Playing house with Roman. Being in public with Roman. As his...

She couldn't even *think* it; it was too insane. She used to dream that Roman Casta would one day propose to her. It had been childish; she knew better now. And she knew that Roman didn't do relationships, didn't do romantic love, knew that he could never learn to love her, and she even knew why. And now she had to *pretend*. She'd have to pretend after knowing what it was really like to have Roman Casta love you, even if it was only physically.

And she'd do it again, if he asked. She'd let him have her however he wanted.

God, she hoped he would ask.

So it would be torture, obviously. But she'd thought she could handle it. Until she'd come walking down the hall, her heels echoing ominously against all that marble, telling herself she'd be fine, and she'd seen *him* standing there, talking to Ford Colson, Volare's lawyer.

Roman.

Holy tap dancing Christ, but the man was gorgeous.

Just the sight of him standing there in the hall, his shoulders broad and relaxed, his aquiline features sharp and intimidating, cutting shadows in the morning light like even the spring thaw was slightly afraid of him—it was enough to take her breath away on a good day. He made standing in a hallway look like an athletic feat. Like the world was waiting on him, and not the other way around. It was always like that with Roman.

He was the Master.

Those kinds of thoughts were *not* making things any easier.

In fact, it was impossible not to think about what had happened the previous night, what had taken them both by surprise. What Lola had dreamed about happening when she'd first met Roman, what she'd worked so hard to *stop* dreaming about since.

Roman Casta, on top of her.

Roman Casta, inside her.

Roman Casta, owning her. *Dominating* her.

She'd thought about all that, when she'd seen Roman, and that was when she'd run away to the broom closet.

Now Lola was starting to feel warm all over again in all the places he touched her. She could have sworn she could actually feel his hands on her again, ripping her dress off, throwing her on his bed, spreading her legs.

*Not helping*.

And it should never have happened in the first place. She kept repeating that to herself, hoping against hope that her body would listen to her mind and stop this insanity. Her last break up had totally fucked her up, and Lola hadn't been able to come with any Dom since. Her ex had lied to her, and then Roman had lied to her, refusing to tell her that he had planted the *Sizzle* article to try to control an inevitable media frenzy, and so she hadn't been inclined to trust anyone enough to submit. She'd contented herself with half-hearted domination of Volare newbies as Mistress Lola, indulging in the Dom side of her switch nature, and she thought she'd gotten used to it.

Until last night.

Until Roman.

It didn't matter that she was furious with him. It didn't matter that she was hurt. It didn't matter that he hadn't seen the need to apologize for keeping her in the dark about the whole *Sizzle* thing. It didn't matter that she'd told herself she could never trust him again. When he touched her, she was absolutely helpless.

Oh God, she was in so much trouble.

Lola groaned, leaning her head back against the door just as someone knocked on it, hard.

She cursed. This was particularly undignified. Hiding in a broom closet wasn't exactly how she wanted to start things off. She was the competent, totally in control, organized Mistress Lola. Mistress Lola did not hide in closets.

"Lola, I know you are in there. I saw you."

That voice, like molten silver. It was Roman. She leaned her head back against the door and whispered again, "Oh, *shit*."

"Open the door," he said. It wasn't a request.

Lola turned around and cracked the door open. Roman glared at her.

"You are hiding," he said.

"No, I'm not."

He cocked his head, as if he were keeping score and she'd just lost a point. Well, it *had* been a stupid lie.

"Step away from the door, Lola," he ordered. "Now."

She wanted to protest, but there was no point. She could feel him pressing on the door, opening it slowly so he wouldn't hurt her, but opening it just the same. It would be useless to resist. She stepped back into the darker recesses of what she was glad was a pretty big closet. Still, when Roman stepped in, all athletic six feet and change of him, it was a tight fit.

He was so close.

She could smell his cologne. Not just his cologne—*him*. All male. He was wearing a three-piece suit for the occasion, an impeccably tailored dark gray suit with a crisp white shirt and a red tie, just a splash of his Spanish color. It set off his dark olive skin and his darker jet black hair in a way that made her want to run her hands through that hair. And then maybe lick his neck.

*Wow. Seriously, Lola, get a hold of yourself.*

She heard a click and a single light bulb overhead flooded the small space with thin, yellow light. Roman towered above her, his broad shoulders rolling beneath his suit jacket, his eyes glittering down at her.

Oh God, that *look*. Like he could control her with just a thought...

He'd looked at her like that last night, right before he'd ripped her dress off. Or was she imagining it? Was she already losing her mind?

7

"I just needed a moment," she said softly, trying to pretend that she couldn't hear the beating of her own heart.

Roman took a deep breath, his chest expanding. His eyes trailed down the length of her body.

"Why?" he said.

Why? *Why?* Did he not remember last night? Lola was pretty sure he'd been there. How was he not completely freaking the hell out, just like her? How could he be so *in control?*

"Do you really need to ask that?" she finally said, beginning to feel tingles on her skin. Roman was dangerous. He was more powerful than any drug—he didn't even need to be inside her to make her crazy.

"Yes," he said impatiently. "You are hiding because you are frightened. That is why people hide. Why are you frightened, Lola?"

Oh shit, could he tell? As well as Lola knew Roman, Roman knew her, too—better than anyone at Volare. Could he tell how she really felt?

A noxious pit of dread coalesced in Lola's stomach. If Roman knew how she felt, that she'd wanted him for so long, that she'd only overcome her infatuation with him by sheer force of will, it would ruin everything. He'd have to let her down easy, and he would never touch her again. And there'd be no way they could keep up the pretense of this ridiculous plan if that happened. Volare would be screwed.

And what the hell, of *course* she was frightened. Defensively, she hissed, "This is not an everyday thing, Roman! It's a big deal, what we're about to do, and we're lying to, like, everyone, *and* breaking the law, and—"

He frowned. "If you are nervous or frightened, especially during the ceremony, it might give us away. It could betray our deception. Remember that this is a performance."

*A performance*. That was the whole problem.

"Believe me, Roman, I know that."

"Then we must make sure that you are not nervous or frightened."

He said it so simply, so calmly, looking at her with that maddening look. What did it mean? He gave nothing away. They stood in silence together for a moment, long enough for Lola to realize their breathing was in tune. Everything about their physical selves felt perfect together, like they were made for each other.

Too bad about the rest—about the person that always came between Roman and anyone else.

Lola swallowed and tried to stand up straighter. "Listen, I am *not*—"

Roman cut her off, getting to the point. "Are you having second thoughts about the arrangement?"

"No!"

"Yet you fled my apartment this morning before we could speak."

Lola didn't have an answer to that, at least not while her brain was functioning on limited blood supply. She could feel her pulse between her legs, and the man hadn't even touched her. Just that commanding tone of voice made her melt.

*Don't look him in the eye. It's your only hope.*

"Speak about what?" she said weakly. Maybe if

she played dumb she could pretend it wasn't a big deal.

Roman's lip curled in amusement, though he wasn't fooled. He never was. "Lola, we are standing in a broom closet. There is a justice of the peace waiting. And you are asking questions you already know the answer to."

"I don't know the answer to anything," she muttered, dropping her eyes. It was the truth. All she knew was that it made her insane to be this close to Roman Casta.

There was a pause, and then his fingers brushed her cheek, and his hand threaded through her thick red hair. His touch sparked through her like a wildfire. She heard him exhale heavily, almost that low growl she's heard the night before, and to her shame she craned toward his touch like a helpless puppet. She suddenly felt like she would do anything to feel him touch her more. Anything.

It was such a dangerous way to feel.

Especially if he felt it, too.

"We needed to talk after last night, Lola," Roman said. "And after this morning. Now we will talk after the ceremony."

*The ceremony.*

"Maybe we don't need to talk," she said quietly, studying the floor intensely. She was still so very aware of his skin against hers. All she could think was that if they actually talked, he might see through her. "We had sex, but we're both adults. It's not like it meant anything. So I don't know what you want to talk about."

Another low sound rumbled in Roman's chest.

He was annoyed. He said, "Don't be foolish. We will have to talk about how this arrangement will work between us. It is clear we will not be able to control ourselves while we must live together and...pretend."

"Maybe we can—"

"*No*," he said sharply, and she looked up in alarm. He licked his lips and his eyes roamed over her body. "You proved that last night. You and I..."

Roman took another deep breath, shaking his head. Roman never hesitated, never cut himself off. Lola had never, ever seen him look so...nonplussed.

His thumb brushed against her cheek, and she thought she could feel his lust in the air between them, like a massive electrical storm brewing on the horizon. It took her breath away. Finally she looked him in the eye.

She didn't think she'd be able to look away ever again.

"I am no longer myself around you," he said hoarsely. "I am not...in control. I have no control around you. Around your body. Now that I have tasted you, Lola, it is all that I think about. And I will not stop until I've had my fill. I know this about myself."

"I know," she said. "You're relentless."

"It is best," he finally said, his gaze resting on her mouth, "to formalize the terms of your submission."

Lola's eyes fluttered at that word. "The terms of my submission," she repeated, almost in disbelief.

11

She'd thought it, but hearing it said out loud was something else.

Roman did growl now, a frustrated sound, and wrapped an arm around her waist, his hand on the small of her back, just grazing the curve of her ass. He pulled her close to him, and his other hand twisted in her hair, tilting her face up. He waited just long enough for her to see the look on his face, to see what it meant, and then he crushed her mouth beneath his.

He was claiming her.

He felt she was his. At least physically. At least as a sub.

Lola's heart thudded out a rapid answer: he was right.

His tongue parted her lips as his fingers effortlessly unbuttoned the conservative blouse she'd chosen for today, his mouth hot and wet and demanding against hers. His hand was just as insistent, just as impatient with the barriers between him and her body; he pushed aside her shirt and bra, and grabbed her exposed breast with a grunt of satisfaction. He squeezed, hard, just like he had the previous night, and Lola gasped.

Finally he let her mouth go, the hand that was at her back moving up to grab her hair again. He liked to grab her hair, to pull on it. It drove her wild.

"Say it," he said. He rolled her nipple between her fingers, his eyes on fire.

"Oh God, Roman..."

Roman buried his face by her neck. "I cannot look at you now without thinking about what you

12

feel like inside, Lola. Without needing to have you. Say it."

He pushed his leg between hers, her skirt riding up her thigh as he did so. The hard length of his thigh pressed between her legs, pushing her now very damp underwear against her flesh.

"You are wet," he said into her ear, and mercilessly rubbed his leg against her. "Oh, God, Lola. You *will* submit to me again. I must have your submission, Lola, or I will lose my mind. *Say it*."

He bit her neck, keeping her right where she was, while he reached down with his free hand, the one that wasn't torturing her breast, to grab a fistful of her skirt and pull it up over her hips.

This was already out of hand. Already out of control.

Lola could barely breathe. Her eyes flew open, and she heard herself moan. Her voice didn't even sound like hers. It sounded desperate, drugged, starved.

"I'll do anything you want, Roman," she said. "Anything."

And she meant every damn word.

Roman released her neck and pulled her head back to look her full in the face. His eyes blazed and his jaw clenched, and he looked utterly triumphant. Roman the conqueror. She loved him like this. She loved that he was like this because of *her*. And she couldn't look away.

That was all the trouble, right there.

Roman took another deep, satisfied breath, and then wordlessly spun her around so her back was to him. Too surprised to speak, Lola reached her

13

hands out instinctively and gripped a shelf in front of her. She tried to look behind her, but Roman still had hold of her hair.

"Yes, you will," Roman said, and she felt her underwear pull against her as he twisted them in his hand. The sound it made as he ripped them from her body sent another shiver through her. "You will do anything I want, whenever I want. And you will thank me for the privilege."

Lola thought she was going to come right there. The pressure between her legs had grown, the dull throb rising to a deafening crescendo, driving out all thoughts except the desperate need to come with Roman Casta inside her.

She wasn't thinking about the ceremony anymore, that was for sure.

Roman slid his hand between her legs, pushing them wider apart. Her wetness had seeped out onto her thighs, and she heard him grunt as he pushed a finger inside her.

"The way you feel inside, Lola," he said in her ear, fucking her slowly with that finger. "It's addicting."

Lola's legs started to shake as her inner muscles clenched around him. She was still a little sore from how hard he'd fucked her the previous night, and she was reminded of it with every stroke. It made her almost dizzy, and she arched into him, unthinking.

He laughed softly.

"Here is what I am thinking, *torronet*. I do not want you to feel afraid. I never want you to feel afraid. So you will go to the ceremony with me in

14

just a few minutes, and you will not be able to think of anything besides how well you have just come for me, and how hard I have just fucked you. You will go to the ceremony with my scent all over you. And you will wonder all that time what else I will order you to do. You will not have time to feel afraid. And everyone will think it is just because you love your husband."

*Husband.*

Roman took his finger away and Lola almost whimpered in protest, until she felt him. *Him.* His rock hard erection, poised just at her entrance. She needed him *now*.

"Oh God..." she heard herself say, and a current of anticipation rippled through her core.

"Say it, Lola," he whispered, gripping her bare ass and spreading her even more. "Say this is mine."

Lola groaned again. She felt obscene, *made* obscene by this man, this man who'd become totally new to her in only the last four days, this man she'd thought she'd known...

"It is," she panted. "This belongs to you. Please..."

"Please, *what*?"

"Please, Roman, just fuck me!"

He surged into her, the thickness of his cock stretching her until she cried out. Roman brought his hand up to her face and gently covered her mouth; she could smell herself on his fingers.

"Quiet," he said, removing his hand and kissing her neck.

He thrust into her hard, shoving her breasts up

against her hands where they gripped the shelving. When he reached around and rubbed her clit with one expert finger, Lola groaned into his hand, spurring him on. He fucked her in hard, definite strokes, the rhythm shaking cans of cleaning fluid across the shelves, until the intensity was almost too much. Tears streamed from her eyes, and he paused, wiping her cheek.

"Don't stop," she said. "Oh God, please don't stop, I can't take it if you stop."

There was a beat, and then he drove himself into her with even more force. He let her hair go and she slumped forward on the shelf, her body incapable of anything but taking what Roman gave her.

Her orgasm didn't build normally, didn't gather slowly in her center and pulse out over the rest of her. It happened everywhere, all at once, a freak storm, like there was just too much energy and it had nowhere to go. She bit down on her hand, and her left leg buckled. Roman caught her, his arm around her waist.

"You are *not* done," he said into her ear. "Come for me again, Lola."

In just a few moments, she did.

And then she did again.

She was dizzy, and when she tried to speak her lips felt numb and her words didn't work. Roman was still buried deep inside her, still thrusting, and she was aware that he was talking to her. Slowly, she came back to herself, like rising to the surface of a lake, and she heard him as clear as day.

"Lola," he said. "*My* Lola."

And he came inside her, his weight on her back, his lips on her neck. She didn't know how he held her up while coming; she could barely remember her own name. And it felt like a long time after that before her brain functioned properly. She just rested while Roman cleaned them both as much as he could with a handkerchief that disappeared conveniently back into his pocket, and she stood there while he rubbed her shaking legs so she wouldn't cramp.

He was buttoning her shirt before she really felt capable of coherent sentences.

"Oh God," she mumbled. "What did you do to me?"

"If you become worried before we finish the ceremony," he said, straightening her skirt, "I will have to do it again."

Lola laughed weakly. "Promise?"

Roman stood to his full height and looked down at her, serious as the grave. "Do not test me, Lola. You will already be disciplined for hiding from me in a...a broom closet."

"Disciplined?" she said.

The corners of his mouth twitched into what was surely a smile. "Yes. I look forward to it."

Lola blinked. She did, too.

Oh. Shit.

Roman locked eyes with her. The two of them stood there like that, again at a loss for words. There were times when the absurdity of their situation crystallized, and there were times when it was clear that Lola, at least, had no idea what they were doing. Like now, in a broom closet, right after

Roman had fucked her brains out.

A dark look flashed across Roman's face, and before Lola could speak he bent down to kiss her. It was more of a brand than a kiss, and it left her breathless.

"Let's go," he said, pulling away. "Before you remember that in reality you would never marry me."

Roman Casta smiled brilliantly, took her by the hand, and led her to their wedding.

# *chapter* 1

*FOUR DAYS EARLIER...*

"You want me to be your *wife?*"

Lola's outrage shone on every inch of her beautiful face. Her green eyes actually seemed to glow, pinning Roman where he stood. Her creamy skin almost glistened, and even her hair, if it were possible, somehow seemed redder.

Every gesture, every breath, every word that passed over those soft lips was infused with passion. No straight human male could help but think about how that passion might manifest in bed. She was just one of those woman who was cursed to be maddeningly attractive when she was angry.

And she was already attractive to start. "Attractive" didn't quite describe her. Roman had always thought there were no words adequate to describe Lola Theroux, even if she was the one woman who would always be untouchable to him.

And she would remain untouchable even if— *when*—he had to marry her.

Roman rolled his neck in an attempt to get his own frustration under control. Lola's reaction to the news that the two of them would have to marry, and quickly, in order to save Club Volare did not cast him in a particularly flattering light. If he didn't know better, he might have been insulted.

"Are you *insane*?" Lola continued.

"Perhaps we could continue this conversation in private," he said evenly.

Had he the option, Roman would not have chosen to approach Lola about the situation surrounding Club Volare in public. He certainly would not have chosen the very small theater space that Jake Jayson had recently purchased for his charity. A space that was currently being used for a rehearsal, and that apparently had excellent acoustics. Everyone present had heard Lola's exclamation.

But Lola hadn't given him a choice—she'd avoided Roman since he'd had to reveal his involvement in the *Sizzle* article exposing Club Volare, and himself as the owner of the club. He'd actually had to track Lola down with the help of Catie, Jake's fiancée, when Lola had announced that she was taking her first vacation, ever, and had stopped answering his calls. This was especially irritating because Lola had apparently already forgiven Catie for her part in the deception involving the *Sizzle* article, when Catie had actually been a planted spy, while Lola's anger at Roman burned as hot as ever.

He had never seen her so angry, and never for so long. Roman had begun to fear it had done permanent damage to their relationship, a relationship that, though he would never permit himself to let it go further than friendship, was among the most important in his life.

But while Lola's stubborn refusal to consider all the facts surrounding his decision to manage the *Sizzle* story by himself had long infuriated him, now that stubbornness posed a risk to Volare. And he could not allow that.

"Lola," he said again, keeping his voice calm. "Let's talk about this somewhere else, yes?"

"I don't want to go anywhere private with you, thank you," Lola said, lowering her voice. The people working in the theater—Jake's people, mostly, and some friends of Catie's—had all very deliberately gone about their business, pointedly directing their attention elsewhere. Even Jake and Catie had departed up the center aisle, giving them a wide berth. It was obvious everyone was trying very hard not to make Roman and Lola the center of attention—which meant, of course, that they absolutely were the center of attention.

It was just human nature. There would be gossip. There was always, always gossip. In fact, Roman's plan to save Volare with this fake marriage depended on it.

And Lola had just tried his patience.

"It was not a request." Roman took her elbow and walked her toward the entrance. Lola resisted, but quickly acquiesced when she saw the look on his face. If she were going to yell at him, it would be in private.

Roman pulled her into the small coatroom he'd seen near the ticket office and shut the door behind them.

"What the *hell*?" she demanded.

Lola was even angrier now. Her chest rose and fell rapidly as she breathed, and Roman couldn't help but notice her breasts, full and ripe under the stylish suit she wore. Roman scowled. The first button on her shirt was low, very low, and showed quite a bit of luscious cleavage. It was a suit that was designed to be aggressively sexual, a power play that reveled in the sexuality of the owner rather than trying to hide it.

It was…unfair.

"Lola, listen to me," he said, and wrenched his eyes away from her chest. He looked into her eyes, and for just a moment he thought he saw more than anger there—she looked hurt. Instantly, he changed tack. If anything were wrong, if anything truly hurt her, he wanted to know about it. He'd failed to protect her the last time she'd been hurt by her ex, that pathetic coward Benjamin Mara; he would not fail in that regard again.

"What's wrong?" he asked.

Lola shook her head, her red tresses waving softly. She gave him her toughest look, the one that said she would be giving nothing away. "You dragged me in here. Please tell me how you could possibly think I'd agree to marry you." After a moment's hesitation, she added, somewhat grudgingly, "And why you're asking."

So she was still going to punish him. He sighed.

"Because Club Volare is under attack, and I have

22

been advised that this is the way to save it," he said. "Do you remember that Ford told us that he received several inquiries from various agencies of the state after the article ran in *Sizzle*?"

"State agencies," she corrected automatically. His English was practically perfect except for random idiosyncrasies, and Lola was the only person who could make him smile with every correction.

"And it was *your Sizzle* article," she went on, her eyes narrowing. "Of course I remember those inquiries; they were nerve-wracking. But Ford said they were nothing."

"One of them has proved to be more than nothing."

Roman paused. He did not look forward to this. Not least because Lola would blame him, not entirely without cause, and become even angrier about the way he'd decided to keep the *Sizzle* article from her. She hadn't even given him a chance to explain his reasoning for keeping secrets from her, and he did not foresee this helping his case.

But Lola looked up at him expectantly. Even in the poor light of this dull room, she was stunningly beautiful. He treasured moments like this just as much as he dreaded them. She couldn't know how much he wanted her. How he had dreamed of having her. How he had dreamed of what she might look like when she came, screaming his name.

Of what she might taste like.

But Roman's obligations remained unchanged: Lola had been his responsibility at the most vulnerable time in her life, when she was much, much younger. It would be a terrible violation of her trust to take advantage of that intimacy and take what he'd long wanted, especially considering Roman's own limitations on romantic relationships. Yet it was becoming harder and harder to avoid thinking about her in a sexual way, harder still because of what they were about to do.

*Try harder,* he thought.

"There is a state senator who has taken an apparent personal offense to us," Roman said. "To who we are, and to what we do. To Volare. He has found a very old law that forbids an establishment with the licenses we hold to be operated by an unmarried woman. You are not married. He will try to take away all of Volare's permits and licenses unless you marry, and he will likely succeed, at least temporarily, because he has what Ford calls 'political juice.' Ford tells me that the political ramifications would be serious. Not even our friends in Albany can afford to publicly support a sex club. Volare will close."

Lola stared at him.

He went on, "Unless you marry *me*, to be precise, since one of my holding companies owns most of the Volare assets."

"What law?" she said. She'd lost the edge to her voice now.

"It is a very old law."

"How old?"

Roman had hoped to avoid this, too. It would only cause unnecessary conflict.

"I believe it dates from the seventeenth

century," he said, as evenly as he could. "The early seventeenth century."

"Are you freaking *kidding* me?"

Roman grimaced. "Yes, I am kidding you. This is all an elaborate joke to trick you into speaking to me again."

He regretted it immediately. Lola's face frosted over, and she looked at him with...he didn't know the word for that look. As though she had just retreated as far into herself as she could go, a place where Roman Casta, in particular, was no longer welcome. The passion he'd always associated with her was gone, and for the first time he truly worried.

Lola only looked away and sighed.

"Look, I get that you don't take this whole thing with *Sizzle* seriously, Roman," she said. "*That* is pretty obvious. But it's difficult to work with someone who doesn't take *me* seriously. Impossible, really. It might honestly be better for everyone if I simply quit."

Roman Casta was speechless. If she had said that in anger, he might have understood. He could respond. But she had not. She'd said it without a trace of emotion. He was stunned: quit? Volare without Lola?

No, not under any circumstances. It was insane.

"It would solve this crazy problem, wouldn't it?" she went on. "And, without getting into it, it doesn't seem like you really need me anymore."

She was serious.

And she was moving towards the door.

"No!"

The word exploded into the small room,

ricocheting off the walls, shattering any pretense of normalcy. Roman's hand shot out to pin the door closed, and Lola turned around in alarm.

"What the hell is wrong with you?" she said.

*That is an excellent question.*

Roman kept himself motionless, breathing deeply while his mind raced. Normally he had an orderly mind, a very analytical mind, but Lola's presence this close to him presented some kind of interference. He could smell her. She always wore Chanel, but it could not hide her own sweetness.

"Lola," he said. "You have not given me a chance to explain my reasoning. It is not like you to make such a decision without hearing all the evidence."

She opened her mouth as if to object, then thought better of it.

"You owe me the chance to explain myself." He took another deep breath and tilted her chin up towards him. She still wouldn't look at him. Why? Had he really done anything that terrible?

Had he truly miscalculated that badly?

"And in the end, Lola, you can always decide to leave if you think that is best. But do this thing *after* we save Volare. Please."

He watched her close her eyes, and he thought he heard his own heart speed up. He hadn't seen her look so devastated, so vulnerable, since the years when he'd first known her, after her father died. She'd been young and naïve in many ways then. That person had been only a shadow compared to the woman he had run into, by random chance, at a BDSM club in the city five years ago.

He knew she was still dealing with the aftermath of heartbreak because of Benjamin Mara; he knew it had wounded her far more deeply than she generally let on. But this seemed more. More even than her anger at him.

"We would only have to be married on paper?" she finally said.

"No, I am afraid not. It would have to be...convincing."

"Convincing."

"Lola, please," he said, reaching out.

He touched her cheek, and everything stopped. She felt hot under his touch, and suddenly he wanted to touch her more, so much more, everywhere. He couldn't remember the last time he'd touched her. Not even for a hug, a small gesture of affection between people who'd known each other for so long. No normal contact. It had become too difficult to keep such contact innocent.

Roman couldn't think of anything besides the feel of her skin.

*She* was the one to pull away. *She* took a step back, and wrapped her arms around herself. She looked so small and hurt, and once again Roman wanted nothing more than to fold her in his arms, but something told him that that would be a terrible idea.

There was something very wrong. Something he was ignorant of. He did not like being ignorant.

"Lola, tell me what is wrong."

"You're asking a lot of me."

"No, Volare is. We need you."

She laughed bitterly. "I have to think about this,

all right? I just need some time to think."

Roman frowned. What on earth was there to think about?

"Unfortunately, we do not have much time," he said. "I have a meeting scheduled with Ford tomorrow. We will have to make a decision then. You will allow me to explain my reasoning and then make your decision."

"Fine," she said, and reached for the doorknob without looking at him. He let her yank the door open. "Tomorrow."

She left without another word.

Of all the many thoughts that swirled through Roman's mind in the wake of that departure, the only one that stood out was this: her absence left him with a dull ache.

He could not imagine Volare without her.

He would make sure that he didn't have to.

# *chapter* 2

"Ok, so what's the emergency, crazy lady?"

Thank God for Stella Spencer. Lola's oldest friend, former Volare employee, and current fiancée to one Sheikh Bashir al Aziz bin Said stood in Lola's doorway, holding a giant tub of ice cream. Lola smiled for the first time in hours.

"You are *not* going to believe this," Lola said, shaking her head, and pulled her friend into her messy one-bedroom apartment.

"What I can't believe is that you're such a slob now," Stella said, chuckling. In college Lola had been neat to the point of disturbance. Her spotless dorm room had given off a highly strung, very controlled sort of vibe, and Stella had been one of the few people to see that Lola's anal retentiveness had more to do with what was going on in her life than who she was. As Lola's father's health worsened and the rest of Lola's life deteriorated into a complete mess, her personal space had become cleaner and cleaner.

Now, it was the opposite: Lola exerted complete control in the rest of her life, and her apartment was a little bit of a disaster area. Or at least she *had* exerted complete control, before she'd discovered that her ex-boyfriend, Ben, had lied to her about sleeping with his ex-wife, and before Roman had lied to her and given an exclusive interview to *Sizzle* behind her back, outing himself to the world as the owner of Club Volare.

Just thinking about Roman's lies made Lola angry all over again. At least Roman had managed to protect the identities of all the other Volare members, including herself. She refused to think about Ben at all.

"So are you going to tell me what the big deal is, or what?" Stella said, rummaging around Lola's tiny kitchen for spoons.

Lola took a deep breath. "I have to marry Roman."

Stella turned her head to look at Lola in slow motion. Her mouth was open.

"Go on," she said.

"You know how we started getting all kinds of heat after that stupid article? Well, some of the heat is from a repressed little jerk who happens to be in the state senate, and is also some sort of freak historical legal scholar. No, I know, don't even ask. Long story short, either I quit, or I marry Roman, or we lose a bunch of licenses. Plus fines."

"Oh shit," Stella said.

"Yeah."

"No, I mean, just *wow*. Roman? *The* Roman? Master Roman? The guy you've been crazy for since forever?"

Lola groaned and confiscated the half-gallon of ice cream, prying off the lid. "Yeah. That Roman."

Not one to be deprived of ice cream, Stella dove in and loaded up her spoon with vanilla fudge swirl. "So wait, is this like, just on paper, or…?"

"Honestly, I don't really know. He said it had to be 'convincing,' but who knows what that means? Roman getting married at all is kind of a stretch, so…"

"Right, Mr. No Strings Attached. What is the deal with that, anyway?"

Lola winced. Roman was not a man who liked to talk about his past; he was, in his own way, ever a cypher. The untouchable Master. Lola only knew what she knew because of Roman's involvement in her life when her dad died, and because her cousin Chance, Roman's best friend, had taken pity on her when her college crush got too serious and told her why Roman would likely never love a woman ever again.

"His wife died," Lola said.

She didn't like to say it. Lola wasn't normally one to betray secrets, but she needed Stella's help to get through this. Stella was the only person who knew how she felt about Roman, how she *really* felt, that it wasn't completely just a college thing, and that she was still very much attracted to the man, and she needed her friend's support. She had to tell her the marriage would be fake. And she had to tell her why Roman was truly off-limits.

"Are you serious?" Stella asked, totally floored.

"Yeah. It was before I met him. It was sudden and totally unexpected, a congenital heart defect or something that no one ever knew about. He just...I don't know. Chance told me he was done in that department."

"And he's always so remote," Stella said. She was obviously lost in thought. Roman had taken an interest in Stella's introduction to BDSM at the hands of her fiancé, Sheikh Bashir, more to make sure that Stella was happy than anything else. While Lola had set them up, Roman had been a presence, the man who seemed to know everything and look out for everyone. Stella had told Lola that Roman was the only guy she'd seen Bashir get weird around, in relation to his woman—the only one who could rile the sheikh. That hadn't surprised Lola at all.

"Lola, that's a really big deal. It explains so much of how aloof he is, even maybe why you guys never—"

"No, don't even say it," Lola said, flopping onto her couch. "I can't afford to think about what ifs, you know? This is already making me crazy. First Ben turns out to be sleeping with his ex-wife—"

"*Asshole*," Stella said fervently.

"Then Roman lies to me, too—which, honestly, I know not everyone thinks it's a big deal, but he's never taken me seriously. Never really respected me. That's how it's always felt, anyway, like I'm still some vulnerable kid to him. I'd thought that after running the club for the past five years, maybe he'd have a little respect—"

"Roman respects you."

Lola shrugged. "You don't lie to a partner you respect about letting an undercover reporter enter the club, and then about doing the *Sizzle* article all on your own, so that she's totally blindsided when the club is exposed."

"Ok, he *did* screw up."

Stella offered the ice cream and Lola dug in just to keep from talking. The truth, her issues actually felt bigger than what she'd said to Stella. Lola had been reeling since she'd discovered Ben's lies, and she hadn't realized how much she'd been relying on Roman until she'd discovered *Roman's* lies. It was like in the wake of Ben's betrayal she'd come to think of Roman as the last upright man, the last man she could trust. And then it turned out that she couldn't.

That didn't stop her heart from fluttering every time she looked at him.

Stupid heart. She told herself it was purely a physical reaction. You couldn't fight the physical.

"What are you going to do?" Stella asked.

"I can't quit," Lola said, frowning. She'd realized it about five minutes after she'd threatened to do it. Truth be told, Lola was a fighter, and what she wanted to do most was kick this Harold Jeels's ass. And besides, Lola believed in protecting her family. And Volare was her family.

"Are you sure you can go through with this, though?"

Lola looked at her friend's face and saw only compassion. Stella was a total bleeding heart, unable to turn away from anyone in any kind of pain. It was one of the things Lola admired about her friend, and one of the things she knew the sheikh had fallen for.

So it was pointless to try to hide from Stella what she was really feeling. In the twenty-four hours since Roman had dropped this bomb on her, Lola had relived everything about the past eight years, since the day she'd met Roman, and she had come to the conclusion that she'd never completely gotten over him. Sure, she'd gotten over her initial infatuation, the kind of thing that happens when you're young and everything's going wrong and you latch on to the one steady person in your life. But God, she wanted him.

Even when she was young, Lola wasn't totally stupid. When Lola realized she was hopelessly infatuated with Roman and that nothing would ever come of it, she'd pulled away to protect herself. They'd pursued separate lives in the city, and a few years later neither of them had been prepared to run into each other at a BDSM club. Lola had been there checking out the scene, and Roman had been there checking out the competition.

In short order, Roman had her working for him at Volare.

It took only a few more months for Lola to realize that her original infatuation hadn't ever quite gone away. But she wasn't the scared, vulnerable young woman who'd just lost her remaining immediate family any longer, and so now she thought it was just that she wanted Roman.

Physically.

She wanted Roman Casta more than she'd ever wanted anything. Even just for one night. Even just a taste. Even while their relationship matured, even while they became close friends, even while they worked together every day.

But the man wouldn't even look at her. It had been humiliating. Heartbreaking.

And she'd just had to get used to it.

And now the prospect of having to relive all of that, daily, while they pretended to be in love? While they pretended to be man and wife? While they pretended...

"Ugh," Lola said, covering her face.

"You've had a really hard time since Ben," Stella said, and nudged her friend with the cold ice cream tub.

"You don't know the half of it."

It was true—Lola had retreated into herself. It had been so humiliating: one of the few men she'd ever let dominate her turned out to have a thing with his ex-wife on the side, for *months*. She hadn't wanted to talk to anyone about it. She couldn't face the vulnerability.

"Has there been anyone since?" Stella asked.

"No," Lola said. "Not worth mentioning. I tried, but..."

Stella's eyes widened. "Nothing?"

"Nothing."

Lola didn't even tell her the worst part: she hadn't even been able to orgasm with anyone since Ben. Mistress of a sex club who couldn't come with a partner: ironic, and not in a good way. And she hadn't even been able to *think* about submitting.

A terrible thought struck her. "Oh shit, I'll have to pretend to be his submissive."

"Well, yeah. *Master* Roman. He's not a switch, is he?"

"No," Lola said, laughing despite herself. "Most definitely not."

"Ok, so in summary: the guy you've been crazy about for almost ten years is now going to pretend to be your Dom husband, and you have to play along while not losing your mind, or the club is screwed?"

"That's about right, although I dispute the 'crazy for' label."

"Whatever," Stella rolled her eyes. "I should have brought you Valium instead of ice cream."

Lola laughed softly, and wiped away a tear. Now that she was talking about it, all of her emotions were coming to the surface. She was really, truly scared. "Seriously, Stella, I don't know if I can do this right now."

"Look at it this way: if after all this you still feel like he doesn't respect you, you can quit."

Lola looked up, shocked.

"Look, I love Volare, but I love you more," Stella said, digging into the ice cream. "And you can't keep hanging around a guy who makes you this crazy, not right now, not after what happened with Ben. You have to eventually move on. So you save the club, and then…"

"I move on."

It actually wasn't the worst idea in the world. It made Lola unbelievably sad, but it gave her some relief, too.

"Hey, I'm sorry I didn't come over last night when you left that message," Stella said, blushing. "Bashir had something…planned."

Lola looked at her friend and smiled. The change in Stella since Bashir had come into her life had been remarkable; she'd gone from having zero self-confidence in the wake of a brutal divorce to being so happy that she seemed in love with the entire world. Lola had wondered more than once what it felt like to have a man love you as much as Bashir loved Stella.

"When do you have to decide?" Stella asked. "Crazy fake marriage or…?"

Lola looked at her watch and cursed. There was no more time to feel scared or overwhelmed or anything else. "I'm supposed to meet Roman and Ford in like an hour."

"Seriously?"

"Seriously." Lola shot off the couch and began digging through her recently delivered dry cleaning for something acceptable. She didn't want to show up to this meeting looking as disheveled as she felt. She wanted the upper hand in at least one way. Roman Casta had the upper hand in everything else. "What the hell am I going to wear?"

Stella's grin was positively evil. "Oh, I know what. That white Dior suit, the one with the boobs."

"White?"

"*Definitely* white. And definitely with boobs. There's no reason to make it easy on him."

Stella was a whiz with hair and make up, at least on other people, and in no time at all Lola looked like a million bucks. She got her favorite red purse—a splash of Roman's favorite color, and the only red item she owned that somehow didn't clash with her hair—grabbed some oversized dark glasses, and rode the elevator down, Stella in tow, finally feeling like she might be back in control.

Which was why she was taken completely by

surprise when she opened the lobby door to find a scrum of reporters, all of them screaming her name.

"Lola! Lola! Is it true you secretly married Roman Casta?"

"Are you the mistress of Club Volare?"

"Who are the other members?"

A dozen flashes went off in Lola's face at once, and she nearly toppled over. How could this happen? How could the press already know? How had they gotten her name?

Stella showed up at her side and helped her fight her way through the crowd to a cab that was stopped at the light. As they piled into the backseat and Lola shielded them from camera flashes with her bag, she had only one furious thought: *Roman did this. Again.*

# *chapter* 3

Where the hell was she?

Roman paced the length of Ford Colson's spacious office, only a few blocks from Club Volare and Roman's own apartment. The club's longtime lawyer, and Roman's good friend, had wisely stayed silent, until now.

"She's just running late," Ford finally said.

"Obviously she is late," Roman said.

"I meant that I'm sure she's coming."

Roman glared. "The alternative had not occurred to me."

Now, of course, the possibility loomed large. Only a few days ago he would have laughed at the suggestion that Lola Theroux would ever seriously consider leaving Club Volare. Ever since he'd brought her into the club she had been a natural fit, and eventually an essential fixture. She managed the place with singular grace, and was central to his plans to open up a second location, though she didn't know it yet.

And yesterday she had seriously raised the possibility of quitting.

It was wrong. He had taken steps to make it right.

But that required that she in fact arrive.

Roman was almost never wrong, but Lola...Lola had surprised him when she'd suggested that she could simply leave. The last time Roman had been that surprised was when he'd discovered Lola in black leather at a now-defunct BDSM club in the East Village. That had been only a few years after Chance Dalton, Lola's close cousin and Roman's partner in the Club Volare ventures, had asked him to take care of Lola in the wake of her father's death. Roman had accepted the responsibility without question and had rushed to Lola's side, a stranger in place of family. He was glad to do it, but he had not expected Lola to be...Lola.

Gorgeous. Smarter than anyone else he knew. Fun. He suspected that Lola and his wife Samantha would have been great friends, if Samantha had lived. In truth, helping Lola helped him get through the most difficult time following his wife's death. But his position as Chance's best friend, his role as surrogate big brother during a vulnerable time—all of those things meant that Lola was, as Chance would have said, off-limits.

Fine. Roman was practiced at self-control, and he'd trained himself not to look at Lola that way. Not to think of her as the beautiful submissive he knew she was. Not to imagine her underneath him.

It was getting harder.

He heard the click of heels on hardwood floors

approaching Ford's office and spun towards the door, his whole body rippling with a singular awareness—it was her. He'd recognize the rhythm of her stride anywhere.

The door opened and she stepped in, her red hair framing her beautiful face and pink lips. Roman suppressed a rumbling in his chest. She was wearing a tight, white suit, some sort of designer item. Roman didn't care about clothing; he cared about the curves underneath. He cared about the way her bottom lip begged to be bitten. He cared about the way her breasts demanded to be mauled.

His cock twitched to life, but he refused to look away. He willed his body under control, and just when he'd succeeded, he realized that Lola was furious.

"Well? Are you going to explain?" she demanded. She took off her oversized sunglasses and he saw her green eyes flash.

"There are many things I could explain to you," he said, his gaze trailing down to her legs. "You will have to be more specific."

Lola glared at him, then walked over to a black leather couch and sat down. Slowly she crossed those long legs, and Roman was mesmerized. When he finally looked up and met her eye, she blushed.

"Excuse me," Ford said, and Roman frowned. He tried to remember that it wasn't Ford's fault he was there. Ford cleared his throat. "I imagine that Lola has encountered the press."

"Explain," Roman said.

Roman kept his eyes locked on Lola. She had dressed like this on purpose. In white, the bridal color, her skin flushed and glowing. Deliberately provocative.

She was playing the sub game with him, whether she realized it or not.

Did she know she was playing with fire?

"There were reporters outside my apartment building," Lola said, her voice finally beginning to falter under the weight of Roman's stare. "They knew I ran Volare. They asked if we were getting married. Actually, they asked if we already *were* married."

Roman cursed, startling them all. Roman had made the decision to deal with *Sizzle*, and with Catie's deception and eventual redemption, all on his own—had made the decision to be the public face of Volare—precisely to avoid this situation. He would always protect the identity of the club's members, but he had wanted to protect Lola most of all. It never occurred to him to ask her to take the risk of being outed for her association with a sex club, and the idea of gossip rags discussing Lola's sex life made him furious, but now it was happening anyway.

And he could never, ever explain why he had made that choice, the choice that so infuriated her, without admitting that he wanted her. That he *had* wanted her, for years. And he couldn't do all of that for a very good reason: he would protect Lola from anything, including himself.

"How?" he barked.

"It wasn't you?" Lola asked, apparently genuinely confused.

Roman was appalled. "I would never do that to you," he said.

Lola's blush deepened, and she finally looked away.

*What the hell is going on?*

"It was me," Ford said from behind him. "I leaked it to the press this morning."

Now it was Roman's turn to be outraged. He whirled around, his protective instincts taking momentary control.

"*Explain*," he seethed.

"I don't think either of you are fully aware of the political situation," Ford said calmly. "Obviously this law is total bullshit, and we could fight everything and probably win — eventually. But this isn't about what's legal or fair; it's about politics and public perception. Harold Jeels is just useful for people in Albany who want to run against the perv club down in the city. We can't give them any excuse. We have to fight this in the media, too, and that means public coverage."

"You should have asked me first," Roman said. "You had no right to do this to her."

"I can speak for myself," Lola said quietly.

Roman looked back at her, and his anger abated. She was standing now, a portrait of elegance and poise, her long, luscious legs spread slightly and her hand on one hip. Her ability to operate under pressure had always impressed him, and it did so again now. Roman was, as he had been when she had discovered Ben's cheating, torn between pride in her evident strength and the desire to utterly destroy whatever had hurt her.

He took a deep breath and tried to remember that Ford was his friend.

"Of course you can," he said to Lola. "Forgive

me."

There was a silence, and he could have sworn he saw her expression soften. She looked down, the slightest hint of a frown marring her beautiful face.

"Ford, you should have warned me," Lola said.

"I couldn't get a hold of you," Ford continued. "You weren't answering your phone. Look, there's nothing pretty about any of this. This has to be a freaking spectacle. We need to get you two officially married as soon as possible, and then after that we need to make a wedding ceremony into a big media event while somehow protecting members who don't want their memberships exposed. Everyone has to be convinced this is real. And in the meantime, there's a possibility that you might need to avoid process servers."

"Process servers?" Lola said weakly.

"That's why you suggested we meet here," Roman said. He hadn't realized this would become such a media circus. "You think they know where Volare is?"

"Nobody can hide from the taxman, and Harold Jeels knows plenty of people in the New York State revenue service. Trust me—he definitely knows where Volare is located."

Roman did not like this. Volare was located on the top floor of an exclusive hotel, a decision Roman had made early on which was always designed to provide cover for the club's members. A wealthy kinkster need not telegraph his tastes; he could just be staying at the hotel. Even so, Roman did not relish the idea of reporters camped out, waiting for Lola.

His brooding was interrupted by the tone in

Lola's voice: soft, vulnerable, yielding.

"Roman," she said. "Are you going to tell me why I'm here?"

He looked at her again, at the softness of her skin, the warmth of her eyes, and was gripped with a sudden, ferocious lust. She stood closer to him now, and was looking up at him through her long lashes, her eyes wide open, her lips slightly parted. He had seen her play the sub with her odious ex-boyfriend and knew that *he*, Roman, could bring out her true submissiveness in a way that bastard Benjamin never had. Knew that she would purr under his hand, that he could make her scream his name and beg. Knew that she would come as many times as he demanded.

"Roman?" she asked.

This was the trouble: he wanted to fuck her until they both lost the ability to speak, but that was all he could give her. He couldn't protect her from his own problems. He couldn't protect her from his grief over Samantha.

"You are here to sign a prenuptial agreement," he said finally. He couldn't take his eyes off her moist lips. "A prenuptial agreement that awards you an equity stake in Volare upon dissolution of the marriage, no matter the reason."

Lola furrowed her brow, and looked at him with concern. *Concern*. God, what he could do with her submission.

"I don't understand," she said.

"I kept secrets from you because I wanted to protect you," Roman bit the words off, his arms tense with the effort of restraint. "And this made you think that I do not take you seriously. That is incorrect. You are...you *deserve* to be part owner. I should have done this years ago. I am only correcting an oversight, but I hope you will understand the sentiment behind it."

Their eyes met, and it was as though the rest of the world fell away, and Roman's entire awareness contracted down into a single, fine point concentrated on Lola. He knew her so well he could see her mind working, could see her running through possibilities and permutations and figuring out how to feel about what he'd just said. Figuring out what it meant. Roman held himself rigid. He found her mind as sexy as her body.

"I see," she said. Slowly she looked him up and down, and Roman's animal lust traced the path of her gaze. Every muscle in his body screamed for him to take her.

"Roman?" she said, and looked up through those long lashes. "Stop protecting me."

Roman's pulse roared in his ears, a primal call that he struggled to ignore.

"Do you know what you are saying?" he asked, his voice hoarse.

"Maybe."

And Lola lowered her eyelashes, her body language unmistakably submissive. Roman had never seen her like this. Had never seen her like this with *him*.

"Lola," he said.

They were interrupted by the telephone. Neither of them turned away as Ford picked it up, speaking quickly and quietly. Roman was transfixed by the sight of Lola, head bowed, in front of him. She was no naïf; she knew what this meant. What her body was saying to him.

She *knew*.

"Guys?"

"What?" Roman didn't turn away from her. Lola didn't turn away from him.

Ford continued, "Harold Jeels is on his way up. You need to avoid him until you're legal. You also need to get your marriage license *today* so that you can make it official tomorrow. And you need to find a way to make this convincing—not just to the press, but to the other Volare members, as well. I don't like telling you to lie, but everyone needs to believe this. Harold Jeels will ask questions and I don't want to give him any ammunition when he's obviously prepared to go to war with a bullshit law that only stands because nobody ever bothered to repeal it. He's fucking nuts."

"We must convince Volare, as well?" Roman asked.

Ford gave a wry smile. "Somehow I don't think it will be that hard. Now get the hell out of here and go to the city clerk's office to get that license. My assistant will show you the back stairs."

## *chapter* 4

Roman kept *touching* her, and every time he did, her brain blew another fuse.

Roman's hand rested on the small of her back, on her waist, on her arm, guiding her, prodding her, telling her where to go. As soon as Ford mentioned that Harold Jeels was on the way, Roman had gone into "determined protector" mode. When Roman had glanced out to the front lobby and seen reporters, he'd gone full caveman. He'd immediately put his body between hers and anyone else. It seemed like he didn't want to go more than a second without some kind of contact.

Lola wasn't complaining. But she *was* worrying.

What had happened in Ford's office? Never mind what had happened in Roman's head—what was behind those smoldering looks he'd given her—what the hell had happened in *her* head? She'd felt herself slipping into a submissive role in a way that she hadn't experienced since Ben. It had just come naturally, just her reflexive response to something Roman was putting out.

In fact, it wasn't really like it had been with Ben. She hadn't had to think about it at all.

Roman had just looked at her and she'd felt warm.

She'd really convinced herself that she could handle this. She'd worked with Roman every day for years and managed to avoid — or suppress — this exact feeling. But the more she thought about it, the more she realized she'd avoided more than a feeling; she'd also avoided almost all personal discussion with Roman. This was the first time in years they'd talked about their relationship, whatever it was.

He'd said he wanted to protect her. She'd wondered what that meant, she wondered how far he'd go, and then she'd wondered if he'd protect her from himself. If he had been protecting her from himself, from his famous sexual appetites and emotional reserve.

Just the thought left her breathless.

His touch, just the slightest touch, lit her on fire. She was sure he must notice. How could he not notice?

But he'd been focused on outward threats. Roman had actually made her wear his suit coat over her head as he put her in a cab, like some kind of white collar criminal doing a perp walk, and he was unwilling to let her go once they arrived at the city clerk's office. He'd practically carried her inside.

"Roman, I'm ok," she finally said, exasperated. They were waiting while the clerk checked out all their forms and identification. Roman was still hovering protectively over her, as though a reporter might jump out from behind the line of people waiting to file for various permits.

"They won't get near you again," he said firmly. "I promise you that."

"Well, they know where I live, so I'm pretty sure they will."

"No. You will move in with me."

Lola looked up to see if he were joking. He wasn't. And she was distracted just by the sight of him. His dark olive skin managed to look good under fluorescent lighting, and the muscles in his neck writhed as he ground his jaw in frustration. She knew he didn't want to wait around out in the open like this. The idea that he wanted to get her back to his apartment…

*Don't read into it, Theroux.*

"Do you really think that's a good idea?" she managed.

"It is the only idea. You will be my wife; of course you will live with me."

"Well, in name only," she said. He looked down at her, his dark eyes unreadable, and a now familiar tingle spread through out her body.

He'd never looked at her like that before. And now, in the past two days…

"Mr. Casta, Miss Theroux? Your license is ready, you just have to wait twenty four hours." The clerk peered up at Roman with owlish eyes and smiled. "Are you *the* Roman Casta? From *Sizzle*?"

Inwardly Lola groaned. The last thing they needed was to have their quickie fake wedding staked out. She still couldn't believe this was of interest to the rest of the world—hadn't anything actually important happened this week? Was a discreet high-end sex club really that big a deal?

The little clerk was looking at Roman with a mixture of awe and lust, so apparently it was. Lola did not like it.

"No," Lola said coldly.

Roman gave the clerk a charming, slow smile, and slipped some money over the desk. "Please, keep our secret. If you do, I will be very grateful."

Lola glared. She had seen Roman flirt before, and she'd even seen him in scenes with other women before. She'd never liked it, and she'd usually found an excuse to be in a different room so she didn't have to see too much of it, but this time she didn't have that luxury. And this time he was supposed to be her husband. Fiancé. Whatever.

"Roman?" she said as he led her out of the stuffy little office. "We're going to have to talk about how we act in public."

Abruptly he stopped and brought her to heel, her hand still in his. He looked down at her fiercely, obviously thinking hard about something.

"Yes," he said. "We will."

And he pulled her into a sudden, simmering kiss.

Lola melted into him, helpless to do otherwise. His kiss was deep and ruthless, his tongue coaxing a low moan from her throat while his fingers weaved into her hair. Before she knew it her hands were on his chest, her fingers grabbing at his lapels, and her clit was throbbing, driving her to get more of the man in any way she could. He took her from controlled and classy to wanting and wanton in less than half a second.

Roman pulled away, his eyes burning in satisfaction. "We will have to do *that* in public," he said. "You will simply have to get used to it."

*Oh God.*

Lola was in a daze as she walked down the broad marble stairs. She ran her tongue over her swollen lips and wondered what that kiss would feel like on other parts of her body. She sat in the cab at his side, eyes closed, sure he could tell that desire pulsed in her, that her clit was painfully swollen from just a kiss. She was afraid to look at him, afraid to talk to him. He would *know*.

He led her in silence through the familiar lobby of the hotel and up the private elevator that led to his apartment, a duplex that was adjacent to and below Club Volare, which was on the top floor. Her mind was in overdrive—would it be so bad if he knew? Was that just the rationalization of an unbelievably horny mind?

He'd done that to her with one kiss.

One. Kiss. And she'd been willing to do anything he wanted. Anything at all. She would have offered her submission right there in the hallway of the city clerk's office, in front of anyone and everyone, if only it meant that he'd fuck her.

Her mind reeled at the thought. She'd been so hurt by Roman's lies, equating them with Ben's lies without thinking, but now she wondered if that was just the break up talking, if her anger at Roman had really been about her anger at being betrayed. Discovering that Ben had been cheating on her with his ex-wife for months had been absolutely devastating, and the resulting break up had haunted her like a damn poltergeist. Just when she thought she was getting over it, the memory would rise up to totally fuck up her day. She'd thought she could never trust a man again, certainly not enough to submit, and then she'd found out that Roman had lied to her, too.

But her body hadn't gotten the message. Her body had just announced that she could most certainly still submit — to Roman.

That she most certainly still trusted Roman, at least as far as BDSM went.

She almost wanted to cry in relief, and then again in frustration. She'd begun to think she'd never trust a man again, that she'd just be broken for the rest of her life, and now, because of a kiss from Roman, she knew she wasn't a lost cause. She wasn't broken.

Too bad Roman was the one man she knew who would never love her.

But it didn't matter — it was like a dam had broken. All of the old feelings that she'd resisted for all these years threatened to overwhelm her. Drown her. She could barely speak.

Roman opened the door to his private apartment and pulled her inside, his shoulders relaxing now that she was finally in the safety of his home.

'Home' didn't really do it justice. Lola had been here a few times before, but she would never get over the shock of the view. The city lay before her, the floor to ceiling windows facing south and west, revealing a beautiful view of the park and downtown with just a hint of blue in the hazy distance. This was only the public area, or semi-public. She knew there was another floor below.

Not for the first time, Lola wondered what Roman felt when he looked at what he'd built here in New York. She didn't know much about where he'd come from, just small snippets over the years, some things filled in by Chance. He'd been on his own as kid, an actual Dickensian sort of orphan, and had worked his way up picking through trash and cleaning gutters in Spain, eventually employing other kids in his business. Twenty hard-scrabbling, entrepreneurial years after that, he'd put himself through school and had the beginnings of a real estate empire, then had sold most of it just before the crash. She didn't blame him for not wanting to talk about where he'd come from, but she never stopped wanting to hear about it.

Lola watched him shrug his suit coat off in one athletic movement, his muscles roiling under his finely tailored shirt. He paced—he always paced when he thought, his body always needing to find some outlet—walking a circuit of the large circular living room, surveying his territory.

He stopped in the center of the room and looked at her, still leaning against the wall in the foyer like an idiot. He made her weak.

"I will prepare the spare room," he said.

The spare room. Lola had heard about this from the women Roman had periodic arrangements with: he was the best Dom in the city, but it was play only. Women could stay over, but he never shared a bed. He would hold them, provide aftercare, but never, ever did he sleep—actually *sleep*—with a woman.

Of course she was to sleep in the spare room. Had she really allowed herself to become so unrealistic? From one kiss and a cab ride?

"Roman," she said, and he stopped in midstride to give her his full attention. He looked like a Catalonian god, standing tall and polished in the late afternoon light. "About…"

"Yes?"

She couldn't do it. Couldn't say "the kiss."

"About being…convincing. How are we going to convince the club?"

Roman cocked his head, a slight smile on his face. The bastard! He wasn't affected at all. It was like that kiss hadn't done anything to him. It was incredibly unfair. Worse, it was humiliating.

"You have been a submissive before," he said. "I am sure you will know what to do."

Lola felt her cheeks reddening. "That's not what I meant. I meant that it's kind of a huge deal, and if we pretend it's not a huge deal, everyone will wonder what's up. We have to actually *tell* people. Make an announcement or something. A big show of it."

He smiled. "Come out of the closet?"

"Yes."

Roman laughed, sprawling his muscular body on the couch. "You truly think they will believe it, just like that?"

How could anyone believe he would be with her? Lola bristled at the insult, secretly grateful to have something to focus on other than the magnetic pull of Roman's body. That sealed it. She would do whatever she had to do to get Roman to take her seriously. To make sure that he was *affected.* That she wasn't the only one who had to endure this torture of pretending to have the man she'd always wanted and yet not really having him. She had a few tricks up her sleeve. She could make him suffer, too.

"I'll *make* them believe it," she said.

Roman Casta had no idea what he had gotten himself into.

# *chapter* 5

Roman enjoyed gambling. Perhaps that explained what he was about to do.

Perhaps that explained what he had already done.

Roman made his way through the private hall that connected his apartment with Club Volare with laser focus, his well-developed muscles twitching angrily under his tailored suit, his whole body screaming at him that he was moving in exactly the wrong direction—away from Lola. His whole being was pulled taught in anticipation, waiting. There was much to do. Much to take care of.

As soon as he'd kissed her, he'd known: he had to have her. He must, or he would lose his mind.

His conscience said otherwise, and the tension between his conscience and his cock had stretched him to the breaking point. The compromise was this: he would have her, if he were convinced it would not harm her. If it would help her.

He repeated the mantra to himself and growled involuntarily. A man didn't need to repeat things that he was sure of. But he damn well needed to be sure of this.

He'd only meant to test himself when he'd kissed Lola in the hallway at the city clerk's office, a test of the sorts of things they'd have to do many times in public, a test he had been confident of passing. And he *had* passed, but barely. It had taken every ounce of self control he had not to take her there and then, and he'd only bought himself time by promising himself he'd have her later. What insanity was that?

She was Lola. His Lola. His charge. Chance's cousin, his family.

But there was no point in going over the arguments again in his mind; no point in rehashing all of the reasons why this was a terrible thing. It changed nothing. It meant nothing, not in the face of what happened when he touched her. It had been instant fire, his higher self burned away, leaving behind something animal. He hadn't felt lust like that since Samantha.

Whatever this was between them needed to be dealt with, before it did real damage, before it threatened their plan to save Volare.

And tonight was the first part of that plan. Tonight, they would have to convince the Volare membership that their relationship was real. It would at least be no challenge to convince them that he wanted her. How he was to determine whether Lola could manage a physical relationship with him... He stopped suddenly; even now the reality of that, of what he contemplated, shocked him. He would never, ever forgive himself if he took her and in the morning she regretted it. Or worse, if she was hurt by it. Damaged.

She had already been hurt by her last Dom. Her only Dom, as far as Roman knew.

The thought of Lola, brokenhearted and humiliated when she'd discovered Benjamin with his ex-wife, brought Roman up short. Lola had actually cried in his office. *Lola had cried.* The memory of it made Roman feel dangerous. He had wanted to punish Benjamin many, many times, but Lola only wanted to forget. For all her worldliness, she was also, in her way, an innocent: she truly believed the best of people. It wasn't in her to understand why someone would lie like that.

And Roman wouldn't lie to her, not about something like that. That was one encouraging fact: if there was any woman alive who already knew of Roman's rules involving physical relationships, it was Lola Theroux. She was, in fact, the only woman who knew the reason for them. She knew about Samantha. He could be confident that Lola, at least, would not expect more than what he could give.

Then why did it still feel like a gamble?

Mother of God, was he really considering this?

"Thank you, Roman, for offering another Casino Night," Sheikh Bashir said, rising from the chair where he'd been waiting in Roman's office. He extended his hand. The two men hadn't seen each other since Roman had interviewed the Sheikh as he spanked the woman who would later become his fiancée—and was one of Lola's best friends—

during a Volare BDSM brunch. That had been months ago. "Stella loved the one we had for our engagement party, and she is delighted that it should become a regular feature."

"I'm sorry I couldn't attend that engagement party, but I have promised Stella, on pain of death, that I *will* be at the wedding," Roman said smiling.

Bashir smiled back. It seemed a particularly knowing smile. "Ah, yes. My fiancée is currently helping your fiancée 'get ready?'"

Roman frowned. "You know?"

"I'm afraid there are few secrets between women, and few people are able to hide things from me. Stella no longer even tries," Bashir said, returning to his seat. "You have my discretion, of course."

"Of course." That made at least four people, aside from himself, Lola, and Ford, who knew. At least Roman was confident in Jake and Catie, and in Stella and Bashir—but circles of trust grew weaker as they grew bigger.

"In that case, Bashir, we plan to announce our 'relationship' at tonight's event. Since you are one of the nominal hosts, perhaps you can help us with any credibility problems?"

"You're joking," Bashir said, then looked hard at Roman. Bashir laughed. "You're not? I don't think that you'll have any problems with that, Roman."

Roman thought about Lola's body crushed against his, and his cock began to throb. "Even so."

"Of course. So why did you ask me here?"

Ah. The question at hand. He'd meant to discuss this with Lola, but recent events had gotten in the way. And now, because of Lola, those plans might have to change.

Roman leaned forward. "I want to talk about another Volare location."

The two men settled into the comfortable realm of business, but Roman was on automatic. He kept thinking about Lola's words: "I'll *make* them believe it."

What could she have meant by that?

~ * ~ * ~

"Something happened, I can tell," Stella said over the mountain of clothing she held in her arms. "Out with it."

"Nothing happened," Lola lied. "Thank you so much for bringing my clothes. I'm over here."

Lola mentally crossed her fingers as she led Stella through Roman's sun-soaked apartment to her designated spare room, hoping against hope that her friend would buy it.

"Yeah, what's with the 'I can't leave the apartment' thing?" Stella said behind her.

Lola cringed, walking ahead and opening the door to the walk in closet, and then went back for the suitcases they'd left by the door.

"It's not so much that I *can't*, it's more that Roman doesn't want me getting mobbed," she said over her shoulder. "He didn't want me accosted by reporters again, at least until we've figured the whole thing out. And, frankly, I'm freaked out after that scrum this morning, so I agreed. Temporarily."

Stella waited until her friend came back lugging the suitcases just so Lola could see the raised eyebrow. "Roman doesn't want you getting mobbed?"

Lola smiled involuntarily. Why was she smiling? It was ridiculous. She should not be smiling about this. "You should have seen him while we were getting the marriage license. It was like that scene from *The Bodyguard*, only...all Roman-like. It was actually kind of sweet."

"Really?" Stella was grinning.

"Protective. And sweet. He's getting me a security detail if it keeps up."

"Are you going to tell me what actually happened?"

"No."

Stella harrumphed. "Pick out your own dress, then," she said.

"Fine, he kissed me. Not a real kiss," Lola added quickly, not wanting to look at her friend. "It's just, we have to be convincing, right? Ford keeps telling us that. So we'll have to do stuff like that in public. And I get that. It's just..."

Stella was never fooled. Her eyes were sparkling. "How was it?"

"It wasn't real."

"Oh, bullcrap. It was *Roman*. The man you've fantasized about for what, ten years? Almost?"

Lola sighed, picking up a dry-cleaned sleeved dress and walking it into the generous closet. "Oh, fine. Of course it was incredible. Of course it was...I don't even have words, Stella. I was floored."

"And?"

"And he *wasn't*. He didn't even seem affected. Like, not even fazed. Just, you know, super-controlled Roman."

Lola joined Stella where she sat on the bed—what would be Lola's bed now, for however long; Lola's huge, lonely bed—and let her friend put a comforting arm around her.

"You ok?" Stella asked.

Lola looked at Stella's hand on her shoulder: there it was, weighing down her friend's finger, the giant engagement ring. Stella must have developed entirely new arm muscles to carry that thing around. She was getting married for real. She had an engagement ring that actually meant something. Lola sighed.

"Well, no, it freaking sucks, wanting him and having these feelings—feelings I'm not even sure of, honestly—and knowing they won't be returned. Look, it's confusing. He confused the hell out of me in Ford's office. I knew it would suck. Like, what did I think would happen when I agreed to this, right? *But*," Lola added, drawing herself up, "One, Volare is my family and my responsibility. And two, I am no pushover. I'm not going to just suffer in silence."

"What are you going to do?"

Lola shrugged and picked up her favorite dress, a gossamer thin, body hugging green dream. "I'm going to show him what he's missing. And if he doesn't want me…well, I'll at least make sure he knows that other guys do."

Stella looked dubious. "You sure about this?"

"Well, it's not like it could get worse, right?" Lola said. "What do I have to lose?"

~ * ~ * ~

Roman lazily flipped a poker chip through his fingers and watched the door, his face expressionless as he watched the members of Volare come and go.

Only one mattered, and she wasn't here.

He would wait.

Stella Spencer's Casino Night had become so popular it seemed it would become a new Volare tradition. The central hall, a large room where most of their big events were held, was crowded with Volare regulars mingling between the many green-topped tables. Stella and Bashir themselves were dancing slowly, out of time, oblivious to the world around them, to some rock/big band fusion group that Stella had found in Brooklyn. Roman glanced at them and smiled. He doubted those two saw anything but each other.

And Roman himself was only interested in one person. The longer he had to wait, the more he felt like a caged animal. He had been thinking about her, about that kiss— and about how the world would be different after he made her his—all afternoon, all night. He was growing impatient.

*No. Remember the conditions.*

Roman was nothing without his integrity. He knew she wanted him. He sensed it with every fiber of his being; Lola had never been very good at hiding her feelings from him. But his concerns of the past ten years didn't simply evaporate because of a kiss; he had to be certain that their past did not turn a sexual relationship into something that could harm Lola. Only, he had to be certain of that before his lust overwhelmed him completely.

It was something of a race.

"Roman, are you even paying attention?"

Annoyed, Roman looked across the table to find Ford grinning at him. Jackson Reed, a man Roman had come to know better since the last Volare Casino Night had reunited Jackson with his own wife-to-be, covered his cards with his hand and tried to look at nothing at all. He had, apparently, raised, and the bet had been met by Salvador Benes, a new member who came recommended by friends. The betting action was to Roman, and he hadn't even realized they'd dealt out a new hand.

"A lot on your mind, Roman?"

Ford appeared to be enjoying this far too much. That good-boy grin was annoying. Roman didn't answer, but checked his hole cards. Jacks. He called.

"Nothing I cannot handle, Ford," Roman said.

He hoped he was right. He was gambling everything on being right.

Alyssa, a pretty blonde sub who'd just been cast in a Broadway revival, dealt out the flop. Normally Roman would have taken in the reactions of the other players, but this was the moment Lola Theroux chose to make her entrance.

God, what an entrance.

The soft bronze light of the natural candles and heavy chandeliers that hung about the room at the Sheikh's insistence, giving off the old time speakeasy vibe that Stella so loved, gave off a warm light that raced through Lola's red hair like a living thing, giving her a soft, tempting halo and an otherworldly glow.

Roman wanted to take that halo and turn it into something more interesting. His gaze slid down her body, which was barely covered in a fine green fabric, a dress that made her seem more naked than clothed. He couldn't take his eyes off of her.

And he wasn't the only one.

Someone was speaking to him, but he didn't hear, didn't care to interpret the words. All he saw was Daniel Billings, a wealthy trader who was always on the lookout for a new mistress, and who had always, *always* looked at Lola with a desire that Roman thought was beneath her. Daniel Billings was moving through the crowd, his eyes locked on Lola.

His Lola.

Roman was already up and walking away from the table, his body propelling him through the crowd, his fists opening and closing, his jaw clenching. There was a group around Lola, people crowding around her, everyone wanting to talk to her—their Mistress, the heart and soul of Volare, the one everyone had missed so much since Roman had driven her away by lying to her. And there was Daniel Billings, swooping in with a gluttonous look, waiting to take advantage of Lola's return.

*No.*

Roman cut in, his arm snaking around Lola's waist. He met her eyes first—her wide, surprised green eyes, eyes that had already seen more of him than anyone since his wife. He might have kissed her there. Would have, if he could have been sure that it wouldn't confuse her more. If he could have been certain of what she could handle.

Instead he turned viciously on Billings.

"Mine," he said.

Everything stopped. All the little pattering

conversations died. All eyes fell to them. Roman's arm tightened around Lola's waist, and Billings put his hands up, stammering out nonsense words.

Roman ignored him. He ignored all of them.

"Come," he said to Lola, and led her across the room to an alcove, a tiny space meant for private moments at public events. By the time he spun her into that private little nook he felt hot, feverish, on edge.

"Roman, was that necessary?" Lola seemed amused more than anything else. He'd let her get away with it—for now.

He said, "It was less than I should have done. You are supposed to be my submissive, remember? My *wife*."

"About that..." Lola paused, looking away as though she were trying to choose her words carefully. "I'm a switch, Roman. And no one has seen me as a sub since—"

"Don't even say his name," Roman interrupted. "Look at me. Do not sully your lips with his name."

The silence between them seemed small, intimate. Not even the music could intrude, and Roman inhaled deeply, breathed all of her in. Her scent, her sly smile, the dull light glinting off her skin, the heat of her burning him through that dress. Then she smiled with wide affection, showing the slight dimple in her left cheek. She said, "Roman, that's a little extreme."

"I do not care. Speak about the relationship, speak about how you feel, but never forget that he is beneath you." He gripped her waist tighter and sought out her hand. "Never."

Now Lola's eyes flashed, and she pulled herself

up to her full height. How did she put it? She could switch gears on a dime? She'd always said it was a redhead trait. He could see that she'd switched into 'angry.'

"You don't have to tell me that, Roman, believe me. That doesn't change my current lack of credibility as a sub. I haven't felt...I haven't been sure of myself in that role, especially not publicly, since Benjamin. And no, you do *not* get to tell me how to speak about my relationships, no matter how disastrous, because they are *mine*."

Roman smiled, unable to stop himself even though he knew it would annoy her. He loved her fire. Always had, and, likely to his detriment, he always would. But now it seemed to be covering something, something more vulnerable, some core of hurt that she still carried with her. The trust that submission required had always put Roman in awe of any true submissive, and Lola was no exception. He could not imagine what it was like to have that trust betrayed, to feel as though you could never be your full self again because someone had chosen to hurt you instead of cherish you.

Something low in him wanted to simply go out and hurt the man who had done this. Something else made him want to stay here and fix it.

He drew her in, wanting to make sure she understood this.

"Lola," he said, "just because you have not found a man worthy of your submission does not change who you are. I see you. I know you. Do not forget that."

She blinked, her red lips parted. Roman didn't know what she had expected, but it was apparently not that.

He went on, "You will find your way. I will lead you. From this moment on, in public, *you are my submissive*. Do you understand?"

Roman put his hand under her chin, and raised it gently. "Answer me."

It was an unmistakable order.

"Yes, sir," Lola said, surprising herself. He could see that it had been an automatic response.

Roman liked hearing those words far too much. For a moment his dominant self gained the upper hand over his conscience, and he had to take several steadying breaths. If they were not very, very careful, they would both find out what happened when the walls fell.

# *chapter* 6

Lola had been having second thoughts about all of it—about risking her own heart playing submissive to Roman's Dom, about tempting Roman until she had proved that she affected him even a little bit, and most of all, about playing with fire—right up until he said those words.

*Just because you haven't found a man worthy of your submission doesn't change who you are.*

*I see you. I will lead you.*

*Mine.*

Every anxious thought rattling around inside her head faded in the face of those words. She melted all over again. She wished he could see what he did to her. Wished they weren't blinded to each other by sheer familiarity. Wished he took her seriously enough to want her for his own.

Did he? She had been crushed when she'd found out he didn't respect her enough to tell her about that stupid Sizzle article, or about Catie's undercover intentions. But he had just said those words: I see you.

She was powerless to say no. Didn't want to say no, even though she knew that would be the smart thing to do.

And so here she was, being led by the hand across the room by Master Roman, feeling every member of the club she'd helped build watch in awed silence. Word must have already spread, and if it hadn't, they only had to see Roman's body language. He was all Dom, and all of it was directed at Lola.

Oh God. Already she felt overwhelmed by him. She was shaky, unsteady. And while theoretically the presence of a strong Dom would be the exact thing she needed, it was Roman, and how he had such a hold over her while she had nothing on him, that made her feel so…weak.

"Roman," she said, pulling a little bit on his hand. He turned, his expression one of concern. Intense concern. She swallowed. "How are we going to do this, exactly? How are we going to…come out?"

"We are going to be," he said, and drew her in to another searing, sealing kiss.

This one could leave no doubt in anyone's mind, at least about Lola's feelings. Her whole body betrayed her and responded to him, as though it had found its true master, and it definitely wasn't her. The warmth spread from his lips to hers, down her neck to her chest, her breasts, to her churning, molten core.

He pulled away, leaving her panting, his head still close to hers, his breath warm on her cheek.

"Like that," he said.

And he pulled her, dazed, the rest of the way to a poker table. As though to put an exclamation point on that very public kiss, Roman sat down languidly in a wide, comfortable armchair and pulled Lola down onto his lap.

It took Lola a second or two to regain her bearings. She wasn't imagining it: everything stopped for a second while the whole room watched them. Slowly normal conversation began again—though it was now hushed, maybe—only with eyes still on them. She turned to the table, hoping for some relief, and was sorely disappointed: here was Ford, grinning evilly, and Jackson Reed, looking astonished and pleased, and a newer member, a man whose eyes she'd felt on her more than once: Salvador Benes.

Great. They were playing poker.

"Does this mean what I think it means?" Salvador asked, reaching for his drink.

Roman's arm tightened around her, and Lola felt herself begin to flush.

"What do you think, Salvador?" Roman said.

Salvador shrugged and gestured to the cards. "We waited for you."

Roman reached over, and Lola could only think about how close his mouth came to her breasts, which were practically falling out of her dress to begin with. It was sort of the point of that particular dress. And now she was sitting on Roman's lap, while men she knew watched, open-mouthed.

She felt dizzy.

"I call," Roman said, and settled back into his

seat, squeezing Lola to him like this was all totally normal. Like this was a thing they did. The new sub who was dealing caught her eye and gave her a commiserating smile, like, Doms, I know.

Lola risked a look at Ford. He was really smiling just way too much.

Alyssa dealt out another card, and Salvador immediately said, "Raise." He threw a bunch of heavy chips in the pot, and held Roman's eye. Ford laughed and folded, and Jackson was already out of the hand.

"Re-raise." Roman threw his own chips in. Lola was starting to feel like a prop, like a plaything—and she liked it.

Really liked it. And she was sure Roman could tell.

Dammit. He already had her. Already. It wasn't even half fair.

Salvador's eyes were on her now; she could feel them. There was something in the air, some hint of male pheromones, the kind of thing you could feel right before men did something incredibly stupid.

And here it was: "I had no idea Lola was a submissive," Salvador said.

Roman corrected, "She's my submissive."

He rubbed his hand up the length of her thigh. Lola inhaled sharply.

"You know, I wouldn't have believed it, either," Ford said, leaning back.

"Call," Salvador said. Alyssa dealt the final card, but Salvador didn't even look. He was staring at Lola.

She took a deep breath and turned slightly to Roman. His hand tightened on her thigh. Each time he moved, she was torn: she wanted it, oh God, did she want it, but part of her was still fighting for self-preservation. After those kisses, she knew: if she gave in, it would be all in. She'd be lost to the way she felt about Roman. And it might be worse than she knew.

"Your action, Salvador," Roman said.

"It's a pity she's off the market," Salvador said, ignoring Roman. "Care to bet her?"

Lola shot him a glare—a decidedly un-submissive glare. "No," she said.

There was a pause.

Salvador chuckled. "Are you very sure that she is your submissive, Roman?"

Lola could hear the low growl in Roman's throat, could feel his fingers digging into her flesh. She closed her eyes and rode the pleasure that all of those things gave her. She opened them when she felt his hand slip inside her dress and cup her breast, his fingers on her bare skin.

"She says no to you because she knows that she is mine," Roman said. "Mine."

He pinched her nipple, and she jumped. She heard laughter.

Oh shit.

She loved it. But she was fighting it. Why? She wanted it, she enjoyed every single second, and fighting it was costing them. It was costing Volare. With their luck, Salvador Benes would be the first person Harold Jeels found, the first one he interviewed, and he'd spin a tale of fraud and deception. For what, her pride? No, not even. Her fear. She was afraid of falling completely into Roman Casta.

"Oh, fuck it," she said under her breath, and bent down to Roman's ear. "Yours," she whispered, and nipped his earlobe.

Roman's hips shifted under her, and the growl became louder. Lola was wet, and she wasn't wearing any underwear. Roman would know just how turned on she was in only a few moments, if he didn't already. Lola closed her eyes against both the humiliation and the heat that that aroused in her.

"Come on, Roman, what is your price?" she heard Salvador say with naked urgency in his voice. "How much to bet a submissive Lola?"

Roman's hand left her breast abruptly, so quickly she was almost hurt by its absence — and then it was there again, on her thigh, rushing up her leg…

"Priceless," Roman said. "If you look at her once more I will throw you out myself, I swear to God."

And, under the table, his hand found her core — and found her bare, and very, very wet.

Lola opened her eyes in shock, and looked at Roman. He met her eyes, and shifted his hips — and then she felt him.

He was rock hard.

For her.

Her fantasy, her unattainable man — he wanted her. He was hard because he wanted to fuck her. She had done this; she could do this. The rush was instant, the adrenaline flooding her brain and drowning what remained of rational, cautious thought.

She bit her lip and moved her hips against him.

His eyes bored into her, a single vein in his

forehead throbbing, and then his hand...his hand kept going. His fingers parted her wet outer lips and slid down the length of her, searching for her opening, stroking her softly, lingering on the pressure points between her inner and outer lips — oh God, of course Roman would know about that...

Her back began to arch, her eyes half closed, her mouth open...

"Roman, I checked. The action is to you."

She didn't even look. She was already spiraling down into her own little world, into Roman...

"All in," Roman said gruffly.

~ * ~ * ~

She felt like liquid silk in his hand, her body responding to every touch, every thought he had. He was mesmerized. Everyone was mesmerized. He hoped they appreciated that he allowed them the pleasure, the privilege, of seeing Lola Theroux close her eyes, lick her lips, and moan...

She stopped.

Her eyes were open.

Her face crashed. Before his eyes, under his hand, she wilted.

"Roman, I called —"

He ignored Salvador. "Lola, what's wrong?"

She didn't answer him, just looked over his shoulder. Roman turned, and the sight he saw filled him with anger.

Benjamin Mara. In his club. Hurting Lola.

Again.

Roman turned Lola's face toward his and said

very quietly, very urgently, "Look at me." She did, and the sadness he saw there sliced through him. "He will not hurt you, Lola. I will deal with this."

He lifted her, placing her gently in the chair, and had not gotten two steps before he realized that Jackson was behind him. Then Bashir joined them, a quick arrow of angry men moving toward one, singular target.

"He's mine," Roman said curtly.

Benjamin Mara soon found himself isolated and alone. This gave him enough warning to turn, face Roman, and speak.

"Roman, please, I've come to apologize —"

Roman kept moving until Benjamin Mara backed up, faltering, flat against a wall, trying to disappear into it. Roman didn't even need to touch him.

He said, "Do not speak. Do not move. If she tells me to, I will harm you — do you understand? You are only safe because of my respect for her. Do not test me."

Benjamin Mara swallowed. He was shorter than Roman, like most men, and thinner. It would not be a real contest. Roman almost regretted it.

Roman's voice was cold. "This is my club. This is her club. Her space. You do not invade it, after what you did. You do not show up uninvited. You indecent, pathetic, uncivilized piece of shit."

"I wanted to explain —"

Roman smelled stale whisky. It was from the man's sweat. He'd been drinking — that was the only reason he'd come. Roman was even more disgusted.

"There is no explanation, you coward. You will

apologize only if she decides she wants to hear it, not because you would like to stop feeling guilty. And now, Benjamin," Roman said, fixing Benjamin's collar and smoothing his suit, just to let him know he could do what he wanted in this place, "you are going to leave. And you are not going to come back unless she asks you to. Do you understand?"

"I—"

Roman's fists closed around Benjamin's lapels, and he lifted him bodily off the ground only to slam him against the wall. Benjamin's head bounced off the hard surface, his arms struggling ineffectually.

"Do you understand?" Roman said again.

"Yes."

"Run."

And Roman dropped him to the ground and watched him scramble towards the exit. Bashir wordlessly followed him, probably to make sure the snake had, in fact, left. Jackson patted him on the back and set about fixing Roman's own collar, and it was then that Roman realized he was breathing hard and his blood was pounding in his head hard enough to hurt.

"You've got a woman to worry about," Jackson said.

Roman didn't even say thank you. He had to find her. The rest of the club, his friends, his business, his life—all of it paled, fell away. His moved through the crowd unhearing, unseeing, until he saw her: just a hint of green, moving towards one of the side doors.

No.

He didn't want her hurt. Not again.

"Lola," he said, her name the best thing he'd said all night. He grabbed her wrist, gently, just wanting contact. She didn't turn her head, but he could still see, hidden under those waves of red hair, the stain of tears on her cheek.

He opened the side door and pulled her out into the dark side hallway. Give her darkness, give her privacy. Give her everything.

"Lola," he said again, putting his hand to her cheek. "Forgive me. I shouldn't have gone so far, I should have known—"

"No!" she said, the strength in her voice shocking him. "Don't apologize. Please, don't…"

He was lost in the warmth of her skin, in wanting her to feel better, to feel good. He said, "Tell me."

He could feel her gathering her strength, and she took a deep breath. Even in the low light he saw her open her eyes. Brave. She was always brave.

"It was…it was good to feel…" She paused, shook her head. Then she made a decision, and looked up. "Roman, with you, I felt it. It felt right, like I could be that part of myself again, that I could submit, even for a little bit… Please don't apologize. I needed to know that. I needed to know that he didn't permanently fuck up that part of me, even if it wasn't…even if it wasn't real."

Roman didn't immediately register the source of her sadness. That last phrase: "wasn't real." Did she think…?

"What are you saying, it was not real?"

Lola bent her head, this apparently too much,

even for his fiery Lola.

"This is a show, Roman, I know that. This isn't... You don't have to explain, I get it."

Roman growled, angry that a man had hurt her so badly that she couldn't think that he would want her for her, that any man would, that she didn't know how beautiful she was, that she didn't know that she was a light in the world for him. That he had never shown her that he wanted her, and allowed her to think of herself as unwanted.

He would correct that now.

"This is real," he said, and placed her hand on his painfully hard cock. "This is for you. All for you. Only for you."

She looked up, her eyes wide, her hand unmoving. He ached underneath, had ached for her for days, for years, it felt like, all of it pulsing through his body like a twisted drug. He needed her. He needed to be inside her, or he would lose his mind.

Slowly he saw the light return to her eyes, saw the sadness recede, to be replaced by that mischievous fire. A new thought: maybe he needed to do this for her. He was worried about sex hurting her, but it was hurting her to lie, and to pretend he didn't want to fuck her senseless.

She stroked him through his pants and he groaned.

"All for me?" she said.

"You were taunting me out there," he said, knowing he needed to get the words out before all the blood left his brain. "Goading me."

"Yes," she said, and stroked harder. "But I knew you'd never go through with it. You'd just go on protecting me. But I haven't needed protection in so, so long Roman…"

He snapped. Pinned her to the wall, kissed her hard. Barely let her catch her breath before he'd lifted her over his shoulder, stepping over a shoe that fell to the ground, not caring even the slightest, and carried her back to his private apartment.

## *chapter* 7

Lola was on fire by the time Roman threw her down on his bed. The look he gave her — pure animal hunger — only made her crazier. She stood up, wanting to strip his suit off, wanting to finally be next to his naked body, and forgot all about his Dom side.

He pushed her back on the bed.

She shivered and looked up at him. Daring him to come at her.

He answered by bending down, looking her in the eye, and ripping her dress off her shoulders. Another vicious pull, another tear, and she was naked, her clothing in tatters.

She moaned, grabbed his arm, tried to drag him down on top her. He smiled at how ineffectual she was; it was like pulling at a mountain. With no apparent effort he pulled her up next to him, and then down over his knee as he sat on the bed.

"What—" She struggled.

"You taunted me," he said, his arm moving across her back, pinning her flat to his legs. His cock pressed up against her belly through the thin fabric of his pants and she writhed against it. Then his hand was between her legs, steadying her. "Manipulated me."

She stopped struggling, guided only by the throbbing between her legs.

"You're going to punish me," she said. She was laughing a little, delirious and drunk with excitement. She couldn't believe this was actually happening.

"I will spank you," he said, his hand beginning to toy with her, moving around just outside — taunting, the way she'd taunted him. "I wonder if you might come like this, over my knee? I think you might. I think you will like it."

"Oh God, Roman, please…"

"Please what?"

"Please fuck me," she said, covering her head with her hands, her naked breasts pushed up towards her chin. "Please."

He spanked her.

Hard.

The sound of his open hand hitting her soft flesh echoed loudly in her ears, each blow deliciously humiliating, each blow reminding her: this was *Roman*. Oh God, Roman. *Roman*.

In just a minute, she was moaning. Writhing under him, arching up to him, craving him. He laughed, moving his arm so he could play with her breasts.

"I want to see your ass red," he said, and spanked her again.

She really was on the verge of coming.

Without warning he dipped a finger into her, found her hot and wet, and she heard him catch his breath.

Then the growl.

He flipped her over and threw her back on the bed as though she weighed nothing at all. "Stay."

He had his clothing off in no time, and then he was moving toward her, his dazzling bronze skin pulled tight over layers of corded muscle, rippling, coiling, like a wild animal on the verge of frenzy. She wanted to remember that sight for as long as she lived.

"You come when I say," he said, climbing on the bed. "You come when *I* say."

She rose to meet him, and he pushed her down again, gently this time, shaking his head. "I have waited so long to look at you," he said. He slipped a hand under one knee, lifting her leg, kissing her calf, her knee, the beginning of her thigh. He rested his face against her flesh, breathed deeply, and then he looked.

Lola was not shy, she had never been shy; she ran a damn sex club. She had been in any number of scenes, had dominated men, been dominated by them, taught them, let them teach her. She thought she'd plumbed the depths of her own kink, her own desires, and only recently had found herself lacking. Wanting. As though she'd run out, as though she'd been spent, and she'd begun to feel herself a bit of a fraud, running a sex club when she couldn't get off with anyone else. When she couldn't submit, when she no longer felt herself capable of the sexuality she'd once known. She'd mourned it, that loss of who she'd been.

But now Roman Casta looked at her with raw lust, with naked power. Roman looked at her like she was the most beautiful, sexual, desirable woman who had ever lived, and the longer he looked at her like that, the more she remembered who she was.

"I have wanted to see what you look like when you come for so long," he said. He was moving his fingers lightly along her skin, setting her to tingling, like he simply couldn't get enough of the feel of her.

His words finally penetrated the fog of sensation, and she rose up again.

"How long?"

"Always."

His eyes locked with hers, and she knew it was the truth.

"Now lie back and let me see you, Lola," he whispered, "or it will be the crop."

She blinked, and then threw her head back laughing. She hoped it would be the crop. She hoped it would be whatever he chose to use on her, whatever he felt like, whenever —

"Oh God," she moaned, and looked down. Roman still knelt between her legs, one hand smoothing the skin down her leg, towards her belly, the other doing something she'd never imagined possible, his eyes on her face.

"Look at me," he ordered.

His fingers worked the outside of her folds in a steady, pulsing rhythm, stroking pressure, on, off, on, off, finding nerve endings she didn't even know existed, sending streaks of fire through her body. Roman's face grew hungry, hungrier. "Look at me," he said again, and pushed two fingers into her as far as they would go.

Lola arched her back, a small sound escaping her as she remembered to keep looking at him. It was so difficult. He felt so good inside her, so right, that it frightened her, and she wanted to hide from him, wanted to feel this on her own somewhere private, where it was safe.

Roman knew.

"You do not hide," he said, and brushed her clit with his thumb, his fingers curling inside her, moving in and out, in and out, slow and strong. "This first one, I see," he said, and picked up the pace, his eyes intent on her face.

She was helpless.

She felt herself caught up in the tide he had created, her hands clawing at the twisted sheets in time to the ebb and flow, each wave stronger than the last, until finally his other hand came down upon her lower belly while he massaged her g-spot from the inside, and she was overcome.

She came in waves, rising up a little further each time, finally crying out his name as he caught her, his arm around her back, his face close to hers now.

"More," he said, "*more*. So perfect, Lola. So beautiful."

She flung her arms around him, terrified at having just let go. He kissed her neck, her face, her arms, her chest, her lips, until she began to calm down again, until she felt it building in her again. Her hips gave her away, and Roman slowly lowered her back to the bed, kissing a path down her trembling body from her lips to her stomach to her pussy.

"God, I have wanted to taste you," he said, his voice more husky, less controlled. She felt the wet warmth of his mouth surround her clit, his tongue dancing with it, his lips sucking on it. He was relentless. He licked her softly at first, and then, as she started to writhe under him, he seemed to lose himself, devouring her, using his hands, thrusting his fingers into her. A man who knew so much technique abandoned it to pure hunger, and it drove her back over the edge, her thighs squeezing Roman's head, her mouth calling his name.

His name, again.

Lola was breathing hard, opening her eyes to a strange ceiling, her extremities feeling numb. She was bewildered. She couldn't remember when she'd last come so hard.

And then there was Roman, looming above her. Roman, turning her face to his, telling her she was beautiful. Roman, stroking her body as she came down from the peak, not letting her settle, but pushing her back up toward another. She heard herself groan, not using real words, just sounds. She wrapped her arms around him again. She didn't even know what she wanted.

He pushed up so he could look down on her, his hand smoothing her hair away from her damp forehead.

"Tell me," he said, and he rose up, his hands sliding under her legs. He lifted them up, resting them on his shoulders, lifting her bottom almost up off the bed. Lola squirmed, suddenly very aware of his erection, poised there.

"Please," she said.

Not enough.

He bent down, his mouth closing around her nipple, and bit it gently. She cried out, feeling his tongue on her, sucking at her. He came up for air, grinning, and said, "Beg."

Lola looked at him, powerless. He would make her say it.

"Roman…"

He rubbed the head of his cock against her still swollen clit, his grin giving way to that intense hunger. "Say it, Lola."

"Roman, please, I need you inside me," she said, reaching for him, trying to pull him down. "Please."

Roman took her hands in one of his, pinned them up above her head, and leaned forward so the head of his cock was just nestled in her entrance. She whimpered.

"Come saying my name," he said. "Come looking at me."

"Yes," she said, more desperate than she'd ever been, "Just *do* – ahh."

He sank into her, so much bigger than she'd thought, stretching her more than anyone else ever had. She closed her eyes, already forgetting.

"Open," he growled, and pushed in deeper.

Oh God.

She hadn't known how deep he could go, and he lifted her farther off the bed so he could push even deeper into her. His eyes fixed on hers as he pulled out and drove into her, dark, deep pools that she had avoided for so long, not wanting him to see how she felt. There would be no hiding now.

Roman still held her hands in his, his

abdominals expanding and contracting with every long, slow thrust, his breath melding with hers. A single bead of sweat gathered on his brow, and still he held her, helpless, his to fuck, love, break.

"Roman," she said, her voice strangled. So much she couldn't say, all of it contained in that word. Her hips were pushing back at him, the two of them crashing into each other

He bent down, caressed her lips with his.

"Come," he said, watching her eyes.

She convulsed, conscious of the effort of keeping her eyes open, aware of his every stroke, still sure and powerful, responding when he paused in her while she contracted around him, her muscles fluttering, trying to draw him in. Trying to consume him, as much as she could. He let her hands go and she grabbed at his shoulders, burying her face in his neck while she screamed and sobbed at the same time, her body not done.

He kept going.

She saw his face again and he looked how she felt: raw, fevered, delirious. The sight of him like that, of Roman Casta mad and frenzied for her, sent her spiraling up and out of control, and this time when she came, he came with her, emptying himself into her with a long, loud cry.

They lay together like that for a long time, Roman still inside her, breathing hard, his weight on her chest both surreal and comforting.

How long would it take her to come around to the fact that Roman had just fucked her? When would she believe it?

Lola let her fingertips play lightly on his skin,

around his muscled shoulders, the hard planes of his back. They were both still slick with sweat, and growing colder. But she didn't want to move. Didn't want to change a thing.

Slowly, Roman stirred. He swiveled his hips, and she gasped to feel him growing hard inside her.

*Again.*

"More," he said in her ear, and pushed himself up on iron arms. She tried to move her legs, and discovered that she was already sore, but those eyes...

Transfixed.

Still helpless.

His.

"I want you to see," he said, his own breath still ragged. He pulled out, and she looked down to protest, saw his cock covered with both of their juices, huge and hard, and became, momentarily, speechless.

Didn't matter. He knelt down, scooped an arm around her, and pulled her up. His large hands handled her as though they'd always known how to, and that thought brought back all of their history—or lack of it—and she was scared again. She must have gone stiff, because he noticed.

"Shh," he said, and positioned her in front of a hastily constructed stack of pillows. She was on her knees, her weight resting on her ankles, the pillows an inviting stack right in front of her.

"Look up."

There was a full-length mirror angled against the wall, an old fashioned thing with a heavy gilt frame. Lola saw them, together. Herself naked, still somewhat flushed, Roman behind her. His hands moving up her sides and around to grasp her breasts. His lips on her neck, his eyes watching hers.

"I want you to see how beautiful you look," he murmured. "I want you to see this before I make you mine."

She shivered. She didn't know what that meant, coming from him, but the dark look in his eyes suggested this was only the prelude. The gentler, softer Roman. She wanted this—and she wanted what came after.

She saw her half-hooded eyes flutter in the mirror. "Yours," she said.

His weight on her back forced her to lean forward, and she braced herself on the pillows, leaning slightly forward. Roman trailed one hand down the length of her back, leaving gentle shivers in his wake. He cupped her bottom in his hands and lifted her slightly, moving under her. And then he just held her there.

"*Look,*" he said.

She saw his hips move in the mirror just a second before she felt him: he impaled her in one swift, upward stroke. The woman in the mirror threw her head back and keened, riding him while he bent over her, pushing her further down. He bit into her neck, one hand supporting himself on the bed, the other reaching for her hip, and drew her down as he pistoned up.

"Look," he growled, and she picked her head up, tired and full and exhilarated all at once, and saw herself.

She saw Lola getting fucked by Roman, saw him

possessing her, taking her, as though he'd never wanted anything else. As though he'd rather have her than anything else on the planet, at that moment, maybe always.

He growled again, a sound she had come to love, and moved inside her mercilessly, his whole body pumping into hers. She watched herself bloom under him in that mirror, and for the first time in months, she felt like herself.

"Again," he said.

Her body obeyed his voice of its own volition, again and again. The last thing she thought as her mind left her was: This. This is right.


Hours later, Lola eased into wakefulness, various parts of her body protesting more than others. She was sore. There was light glinting off of something, directly in her eyes. She moved and stopped: holy shit she was sore.

It came back to her in a slow trickle, and then all at once, in a flood.

Roman.

Oh God, she hadn't dreamed it. She hadn't dreamed any of that. The party, the lies, the lies becoming true…or not true, but half true. Roman nearly killing Benjamin just for showing up, Roman chasing her down, Roman showing her what she was.

Roman inside her.

She shivered at the memory. And then came the worry: this wasn't any man. Any dom. Only he didn't know it, didn't know how long she'd wanted him, didn't know how this could feel for her.

Or did he? He'd said he'd wanted her always. She hadn't dreamed that, had she?

Lola kept her eyes closed, not wanting to face the day, or the differences she was sure it would bring. But she had to. She had to at least face him. Maybe it wouldn't be so bad. Not so different. Maybe it would work.

She opened her eyes and rolled over to find an empty bed.

And then she remembered: of course, Roman Casta never sleeps with his conquests. Never in the same bed. He'd brought her to his bed, fucked her unconscious, and then left.

She was no different after all. She should have known that. She *did* know that—so why was she so disappointed?

Lola sat up, pulling the soft red sheet with her— not silk, not satin, just some impossibly high thread count cotton. Softer. More comfortable. And of course, red. She looked around the room, taking it in as she couldn't have the previous night, trying hard not to dwell on the fact that he was very much not there.

It was…less showy than his office in Volare proper. Not quite so ornate. The mirror looked like an antique—oh God, the mirror; she couldn't help but remember the sight of him taking her from behind. Looking into it now she saw herself blush, her pale skin reddening to match her unruly hair.

She looked away, saw a dark wood bureau with photographs. An old one, back in Spain: his mother? A grandmother? She thought his parents had died, that he had no family. Another picture, this one of a young, pretty woman, smiling blissfully into the camera, brown hair, blue eyes, an unaccountably kind expression.

*Samantha.*

Lola was very sure now that she was the only woman who'd seen the inside of this room in years. He wouldn't let anyone see that picture. She didn't know what to do with this information. Roman left no clues. He didn't stay to explain.

Lola got up, propelled herself off the bed, wrapping the sheet around her. It hissed as she pulled it from the bed, chasing her as she made a foolish tour of the room, looking for clothing. *No, he destroyed the dress.* She smiled. She'd be able to feel that memory for the rest of her life.

She'd be thinking of this night when she was old and grey. She'd remember it long after she'd forgotten everything else.

"Ok, no time to be maudlin," she said.

If she were any judge by the light streaming in, they had an appointment with a justice of the peace in only a few hours, and Lola did not want to show up for her first wedding, fake and rushed and calculating though it may be, with a head full of confusion and fear.

She needed time to think.

She opened the door, ready to charge through and get changed, and stopped in her tracks.

There was Roman. Asleep on an expensive, uncomfortable looking modernist divan, a piece of furniture that looked more decorative than functional, but that happened to be located directly across from what was undeniably *his* bedroom. The bedroom where he'd fucked her, and where he'd allowed her to sleep. He was sprawled out, barely covered by a fleece blanket, his heavily developed pecs rising and falling slowly in the soft light. He looked peaceful.

She had never seen him like this before, had never seen this side of him. And yet the man she watched while he slept looked like someone she had known, had cared for, forever.

*No. That is a dangerous way of thinking.*

It was just sex. It is always just sex with Roman. And she was not some inexperienced dummy who confused an excellent fuck with love.

"Get your shit together, Lola," she muttered, and proceeded to do exactly that.

# *chapter* 8

Roman came awake all at once, as though he'd only just closed his eyes, and looked immediately at his bedroom door.

It hung ominously open.

She was not there.

She was not anywhere.

He checked the entire apartment, all fourteen rooms and two floors of it, his sense of foreboding growing with every empty, untouched room. She had rifled through her suitcases and used the shower and somehow he had slept through all of it.

And she was gone.

Roman returned to his stupidly expensive divan and sat, running his hands through his hair. He had specifically chosen this spot to avoid this very scenario. He did not want Lola waking up and wondering too long, or having to chase him down. She had fallen asleep—passed out, more accurately—before he'd had a chance to explain, to the extent that he could explain this…situation, and he hadn't been able to bring himself to wake her. She'd looked happy. Content. Peaceful. For the first time in months. So much so that he hadn't realized how accustomed he'd become to lines of worry on her face, to anguished expressions that she thought she'd hidden.

It had made him angry at Benjamin Mara all over again.

He had even thought, for just a moment, of staying. Of letting himself fall asleep next to her. It was the only time he'd considered it seriously, in all the years since…

But he could not, in the end: the risk was too great. Whatever happened, he did not want to lose Lola. Did not want to think of anyone else when he looked at her. Did not want to fill those moments that they had together with grief.

Instead, he'd dragged a piece of furniture halfway across his apartment and fallen asleep like a dog waiting at the end of the bed. And he'd *still* missed her.

He was so preoccupied with these thoughts, with rushing to get dressed so that he wouldn't miss their first fake wedding, knowing that she would be there because she was Lola and she would never fail the people who counted on her, that it wasn't until he was already walking up the steps of the city clerk's office that he allowed himself to think: *Christ, Lola.*

He'd had Lola.

He stood there, frozen, a huge monolithic statue in the way of any number of people on their way to and from demanding jobs, that one thought echoing in his head: he'd had Lola.

He was certain of nothing except one thing: he had to have her again.

Ford was waiting for him outside the appointed room with that same evil grin that Roman had noticed the previous night.

"Where's Lola?" Ford asked, doing his best impression of innocence.

"She'll be here."

The grin faded slowly. Ford stepped closer, his voice lower.

"Roman, did it go badly? Did something happen?"

Roman stared at him. There was no way to answer this, not without talking to Lola herself. It had not gone badly for him, of that he could be sure. But his worry for her, and his irritation at her disappearance, grew with every passing moment.

Roman's silence, however, spoke volumes.

Ford stepped back. "Holy shit."

"Do not say anything, Ford," Roman warned. "Do not intrude on her business. Leave her alone unless she asks to talk to you."

"It's not just her business, Roman, or yours. I'm Volare's lawyer. I have responsibilities. Hey—"

Roman brushed past him, unhearing. He'd just seen Lola approach from the other end of the hall, look at him, and dodge into a side door like she was in some screwball comedy.

Not just a side door. A utility closet.

He sighed, and knocked on the door.

"Lola, I know you're in there."

She opened the door a crack, and he stifled a

laugh at her bashful expression. He pushed his way in and somehow managed to keep his face stern. Even in the terrible light of a — a broom closet? Lola was beautiful. She had the look of someone who'd just been caught doing something she shouldn't, and it made him hungry for her. Again.

Well, truthfully, she could read the phonebook, and it would turn him on.

He demanded to know why she was hiding in a broom closet. She evaded, disassembled, avoided his eye. Roman realized they would have to formalize this arrangement. They needed rules, explicit rules, like any D/s arrangement. It had been foolish to have sex without taking care of that first, but it had happened.

Still, none of that accounted for Lola, unflappable Lola, choosing to hide in a broom closet. Lola, frightened. A terrible thought struck him.

"Are you having second thoughts about the arrangement?" he asked bluntly.

"No!"

He should not have felt such relief.

He should have been able to keep himself from touching her.

So many 'shoulds.'

He could do two things for her: give her certainty about their arrangement, and give her something to feel besides fear.

That was when he kissed her. And once he kissed her, he had to have her. His hands seem to move on their own, undoing buttons, stripping away clothing. Her nipples was already hard and pointed, already so sensitive.

"Say it," he heard himself say. "*Say it.*"

Her face, gorgeous and glowing with the flush of excitement, an instant reminder of how she'd looked when she'd come for him the night before, and he thought it had been the most beautiful thing he'd ever seen.

"I'll do anything you want, Roman," she said. "Anything."

She made him *insane*.

He spun her around, her back to him, and pushed her towards the shelves to give her something to hold onto. He could make sure neither of them thought of risks or dangers or fear when they walked into that room. He could make sure she felt only aftershocks.

She felt even better, coming around his cock, than he'd remembered. They both made it through the ceremony with dazed, blissful looks, and it was only as they were leaving that Roman thought: man and wife.

Now it gets complicated.

~ * ~ * ~

"Why does it have to be so complicated?" Lola groaned.

"Wait, wait, wait—you had sex in the broom closet? At city hall?" Stella said. She was gesturing with a fork full of salad while the two of them sat outside at their favorite Italian place. It was unseasonably warm, but it was still March, and they were the only two New Yorkers brave enough (or stubborn enough) to insist on eating outside.

Lola closed her eyes. It was like she lost all

ability to think around Roman, now. Like she'd broached security, and now there was no holding back years of pent up desire.

"Yeah."

"And, just to clarify, this is after you had sex last night? After he threw the Bastard Ben out of Volare? Which, by the way, what the hell with Ben showing up." Stella's expression became grim, but then she remembered the real reason for their meeting. "Holy shit, it's not totally a fake marriage anymore, is it?"

"Hey!" Lola opened her eyes in alarm. She had to stop that kind of talk at all costs. "No, nothing has changed. We're...I don't know. But Roman is still Roman, and if you let me forget that I'm going to get my heart broken, so could you please...?"

"Right, sorry." Stella chewed thoughtfully. "I'll just pretend like that has ever worked, ever."

"Gee, thanks."

"Do you guys have a plan?"

"We're going to dinner tonight to discuss 'terms.'"

Stella's eyes went wide. "Like...a contract?"

"I mean, probably not, you know. So formal. But yes. Those kinds of terms, what else?"

"Actually, I was asking about, like, wedding plans, but what you're doing sounds *far* more interesting."

Lola cringed. Of course she'd been thinking about negotiating the terms of her submission to Roman freaking Casta instead of...well, anything and everything else. "What do you mean, wedding plans?"

Stella gave her a practiced side-eye that said 'I

know you're evading the real issue, but I'm gonna let you do it because you're my friend.'

"Well, your picture was on the gossip sites, and that politician weirdo isn't letting up. This is, like, a public thing. And didn't you say you guys had to do public relations on the whole situation?"

"Yeah. You remember what it was like with the reporters outside my apartment."

"Weeeellll," Stella said with relish, "what's better public relations than a big ol' Volare wedding?"

Lola almost choked on her diet soda. "Are you kidding? Do you know how long it takes to plan a wedding? Ford suggested this, but, I mean. It's not realistic, is it?"

Stella scoffed. "Um, I know *exactly* how long it takes to plan a wedding, it's like all I've been doing. But, I bet I can get my wedding planner to do this on the quick. She'll love the publicity, too. Plus, a Volare wedding? Please—everyone will love this."

Stella was such a picture of innocence that Lola knew her friend was up to something. She know Stella the romantic wouldn't give up on the idea of Lola and Roman living happily ever after, no matter how much Lola tried to convince her that Roman was not interested in real love, and so Stella was probably planning something. Lola was about to object when her phone buzzed with a text message. She grabbed at it, half expecting it to be Roman.

BEN: Lola I'm so sorry. I'm sorry for coming to Volare and...I'm sorry for everything. I wanted to try to explain why I fucked up so badly—you deserve that. If you never want to hear from me again, just say the word. I love you.

Lola didn't know whether to cry or to scream.

"So is that Roman?" Stella said, smiling over her straw.

Lola blinked, shook her head. "No, it's nothing." She looked up, and it was obvious Stella didn't believe her, but this just was not something Lola could talk about while still holding it together. She was just stretched too thin—the combination of Roman and Ben was *still* more than she could handle. She wasn't ready to think about all the ways Ben's betrayal had hurt her, not when she had this new danger in her love life.

Roman.

Lola forced a smile and said, "So tell me about this wedding scheme."

~ * ~ * ~

Roman did his best not to grin as Harold Jeels inspected his brand new marriage certificate. The redder Jeels' face became, the more Roman struggled not to smile.

Eventually he stopped struggling.

"Everything satisfactory?" Ford asked. Jeels grunted.

They were meeting in Ford's midtown office this time, Roman preferring that Jeels not get anywhere near Volare or Lola if it could be helped. There was something about the man's obsession with Volare that made Roman very wary—Jeels obviously considered his crusade to be a personal one, and that meant he was crazy. Crazy people were dangerous, and this crazy person had Lola in his sights.

Still, it was fun to see Jeels lose his temper.

"This is outrageous," he sputtered.

"No, it's legal," Ford pointed out.

"This is an obvious attempt to circumvent regulatory issues. It's dated *today*. It's a fraud. You only married that woman—"

"Mr. Jeels," Roman said, standing up to tower over the angry politician, "Watch how you speak of my wife."

The silence was frosty. Roman didn't often make conscious use of his physical stature to intimidate other men; he felt it was beneath him. This time, he made an exception. Let Jeels feel as small as he was.

"You have lost, Mr. Jeels," Roman continued, buttoning his suit coat. "Whatever fixation you have with the society I have founded, and with my wife, is your own business. But I promise you that if you try to hurt either Volare or Lola again, I will make you suffer."

"Are you threatening me?"

Roman stared at him. In different circumstances, Roman might have tried to help a desperately unhappy little man such as this. Jeels was one of those men who projected his dissatisfactions and fears onto the world around him and then spent their lives fighting shadows and leaving innocent casualties in their wake. In different circumstances, Roman would have pitied him. But he had gone after Volare. He'd gone after Lola.

"Get out," Roman said.

Jeels cowed, his face twisted up in fury. Without another word he waddled out of Ford's office.

"You know," Ford said, "it is, technically, my office that you just threw someone out of."

Roman rolled his neck, surprised to discover that he was quite tense, and turned back to his old friend.

"Yes, but we won, so it is unimportant, no?" he said, moving to make himself a drink.

"Actually, no. Very important."

"How?"

"Roman, this isn't over." Ford got up and joined Roman at the little-used wet bar. "Fuck it, it's a special afternoon. Here, try this, it's single malt."

"Why do you say it isn't over? Lola and I are married — we won. Over."

Ford sighed, swirling his whisky. "So you know my firm does some lobbying work in Albany?"

"Yes, one of the many reasons we hired you."

"That, and I donated the St. Andrew's Cross," Ford said smiling. "My Albany contacts say Jeels was getting support from another state senator who's got a serious primary challenger. If they want to make Volare into a political issue, they don't need ridiculous laws to do it. They can go after health certificates, zoning, whatever the fuck they want."

Roman frowned. "You think this is what will happen?"

"I know."

"So what do we do?"

"Politics is about public perception," Ford said. He had that hard look in his eye that told Roman he was ready to fight. Roman liked that look. "You win public support, and you don't become a punching bag during a political campaign."

"Public support for a sex club?" Roman laughed.

"It's not as crazy as it sounds. You do all that charity work, you're married now, and…"

"And?"

"And people love weddings. I've already gotten press requests. Here, check this one out."

Ford handed him a slip of paper—*Denise Nelson, Tattle*. The biggest gossip site to rival *Sizzle*. Roman thought he recognized the name. Nelson would be a pretty brunette who always looked like she was hunting something or someone.

"You can even use the opportunity to talk up the second Volare location," Ford continued. "Speaking of which, have you talked to Lola about that yet?"

Roman frowned. No. It wasn't something he particularly wanted to bring up. His plan to move to L.A. to set up a second Volare location, while leaving Lola in charge of the New York club, seemed less and less workable by the day. It simply didn't sit right with him, and yet he hadn't come up with an alternative—even though construction on the L.A. club was already nearly completed.

So. A publicity wedding, a political minefield, and cross-country moves.

"No," Roman said, finishing his drink. "Lola and I have more important things to discuss at the moment."

Like the terms of her submission.

# *chapter* 9

Lola perched nervously on a stool at El Sol Vermell and ran her finger up and down the stem of her wine glass. This was Roman's place. He'd picked it, sent her the address, time, everything. It was hidden in a side street on the Lower East Side, the part that had been long gentrified and was full of money, right next to the parts that, well, weren't. It had lanterns hanging out front and a low-key, fashionable sort of crowd — a crowd that didn't include Roman, yet.

She had spent the day hanging out with Stella, afraid to return to her own apartment because of reporters, which pissed her off, and afraid to go back to Roman's place because, well, Roman. If she saw him in the privacy of his apartment, she was a goner, no questions asked. She hadn't been able to resist him in a freaking broom closet at city hall. Her only, minuscule hope of having a substantive discussion was meeting him in a public place.

And in the end, that might only make it worse.

She shivered, already enjoying the thought. That was not a good sign.

They were supposed to meet to discuss, as Roman had put it, the terms of her submission. Lola was no stranger to D/s, nor to relationship contracts, but she was a stranger to Roman in those contexts, and she found, to her chagrin, that it made her feel like an inexperienced virgin all over again.

"This is stupid," she muttered into her wine.

They needed to discuss a lot more than the terms of her submission. He was kidding himself if he thought that was all that was on the menu. Their relationship had evolved—hell, it hadn't evolved, it had wandered into some radioactive goo and sprouted wings. And Lola needed to know what that meant.

Or at least, she thought she did. Maybe. The deeper she got into that glass of wine, and the more she thought about Ben's text, the more she wondered if what she needed was more emotionally baffling men in her life. More men that didn't appear to respect her until after they'd screwed up, who thought it was ok to keep secrets.

How is it possible that both the men in her life didn't seem to respect her at all? Did she somehow make that easy for them?

And oh, God, how was she supposed to *submit* to Roman when she couldn't be sure about that? Never mind that she'd had no problem with that the other night. Or earlier today. She obviously wasn't in full control of herself around him, and there was no way she could do this under those circumstances. She didn't understand why she was able to submit to him if she couldn't trust his feelings, or her own. She just couldn't handle it if yet another man treated her like...

"Lola, where are you going?"

She had left a twenty and jumped down off her uncomfortable stool, totally ready to leave and go do some serious drinking / thinking at Stella's place, and...there...was...Roman.

Like an immovable, muscular wall of hot.

"Oh shit, I think I'm tipsy," Lola said, steadying herself with a hand on his chest.

His broad, hard chest.

Roman frowned. God, even his frown was sexy.

"We will have to sober you up first," he said. "I have reserved a private room."

"I only had one glass of wine," she complained. "It...might have been a big glass."

"And what have you eaten?"

"Shut up," she said. She'd had that salad.

His arm stiffened around her waist, and drew her close. She stopped breathing momentarily, and that heated feeling swept over her. "No, Lola, you do not tell me to shut up," he said. "And you do not abuse your body. That," he said, leaning down to whisper in her ear, "is *my* right."

Lola thought she would lose it all over again, right there. She closed her eyes and tried to remember all the very rational reasons she'd come up with to avoid this situation, but now she was drawing a blank. Her mind just kept coming back to how good he felt next to her. Stupid mind. Stupid body.

He didn't wait for an answer, but took her hand

and led her right past the hostess stand, where he waved blithely, and kept going. The restaurant was an eclectic blend of Catalan and Japanese—hence the wine, the tapas, the seafood, and the private rooms, or tatami rooms. The rice paper walls were decorated with ink painted scenes from Don Quixote, though Lola was pretty sure that wasn't Catalonian, and there were generous wine carafes, chopsticks, and communal plates on every table. Roman led her to the last room at the end of the hall, far from the noise of the main restaurant area—a veneer of privacy, belied by the rice paper walls.

Roman slid the door aside and gestured. "After you."

He had that look again.

That…look.

She was in trouble.

Instead of the usual flat cushions you'd find in American tatami, these rooms had a series of plush throw pillows, almost like a high end college dorm—like really expensive bean bag chairs, with the usual low table. Lola looked around, puzzled, and then collapse into a cloud of pillows. It was incredibly comfortable.

It was also incredibly suggestive. Like even the furniture wanted her to get laid again.

"Is this supposed to be…Moorish?" she asked, desperate to distract herself. The fabric designs had a definite geometric bent. "Wasn't that, you know? Southern Iberian peninsula?

Roman grinned at her. "Of course you would notice. This restaurant, they are not so…how would you say? Historically accurate, as far as decorating goes."

"Is the food good?"

"Excellent."

He was still looking at her with that same dark intensity. She wanted to look away, but found she couldn't. The man had super powers.

"So we have things to talk about," she said softly.

"Indeed."

A waiter knocked on the wood frame of the ridiculous rice paper walls, and slid the door back. He had another carafe of wine, a basket of fried little seafood critters, and some coffee. He set it down without a word, and Lola downed the coffee, black.

"Good decision," Roman said.

"I figure I should be at my best."

"You are always your best."

Lola squirmed a little on her cushion. She was sitting with her legs folded under her, weirdly modest in front of Roman all of a sudden, and yet still she felt vulnerable. The heat rose from her chest to her cheeks, and she knew she was starting to blush. She was painfully conscious of Roman's smooth skin, his dark eyes, his heavy shoulders straining the best intentions of his shirt. She would not be negotiating from a position of strength if this kept up.

Especially not if he kept saying things like that.

"Roman, this is hard for me," she said. She didn't—couldn't—tell him the full truth. She didn't even know what the full truth *was*. Was she still in love with him? Oh shit, she'd been denying all this time that she'd ever been truly in love with him.

Could she be, if she didn't know him well enough to know what was going on with him now? Had she ever known him well enough?

"It is hard for me too," he said, and picked up a carafe of wine. Lola held her breath, not daring to believe he felt the same way she did, while he carefully aimed a stream of wine into his mouth from a foot or so away.

"Really?" she finally said.

"Yes. It is hard for me to keep my hands off of you. It is hard for me to restrain myself, and keep to my side of this table. It is hard for me not to tear off every dress you attempt to wear."

She stopped breathing.

"Lola, I have a confession to make."

Screw not breathing. She would love to be just not breathing. Now she was negative breathing.

Roman leaned forward, and took her hand in his. He turned hers over, and began to rub her palm with his thumb, his expression one of intense concentration, his touch unbelievably sensitive. "I have wanted you for a very long time. A very, very long time. It has been…inappropriate. Wrong. But I don't care anymore."

Roman held her motionless with his stare — with all the things it could mean. With all the things it reminded her of. He was the most intense man she had ever known, and being on the receiving end of that intensity, even fully clothed, was intoxicating. Lola knew she had to be careful, so careful, and yet it was so hard to remember how to do that. She could already feel her body giving way, no matter how much her mind screamed at her that this was how you got hurt.

Ben really had messed her up. That text had only reminded her of how easy it was to get hurt.

"What does that mean?" Lola managed.

"It means I need to have you," he said very low. His hand closed around hers. "It means I need to have you as my submissive, Lola. I have never wanted anyone the way I want you."

Anyone?

Even his wife?

She couldn't bring herself to say it. The thought alone seemed terrible, something she should banish from her mind. No good could come of thinking that way.

The noise of the restaurant behind them faded away, and left only a pulsing thud in her ears. Her heart was going insane. Her mind was going insane. Her entire body, every nerve ending, every sense, every muscle fiber: all of them screamed YES.

She had to close her eyes.

"I have to know you won't lie to me again," she said. "I know it sounds dramatic, but I just…I can't go through that again."

She opened her eyes to find Roman's classical face screwed up in agony. What had she said? She hadn't—

"You include me with Ben?" he said, his voice rough.

Oh shit. She hadn't meant to make that connection explicit, but, well, Roman was smart. The smartest man she'd ever met. The only one who could match her on the New York Times crossword—and English wasn't even his first language.

Of course he'd figured that out.

"That's simplistic," she said carefully. "But you lied to me about Catie, and the whole Sizzle thing, and after Ben, that's just a really raw wound. I—I don't think I can resist you if you really want me, Roman, but I know that you can hurt me. Please don't."

There was a silence. She couldn't bear it.

She broke first, and said, "Oh God, I'm sorry. I don't know what I was thinking, I don't know what *we* were thinking, obviously this is completely insane—"

She didn't get to finish, because Roman stood up and walked around to her side of table. He knelt in front of her, his hands immediately framing her face, his body heavy over hers, all of it feeling so treacherously *right*.

"Lola," he said. His eyes searched hers, and his voice was thick. "Please, believe me. I lied to you, but because my thought was to protect you. I know that was wrong. *I am sorry*. The idea that I would hurt you…" Now it was Roman's turn to close his eyes. Lola had never seen him like this. She'd never seen him look…devastated.

"I didn't mean you'd done it on purpose," she said.

"*No*," he said, fiercely. "Do not make excuses for my behavior. But what we have done…what we have known of each other…already, it is changed, Lola."

She couldn't hold back any longer. She raised her own hand, her finger tips touching the base of his neck, the dip where his collar bones met. He had changed into a more casual suit, no tie, his collar open.

He was so effortlessly gorgeous.

"Yes," she choked.

"You are my submissive now, Lola, while we are in…this situation. For however long. I do not know. But it *is*, whether or not we acknowledge it. It will keep happening."

His fingers began to move now, tracing the line of her jaw, down to her neck, down the center of her chest, until he met the fabric of her dress — another dress she found she wanted him to ruin.

"Yes," she said.

"Remember you have the ultimate power, Lola," he said, his hand trailing down her stomach, circling back to graze her breast. She closed her eyes, again, and tried to concentrate: she knew that to be true, intellectually, knew that the submissive held the power, the ultimate ability to say no. But did she really believe it, in this case?

Did it matter?

It was her one chance to have any semblance of power in this situation. Because otherwise she was defenseless against Roman Casta.

"Yes," she said, eyes opening, Roman's face hovering over her. Gently, so gently, he was pushing her down amongst the cushions, his body poised over hers. She said more forcefully, "Yes, I will be your submissive. Formally."

"Club safewords?" he said, pushing her flat on her back.

"Red, yellow, green. Yes."

"Hard lines?"

"None."

Roman hissed, and his hands, once gentle,

became rough. He roamed over the surface of her body, clad only in her form fitting cream sleeve dress, as though he was surveying a land that now definitively belonged to him.

He said, "Everyone has hard lines."

"Don't lie to me. Don't...don't be with anyone else."

Roman let his fingers fan out, moving away from her breast to her stomach, the whole of her body available to him as she lay, ridiculously, on those cushions. She was breathing hard, each gasp, each catch of her breath obvious to them both with the rise and fall of her chest. He knew exactly what he did to her.

"Agreed. And for you: you are mine, only. You are *mine*. No one else touches you."

She breathed deeply. She didn't want to admit it, but the idea of Roman with anyone else made her feel sick, and not because of STDs—they both had access to each other's medical records at Volare, and she knew they were both fine, and he knew she was on birth control.

"So, exclusivity," she said.

He slid his hand down the length of her to her thigh, and then up between her legs.

"No one else," he said savagely. "I cannot bear the idea of anyone else..."

His fingers came into contact with her underwear, a thong with this dress, and he cursed just as she arched into him involuntarily.

"What are *these*," he said, already beginning to pull them over her hips. "Nothing between you and me, if I want it. Wear them at your own risk."

He was taking her underwear off. Again. Lola

put her hands up to cover her face, and lifted her hips to help him. She was incredibly turned on, incredibly wet, and somehow ashamed.

"Roman, please, we need terms," she managed to force out.

"We have them."

"I'm not a slave."

"I've never wanted a slave. I want you, beneath me."

Oh, Jesus.

"And this is…this is just sex."

He was silent for a moment. A terrible, terrible moment, when she almost hoped…

"There is nothing 'just' about the sex we have."

She shuddered. Well, that was true.

He came closer, his voice low and urgent. "Lola, do you agree?"

As though there was ever any question. As though she had a choice.

"Yes."

"Good. Now strip."

## *chapter* 10

Lola's eyes flew open. Roman had just ordered her to strip, in a semi-private dining room in a very public restaurant.

"Wait, what?" she said.

His eyes sparkled, and there was a devilish smile at the corners of his mouth. "Take off your dress. I told you this morning that I would punish you for hiding from me. I meant it. You will eat in the nude."

"But we have other things to talk about."

"Being naked does not prevent your mouth from working," he said, smiling in obvious amusement. "In fact, I'm rather counting on that fact, in more ways than one."

"But there are waiters —"

"*Now.*"

The tone in his voice was unmistakable. Even the party in the next room heard it and automatically stopped their conversation. It was the Dom voice, not to be disobeyed.

It made her quiver.

It had been so long since she was on the receiving end of an order like that.

She swallowed hard and said, "Yes, Master Roman." And found that she enjoyed the way it sounded.

His eyes narrowed, and she could tell she'd gotten to him. She liked that even more.

Slowly Lola sat up, letting her red hair fall down around her shoulders. She arched her back and reached behind her to unzip, and saw Roman's eyes immediately drawn to her breasts. He had retreated slightly to give her room, but was still within easy reach of her.

They hadn't touched the appetizers.

She unzipped her dress as slowly as she dared, never taking her eyes off Roman. She wanted to see if the heat built in him the same way it did in her. She wanted to see that he had meant what he said. That she could feel safe, knowing he was as addicted to this as she was.

Her dress fell over her shoulders, and he crushed a pair of chopsticks in his fist.

"Keep going," he demanded.

She tugged the fabric down to her waist, baring her breasts. She paused at his sudden intake of breath, relishing the moment: she was past the point of no return now. A waiter could come by at any moment. The people in the next room could be listening. She was getting naked for Roman in the middle of a restaurant.

"Keep. Going," he said again.

Lola took a deep breath and raised her bottom

up off her legs, just enough to shimmy the dress down to her knees, and then a quick pull and she was naked, but for her shoes.

"Give it to me," Roman said, hand out.

Lola hesitated. He'd have her clothes. No way for her to cover up at a moment's notice, no place to hide.

"I *will* spank you again," he said. "And I will do it here. Give them here."

She handed over the dress.

He smiled, folding the dress neatly and placing it behind him. He looked her up and down very slowly, his face an open display of appreciation.

"My God," he whispered. "I may need to have you photographed."

Lola bit her lip. She could feel her nipples hardening into fine little points, and she was sure she was blushing in more than once place.

"Now, what else did you want to talk about?" Roman said, brandishing the remaining set of chopsticks above the platter of appetizers. It wasn't just fried little fish and crabs, there were cuts of sashimi, figs wrapped in cured meats, and about four things she couldn't immediately identify.

A peal of laughter from the next room cut through the momentary silence, and Lola was suddenly reminded of her predicament. She hadn't ever submitted like this, in public, to anyone. She was unbelievably turned on, but also…frightened.

"Roman," she whispered, "Is this really a good idea? I'm naked, and —"

He silenced her by reaching across the table and pinching her nipple with his chopsticks as though it were just another morsel. It was a sharp sensation, the kind of thing that balanced deliriously on the border between pleasure and pain, and thus intensified both. Her pulse quickened.

"I do not think you have had very good doms, Lola," Roman said. "You are such a natural submissive, and you have not even known it. There has been no one to show you."

"Roman…"

"Yes, they might hear you."

Lola listened: the silence indicated that they had. Hadn't it?

"We said we'd be exclusive," she breathed.

Roman smiled, and tweaked her nipple with the chopsticks. "No one else will touch you as long as I have a say in it, Lola. But I am only human. I will show you off."

Lola felt drunk. She'd chugged coffee, just in case she'd been tipsy, but nothing could sober her up from this. Roman Casta, talking about showing her off. About how much he wanted her. About the things he was going to do to her.

"Lola," he said, beckoning with his free hand. "Come here, and tell me what you wanted to talk about."

She crawled over to him—*crawled*, where did that come from? It was instinctive, naked, on these ridiculous cushions—and he quickly pulled her onto his lap. Her nakedness felt all the more total next to his expensive clothing; it was like an outward expression of their power arrangement. She felt like a coveted possession.

"Um. I wanted to talk to you about an idea," she said. He had threaded one arm around her and had abandoned the chopsticks and appetizers to fondle her absently while she talked. It made talking about even simple things a bit of a challenge. "Stella thinks we should have a big wedding ceremony. For the papers. For publicity."

He was rolling her nipple between his fingers again, and smiling at the evident effect it had on her.

"What a coincidence," he said, not bothering to hide his amusement. "Ford thinks we will have to run a public relations campaign. That should serve both purposes."

"Hmm?"

He dropped his hand to her thighs, and pushed between her legs, flicking at her vulva. She started, and tightened her arm around his neck.

"Roman…"

"Do you agree?"

"What?"

He laughed outright now. "Tell Stella to make it the greatest show on earth. We have to fight a publicity war now. You two can organize, simply give us the dates."

"Sure," she breathed, and moved her leg to give him better access. It didn't matter: he was just torturing her. His finger teased her, grazing her flesh at will, giving her no release.

Some part of her was amazed. Some part of her kept thinking, *He can make you do anything*.

"Give me wine," he said.

She looked around—there were just the specially shaped carafes, like scientific beakers with long spouts. Roman had poured an elegant stream of wine into his mouth from a great distance. Lola didn't want to be outdone.

She picked up the carafe and tipped it from a few feet, pouring the wine in a long arc into Roman's open mouth. She even knew when to stop. She felt somehow even more servile, even more…

His submissive.

"Very good," he said, and the arm he had wrapped around her waist moved briefly to give her a pat her ass.

"You shmuck," she said, smiling.

"You liked it," he countered, and tweaked both her nipples. "There. That's better. I want you to be properly adorned when the waiter arrives."

"The *what*?"

But there was already a knock on the wooden frame. Lola startled like a frightened bird, and looked at the flimsy rice paper door that separated them — and her nakedness — from the rest of the restaurant.

Of course the waiter would be coming by. *Of course*. It was a freaking restaurant.

"I know this place," Roman said.

The door slid open. The young waiter gawked. Roman said, very calmly, very firmly, "Come in and close the door."

Lola clung to Roman. She was simultaneously furious and thrilled. She felt like she was on display — well, not felt *like*, she absolutely *was* on display — and at the same time completely safe. She didn't doubt for a second that Roman would break any number of laws to protect her.

"Give us the Catalan *omakase*," Roman said, handing the speechless young waiter a wad of cash. "And tell the rest of your colleagues not to come by this room, yes?"

The young man, all of about twenty, stared open mouthed at Lola. Somehow it made her feel...powerful. She tightened her grip on Roman's neck, and extend one leg across his lap.

He squeezed her leg in approval.

"Yes sir," the waiter finally said.

"You won't want to draw attention to us, will you?" Roman asked. It was technically a question, but he used the Dom voice. So really, no human mortal could actually question it. Lola smiled into his neck.

"No, sir," quavered the poor waiter.

"Good. Close the door behind you."

Lola heard the door slide shut. The room next door was full of chatter, oblivious to what Lola and Roman might be up to. They were alone.

"Dinner will arrive in twenty minutes," Roman said, unwinding her arms from around his neck and pushing sideways onto the cushions so that she lay down, her exposed pussy facing him. "I want to work up an appetite."

Lola started to protest, but felt his big hands pin her one useful arm uselessly behind her back. She looked back at him, unable to keep herself from smiling. "You are unbelievable," she said.

"You have no idea," he said, unzipping his fly.

"You are really going to fuck me here," she gasped.

"Yes," he said. "And I'm going to fuck you well."

One hand came around her front, greedily fondling her breasts, as he came into position.

"Don't make too much noise," he said with a smile.

And then he pushed into her. She gasped, not quite believing he would do it. He was fucking her sideways in the middle of a restaurant. He expected her to keep quiet, while all of him — *all* of him — thrust into her.

He thrust again, even deeper, feeling larger than he ever had because of their position, her legs nearly crossed in front of her, and she couldn't help it: she cried out.

The conversation in the adjacent room stopped. Lola bit the soft flesh on her upper left arm. Roman pumped harder. He leaned over her, and whispered in her ear.

"If I have to pay more in bribes because you were too loud," he said between thrusts, "I think we will have to do this all over again."

Lola buried her face to keep from crying out, smiling despite her best efforts. No other man had been able to make her laugh and come at the same time.

# *chapter* 11

Roman checked his watch for the third time, and wondered again what Lola was doing.

Rather, he wondered about various ways he could do Lola.

It was *maddening*. Here he was, having lunch with the very pretty, very obviously curious reporter that Ford had set him up with, and still all he could think about was Lola. Lola's eyes. Her legs. Her ass. The way she looked when she came.

"So tell me about your wife," Denise Nelson said.

Roman felt like he'd been hit.

That word — wife. It was a word he hadn't used much in recent years. It was a word that made him think of Samantha. It always took him a moment to realize that now people meant Lola.

"Did I say something wrong?" Denise asked.

"No, of course not," Roman said.

Denise Nelson gave him a long, thoughtful look.

She was sharp—her questions so far had indicated that she knew exactly what the situation was with Harold Jeels, and she knew exactly why Roman had agreed to an interview. She wouldn't be an easy ally, nor would she allow herself to be manipulated. Roman had to make sure that it was genuinely in her best interests to write stories that helped Volare.

He got the sense that she smelled blood.

"You were married before, weren't you?" Denise asked.

Roman tensed. This was exactly the sort of conversation he wanted to avoid. "I do not think that is relevant," he said.

"Of course it's relevant. It was a tragic story."

"You do not think it is poor taste to discuss my late first wife when asking about my current wife?" He was beginning to lose his patience.

"I think it's interesting that when I asked about your wife, you thought of Samantha Casta."

Roman laughed bitterly, even though he felt like he'd just been punched in the gut. He couldn't help it. He'd just wondered how he could get himself to stop thinking about Lola constantly, like it was some sort of addiction, a weakness, and here was a journalist claiming that he couldn't stop thinking about Samantha.

The terrible thing was that he hadn't thought about Samantha as much, since he and Lola… No. Samantha was never far from his thoughts. But it was true, undeniably true, that he hadn't felt the weight of grief and guilt as heavily as he once did. What did that mean? What did that make him?

Why did it take a nosy journalist to point that

out to him?

Roman shifted in his chair. He didn't know what to do with that realization. He felt nauseous with guilt.

Why?

"Have you ever lost someone close to you, Ms. Nelson?" he asked.

"Yes."

"Are they ever completely gone from your thoughts? Do they just vanish?"

Denise looked at her uneaten salad and said, "Fair point. But this is a human interest story, Mr. Casta—"

"Call me Roman."

Denise smiled, the first sign of pleasure he'd seen from her. She was trying too hard to be the hard-nosed journalist, and then in moments like this she revealed...something. Perhaps more than a professional interest in Volare.

"All right, Roman," she said. "Samantha's death is part of the public record, because it was so sudden. There was that inquest. A congenital heart defect, something no one could have known about, if I remember correctly. But there were reports that just before she died—"

"You may call me Roman," he interrupted, "But know that if you ask me about my first wife's death again, this interview will be over, and I will speak candidly with your toughest competitor instead."

The silence fell thickly, leaving Roman's threat hanging in the air between them. This was a very real boundary. He would not tolerate speculation on the circumstances surrounding his wife's death. He did that enough on his own, and he knew the answers would only cause more pain. Nobody else needed to feel responsible, and he certainly didn't want Lola to have to endure this kind of comparison. He could shoulder that burden himself.

Denise nodded her apology, raising her hands in mock surrender. She said, "I thought you hated Sizzle now."

A peace offering.

"I do not have the best of luck with journalists, it seems."

"Maybe I can break your streak," Denise said. She smiled at him over her glass of wine.

Roman sighed. Yes, she definitely had more than just a professional interest. He would have to manage this carefully—he didn't know what the best protocol was when a flirtatious journalist interviewed one's new, fake wife who was also one's new submissive, but he'd better figure it out before he put this woman in the same room as Lola.

*Lola.* Damn. Again, an image came to mind, unbidden: Lola naked, looking at him over her shoulder, while he...

"Roman?"

He shook his head. He couldn't believe it. He'd gone from grieving thoughts of Samantha to...

He was gripped with a sudden certainty: he had to get out this restaurant. He had to find Lola.

He said, "Ms. Nelson—"

"Denise."

Roman rose. "Denise. We will have to finish this interview another time."

"What? When?"

"Soon. And I will make sure Lola is present as

well. You will get a better story that way, no?"

"I don't know what kind of story I'm going to write yet, Roman," she said.

"I hope that isn't a threat."

"No, just a fact."

Roman laughed again, though his mind was spinning. In spite of himself, he liked this woman Denise Nelson. The combination of strength and intelligence reminded him of the two women he could not apparently stop thinking about: Samantha and Lola.

Samantha and Lola. Roman gripped the back of his chair so hard his knuckles turned pale.

"Very fair, Denise," he said, taking her hand. "I promise you will get a better interview."

He didn't wait for a response. He needed fresh air, needed something to ground him, something to put what he was feeling into context. He was already out onto the street, striding up the avenue just to keep moving, barely noticing the other pedestrians who hurried out of his way when his phone rang.

It was a call he had to take.

"Chance," he said.

"Hey buddy, how goes?" Chance Dalton's voice was punctuated by static, a sure sign of a bad connection.

"You have not been keeping up with New York news," Roman said dryly.

"Nah, should I? Listen, I only have a minute, but I wanted to tell you I'm wrapping up here early. I have some maybe big news for you, but I don't want to blow it until I'm sure. Just tell me the L.A. Volare is still on," Chance said.

Roman knew that this was where he should tell Chance about Lola. About the sham marriage. There should be nothing difficult about explaining that situation to Chance.

But that would be dishonest, because it wasn't entirely a sham. He was fucking Lola. He was fucking his best friend's cousin, the woman he'd been charged with looking out for. He was apparently obsessed with fucking her.

It was *still* all he could think about. If he let his mind wander, there she was. Lola. Even when he should be grieving his dead wife, even when...

And that was not something he cared to explain over a difficult satellite connection while Chance was on a break in some desolate warzone, doing God knew what to provide security. That was something he needed to say in person. He could at least give Chance the opportunity to beat the shit out of him.

"The L.A. location is proceeding ahead," Roman said.

It was a lie of omission, the kind that offended Roman the most, since it seemed cowardly, and yet necessary under the circumstances. Roman couldn't imagine leaving Lola in New York under the present circumstances, and yet there was no one else to run the L.A. club.

"Good! We're gonna have to talk about that when I get in."

"When you get in?"

"I'm coming to New York, buddy!" Chance shouted. "I'll see you in a couple of weeks!"

Roman stopped in his tracks, forming an immovable island in the current of New York city pedestrians. The connection was gone; Chance had hung up.

The hunger came upon him like a brutal, unreasoning tide, and he no longer cared that it didn't make sense, or that he should feel guilty about it. Right now, he had to see Lola.

He took off running.

# *chapter* 12

Lola was vaguely aware of a maelstrom of activity around her, with her at the relatively peaceful eye of the storm, but she wasn't paying much attention. Luckily, she didn't have to; the wedding planner Stella had brought in, a tiny blonde woman named Dagmar who never smiled, constantly talked into her headset, and probably could have organized an invasion of Europe in an afternoon if a client asked her to, was a blur of activity. Dagmar and Stella had herded her into some fancy wedding dress place, and were in the process of winnowing down dress choices. They barely needed Lola at all.

Which was good, because Lola had a lot to think about.

Three more texts from Ben.

Each more apologetic than the last.

Each one saying exactly the things she wanted to hear.

Each one begging to see her.

Rationally, she should tell him to go fuck himself. Maybe. On the other hand, Lola had been making herself crazy for months, wondering why he'd done it, why she'd been so easy to lie to, why, why, why. And there had been no answers. She had finally accepted that she would never get any answers.

And then here came Ben, offering to give her those answers.

Maybe.

And she couldn't help but think that maybe if she got those answers, Roman wouldn't be able to drive her so crazy. That maybe, if she got that closure, she wouldn't be so vulnerable to Roman.

Because she was sure feeling incredibly vulnerable.

"Hey, bride lady!" Stella said, waving a hand in front of Lola's face. "You know we're picking out your wedding dress over here, right?"

Lola snapped out of it. She looked down at Ben's last text—*Please just for coffee, you don't even have to speak to me. Just let me apologize*—and thought, *fuck it.*

She typed: *Ok. Coffee.* And hit send.

"Sorry," Lola said. "I just had something I had to take care of. It's not a real wedding, Stella, so, you know. Whatever. Where are we?"

"Dagmar has narrowed it down to a couple of choices," Stella said.

Dagmar's head snapped up from her tablet. "Also you must choose a theme. I will pick location, decorations, etcetera. You leave it all to me. I get press, I get magazine pictures."

Dagmar waved her hand in the air like a

conductor, and went back to her tablet, muttering something into her headset.

A terrible thought occurred to Lola, and she groaned. "Um, guys—I know the point is publicity, but we can't compromise the identities of our members. How...how is that going to work, exactly?"

"Is no problem," Dagmar said, not even looking up. "Mask. Costume. Venice. Carnival."

Stella giggled. "*Eyes Wide Shut.*"

"Very hush hush," Dagmar said, apparently not getting the joke. "Very exclusive. Magazines love."

Lola marveled. The woman didn't even have time to speak in full sentences. "Stella, where did you find her?"

"I know, right? She's like the special ops of wedding planners. She's already picked out something for you to try on. They'll have it out in a minute."

"I don't even need to be here do I?"

Stella smiled. "Well, except for the tiny detail of actually trying it on, no. Hey, listen, you ok?"

Lola tried to laugh it off. "Yeah, I'm fine. Why?"

"I just thought, you know, this wedding stuff, with the way you feel about Roman..."

"The way I *used* to feel," Lola corrected. She even hoped it was true. She had trouble figuring out how she felt about Roman now—her mind usually stopped working completely as soon as she saw him. It was maybe better to just rush ahead and not stop to think too much, like the way circus people ran across tightropes. If she stopped to think, she'd plummet.

*Ok, so keep moving, then. Change the subject.*

"I was just distracted because I keep getting these texts from Ben."

"Oh, honey." Stella gave her a one-armed hug. "Bad?"

"I don't know. He wants to talk."

"Do you?"

"I think so. Is that a terrible idea?" Lola asked. She really had no idea if she was making a mistake.

Stella shrugged. "I dunno, I'm not an expert. I was kind of a disaster before I got lucky and you hooked me up with Bashir. But it does seem like some break ups are tougher than others, and this one is, um, pretty bad. Maybe it's like tipping over a vending machine—you have to give it a few shoves and build up some momentum before it really takes."

"So you're saying talk to him and give him one final shove?"

"Metaphorically," Stella said. Then she thought about it. "Or not. I'm ok with literally shoving him, too."

Lola laughed and gave her friend a big two-armed hug. "You are basically the best, you know that?"

"Tell me that after you go through with this wedding."

"The dress," Dagmar said, looking up from her tablet.

Two smiling assistants had indeed come back with a dress. Lola was overwhelmed by yards of sculptured white silk, afraid to even touch something that pretty. She couldn't imagine actually *wearing* it.

Oh, who was she kidding? Once she put it on,

they'd probably have to knock her out to get it off. She'd try to wear it everywhere if they let her. She'd wear it to freaking Starbucks.

"Oh boy," she said under her breath.

"We help," Dagmar commanded. The assistants left them at Dagmar's insistence, albeit somewhat reluctantly, and Dagmar and Stella went to work. Which was good, because Lola had gone into a weird trance state as soon as she'd looked at that dress.

Which was crazy. It was just a dress. It wasn't magic.

Lola hadn't ever been one to plan her fantasy wedding without having a groom in mind, since it just seemed like a way of tempting fate, but now, in this place, looking at an actual, real life, beautiful wedding dress...

"Lola, you all right?"

"Yup. Fine. Great."

"Let's get this thing on and see how it looks."

She was zipped, cinched, and pinned. Lola took a deep breath—it felt perfect. She'd never worn an item of clothing that had felt this perfect before.

She was totally afraid to look.

"Oh, Lola," Stella whispered, her hands covering her mouth.

"What? Is it wrong? What? Did I rip—"

"Look," Dagmar said gently, and turned Lola toward the bank of mirrors. "It's perfect."

Lola looked.

She never thought she could look like that. Had never really dared to dream of herself, looking like that. The dress was sculptured; form-fitting layers off of one shoulder, an asymmetry that somehow brought out her coloring, her eyes, her hair. Each layer accentuated her curves, turning even her insecurities into assets. The silk almost seemed to glow. She felt like she was looking at a fairytale. Like an actual magical being had created this dress just for her. Like she had been born to wear this dress and have a happy ending.

And it was all a lie.

It hadn't really hit her until that moment. Until she was confronted with the image of what should be the happiest moment of her life, with something she hadn't even been able to admit to herself that she wanted—but the way she felt in this dress, this stupid, beautiful, perfect dress, didn't lie. And it meant that she couldn't lie to herself anymore, either.

She was marrying the right man for the wrong reasons; only he didn't even love her. Couldn't love her. Not the way she loved him.

It was the cruelest lie she could imagine.

"Lola, sweetie, are you ok?" Stella asked.

Lola wiped at her eyes. "I'm fine, really."

"No crying on dress," Dagmar said, patting her arm affectionately. "Is silk."

They thought she was crying from *happiness*.

Well, what could she do? She couldn't back out. She didn't want to back out. And she didn't want to stop having sex with Roman. Or, rather, even though she knew it would be good for her to stop having sex with Roman—probably—there was no way in hell she could actually stop. She didn't even have the strength to try. She didn't *want* to try.

In a situation like that, what was she supposed to do?

"I've got to get this out of my system," she muttered. "The next time I see Roman, I—"

"Lola."

All three women turned to see what man had invaded this very feminine place. But Lola recognized the voice. Lola would always, always recognize that voice.

Roman.

~ * ~ * ~

Roman was stunned speechless, except for one thing: he could still say her name.

"Lola," he repeated. He didn't even care that Stella and some other woman were staring at him like he had just escaped from the asylum.

He couldn't tear his eyes off of Lola.

Lola, in that dress.

He knew people used words like "radiant," and "glowing," and "gorgeous" all the time, but those people had never seen Lola like this. She looked as though she had been born for this moment. As though she had been made for him, and this was the proof.

He shook his head, bewildered. He had come here because he needed to be near her. Had needed to feel what he felt when he was near her, to have some sense of familiarity, some sense that things were still in control, even though their sexual relationship felt anything but. Because the truth was that Lola was the most important woman in his life, and had been, for a very long time. The idea that that might change by the choices he had made…

Except he'd never really felt like he'd made a choice. He felt like he'd been pulled along, compelled by forces outside of his control. Like his attraction to this woman he should never have had was a force of nature. For a Dom, this was a terrible thing.

He'd wanted to feel in control again. He'd wanted to feel like he knew his own mind, like he understood what existed between them, and the only way to be certain, in that moment, was to be near her. So he'd called Bashir, found out what Stella had planned, and tracked her down.

The sight of Lola in that white dress, her red hair spilling over her shoulders, her eyes wide and shining, her lips parted in surprise...

He wasn't in control. He wasn't in control at all.

"Everyone else leave," he said.

"No, no, no," a tiny blonde woman said, looking back at her tablet. "Is bad luck!"

"Get everyone out *now*," he said, his voice a crazed, wild version of his Dom voice. "Close the store. Charge me for the day. Get. Out. Now."

He hadn't taken his eyes off of Lola. In his peripheral vision, he saw Stella herding the blonde woman out, whispering to the shop girls, followed by some opinionated arguing, and then it all faded away. He heard a door close.

He heard Lola catch her breath.

"I was just thinking about you," she said.

He didn't have words. Didn't really know what he was feeling, only that it was strong. Only that he needed — *needed* — to touch her.

The closer he got, the more he felt the pull: this woman, his, *now*.

"Roman…" she said.

He stopped. With the remaining self-control he had left, the most he could manage was to pause for just a moment. He knew he'd come here with a more coherent purpose, with an actual idea, but it all faded away in the light of Lola standing before him.

Lola's words failed her. She looked at him helplessly and shook her head, ever so slightly. Then she reached out for him.

Roman broke.

He pulled her hard and fast against his body and kissed her. She kissed him back, harder, hungrier, and it drove his own need higher. Neither of them wanted to speak; Roman didn't even want to tear himself away long enough to breathe. She ran her hands through his hair, he pawed at the back of her dress, *that dress*, that thing that made him think…

No, he wouldn't, couldn't think: he had her in front of him. That had become the only important thing in the world.

It came off so easily.

She stepped out of it. He ripped at her underwear. Bent down, lifted her up. She clung to him as he carried her to the leather bench in the center of the room, surrounded by mirrors; he only pulled away to free his cock.

He thrust hard inside her, and they both shuddered with relief. He felt calmer now that he was inside her again, more right with the world: he built up a rhythm, long, deep strokes that had her rising to match him, her hips coming off the bench while her hand cradled his face. He looked down to see her muscles straining with him, sweating with him, and wondered how he'd ever gone without this.

"Roman," she whispered. He couldn't even speak. Just drove into her more and more, desperate to feel her come around his cock.

"Look at me," he said as she came. She did, and it leveled him.

# *chapter* 13

"Roman, you're a mess."

Roman glared at Ford. He had not come here for a makeover. Or an opinion, for that matter. He'd come here to talk about the logistics of the L.A. Volare expansion.

"Not relevant," Roman said brusquely.

"Bullshit it's not relevant. What the hell is wrong with you?"

Roman ran his hands through his hair. "I haven't slept well lately," he admitted.

His physical need for Lola had become all-consuming—she was never far from his thoughts, and if he thought about her for too long, he would inevitably have to have her. He had tracked her down while she was trying on wedding dresses. That was not normal behavior.

His reaction to her, in that dress, had not been normal behavior.

It had been like flashing red in front of a crazed

bull. He had not wanted to think about why.

It was not a sustainable state of affairs for a professional man. It was even worse for a man who couldn't allow himself to fall asleep in the presence of a woman, any woman, because of what would inevitably happen when he woke up. He only wanted good things with Lola. He didn't want to associate that terrible grief with her, not even once, and yet he couldn't bear to be far away from her, so he slept on that stupid couch.

The result was that he couldn't remember the last time he'd had a good night's sleep.

It was unlikely he would have been able to sleep much, anyway. A few hours away from her and he became hungry for her again. It was insane. He had taken the overindulgence approach, thinking that if he had Lola as much as humanly possible, it would sate him. They would work it out of their systems, and their lives could return to some semblance of normality.

In his case, that had been a grave miscalculation: it had only made things worse.

"Are you sure you're all right?" Ford asked.

"No, but it does not matter," Roman said. "You were reviewing the requirements for the expansion site with me."

He felt Ford's eye on him and rolled his neck, feeling the pull of each individual muscle on his back and shoulders, already wanting to get out of here and get back to Lola. Jesus Christ, this could not be healthy. Roman didn't even know if Lola was as perturbed as he was; by tacit agreement, they didn't speak of it. They both pretended this level of physical chemistry, of *need*, was normal.

Roman knew it was not.

"Ford, ignore whatever you are thinking, and get on with it."

"Sure, you're the boss. Everything's set to go, whenever you can pull the trigger. The major issue right now is whether this political situation with Senator Jeels is stable enough for you to leave Volare NY in Lola's hands while you go to L.A."

Roman winced.

"You still haven't talked to Lola about this, have you?" Ford said. "Damn, Roman, this is not like you. What the hell is going on? Ever since the two of you—"

"Don't, Ford," Roman said, collapsing into the chair opposite Ford's desk. "It doesn't matter so long as Senator Jeels continues to make our situation unstable, yes?"

"Yeah. How is that going, by the way?"

Roman shrugged. "Stella and a wedding planner are making the ceremony a publicity event. I gave that reporter an exclusive, so she is happy to be the only one with access. Exclusive photographs, all of that."

"Good idea. You doing an interview?"

"Eventually," Roman said. He had made that promise. And he'd promised that Lola would do it, too.

"That doesn't quite settle everything, though. We need more."

"You have private investigators, yes?" Roman said. "Hire them. Send them after Jeels. I do not want this man posing a threat."

He finished the sentence in his head: *to Lola*.

"Understood," Ford said. "But if you want my

advice, as a friend? You need to talk to Lola about moving to L.A., and you need to do it soon. You can't just spring that on her, Roman."

Roman nodded. The trouble wasn't that he didn't know how to tell Lola that he would be moving to L.A., leaving her in New York to run the original Volare club; the trouble was that he no longer wanted to go to L.A., or anywhere in the world, without her.

And he didn't know what that meant.

~ * ~ * ~

Lola stacked packets of sugar into little piles, little forts, little castles. Then she knocked them over and did it all over again.

She was early. She was early because she was nervous. She was nervous because she had started to think, more and more, that she was making an incredible mistake.

"It's just coffee," she said to herself.

The smarter part of her brain screamed, *No, dummy, it's coffee with the man who said he loved you, and showed it by screwing his ex.*

But she had to figure this out. As she'd explained to Stella, she had to confront this, get some kind of closure. Maybe then she'd get over this thing with Roman.

"How does that make any sense?" Stella had said. "What does Roman have to do with Ben?"

"It's complicated," Lola had answered.

Now, sitting in this coffee shop, waiting for Ben to walk in and fuck with her head, Lola wondered if she was lying to herself — again. The thing was, she had no ready explanation for what was happening with Roman. It was as though they were both incurably addicted to each other, to the point where Lola seriously wondered if she were just filling some vacancy, tending some wound, with sex. Not just any sex, though — sex with Roman.

There was nothing else in the world like it.

She was willing to bet there had *never* been anything else in the world like it.

She had never felt closer to the man, or farther away. They had stopped trying to articulate things with real, actual words, had just reverted to madly tearing at each other's clothing when alone. They at least understood each other physically. But Lola was almost grateful that neither of them could ever seem to find the words to express what was happening, because she didn't want to think about what it meant that Roman would never sleep next to her. And she didn't want to have to think too hard about her own feelings, especially after what happened in the dress shop.

"This can't last," she said to herself.

"I have to agree. It doesn't look too architecturally sound."

Lola looked up and the latest iteration of her sugar packet fortress crumbled. Ben stood over her, his hands in his pockets, sandy colored stubble on his chin.

"Hi," he said.

Lola took a deep breath. "Hi."

"Thank you for meeting me," he said, and sat down across from her.

It was such an uncharacteristically Ben thing to say, and in such an uncharacteristic tone for him, that it threw Lola off. Ben wasn't such a natural Dom all the time the way Roman was, and so it wasn't ever something he took casually. He was usually so deliberate in his intentions, so careful— which was maybe why she'd been able to trust him in that role.

*And that turned out to be a huge mistake*, she reminded herself.

Sitting across from him, looking into his sandy blond hair and his disarming blue eyes, Lola remembered why she had *wanted* to trust him in the first place.

"You look uncomfortable," he said.

"I'm wondering if this was a mistake," Lola admitted. She was feeling queasy. The last time she had seen this man, apart from his stunt at Volare, he had been balls-deep in his ex-wife, on a night when she had planned to take him to dinner. He had left the front door open at his apartment, almost like he wanted to get caught. Now Lola watched him take a sip of his coffee and remembered looking around his apartment for bottles after that night, even half-full glasses, anything that might say he was only cheating because he'd started drinking again. She'd felt terrible about it later, but at the time she'd just wanted there to be a *reason* besides "he doesn't give a shit about you."

"Lola, please," Ben said, leaning forward. "Please let me try to explain—"

The word "explain" made her see shades of red. She said, "You know what? There's really no way to excuse—"

"Shit, that's not what I meant." Ben pinched the

bridge of his nose the way he did whenever he needed to concentrate. "I don't want to make excuses. I just...I meant that I wanted to try to explain *why* I fucked up so badly, just to make sure that you knew it had nothing to do with you. That it was me. All me. And that I'm more sorry for this than I ever have been about anything in my entire life."

He looked at her, his eyes pleading. And he was saying things that, truthfully, she was desperate to hear, because no matter how many times she told herself that it wasn't her fault, there was always some part of her that wondered. She knew it was stupid. But hearts were stupid. And hers was still seriously damaged.

"Ok," she breathed. "Shoot."

Ben sighed, and gave her a tired smile. "This is harder than I thought."

"I'm not all that sympathetic to that, Ben. I really—"

"You are the most amazing woman I have ever met, Lola," he said, his blue eyes clear and steady, refusing to let her go. "Every day you blew me away, and every fucking day I couldn't believe I was so goddamned lucky as to even know you. That you would look at me, and smile. That you said you loved me, too. Christ, Lola, it felt like I was dreaming. I felt like it was a miracle that you could love a fuck-up like me. And the longer it went on... No, Lola, please don't cry. Look at me."

He reached out to touch her face, and she jerked back.

"No, Ben."

He didn't get to comfort her anymore. He didn't

get to be the one to tell her things that made her feel good about herself, or at least less badly, even if she so desperately wanted to believe them. It wasn't fair.

"I'm sorry. Lola, I am so, so sorry. I did this—I know I did this. Apologizing and taking responsibility is part of my recovery; I've been talking about it in group—"

"Did you start drinking again?" She felt terrible asking. Would that make it better, if he'd broken her heart as part of a relapse? Or worse?

"No," he said, shaking his head. "But I think that's why I...did what I did. I was so sure that I was going to fuck up eventually, Lola, I was so sure I didn't deserve you, that I sabotaged everything. I just...I couldn't take it."

Lola wiped at her eyes, willing herself to stop crying. Why was she crying? She should be past this, over this. Done.

This man shouldn't have the power to make her feel anything anymore.

"Why did you come to Volare?" she demanded, taking refuge in anger. "Why?"

Ben at least had the decency to look ashamed. "Because I saw your picture online on a gossip blog. It said you were marrying Roman. I...couldn't believe it."

Lola leaned back and just stared at him. Ben looked miserable. He looked like he hadn't slept in ages, like he hadn't shaved, like he hadn't taken care of himself at all.

"Is it true?" he asked. "Are you two really...?"

"It's none of your business," she answered. Besides, it's not like she really knew the answer herself.

"Please don't take offense at this, Lola, but I have to disagree."

There was a silence between them while Lola checked and double-checked what she'd heard.

"You *what*?" Lola finally said.

"It *is* my business. I might not have any right to any of this, but the fact is, Lola, I love you. I'm not going to stop loving you just because I screwed up. And that makes it my business. I just wanted you to know that I *know* how wrong I was, that I know what I've lost, that I know you are the most amazing woman who ever lived. That I want to make all that up to you. That I want to fight for you."

Ben rose, taking his coffee cup with him. Lola was speechless. Angry, shocked, ashamed that she was glad to hear some of it, and speechless.

"At the very least, Lola," Ben said, rising from his seat, "I want to make sure you know that you deserve the absolute best in everything. And that includes a man who will protect you from idiots like Harold Jeels, making those dumbass statements to the papers, especially when protecting you from him is so goddamn easy to do."

"What?" Lola said, truly confused. He was throwing a lot of curveballs all at once, but this one needed special attention. "What are you talking about, 'easy to do?'"

Ben leaned down and chucked her under the chin. "I can't believe you don't recognize him. You don't remember Harold Jeels from the scene before you joined Volare, all those years ago? That man is a switch, and he likes his leather. Someone's got to have photos. I'll be seeing you, Lola."

He gave her a two-fingered salute and walked out.

## *chapter* 14

"You look distracted," Jake Jayson said.

He was not the first person to mention this to Roman. It was starting to become annoying.

"A lot on your mind?" Jake continued. He was smiling.

"What are you smiling about, Jacob?" Roman snapped.

Jake laughed out loud as they walked through the Volare lounge, sparsely populated at this relatively early hour. Roman had come by to check on the operation of the club, something he'd asked Jake to watch over while Roman and Lola dealt with the wedding preparations, Harold Jeels, the publicity push—and while Roman secretly dealt with the preparations for the LA location. Jake was eager to do it; he had time on his hands while his fiancée Catie visited her grandmother in California.

"I'm smiling because not a few months ago, you laughed at me when I had the same look on my face, and for the same reason."

There was no question; Jake Jayson was relishing this. The heir to an industrial fortune who had devoted himself to charity had, a few months previously, found himself a pawn in one of Roman's better plots. Roman had set him up with Catie without informing anyone that Roman knew Catie to be working undercover for a gossip magazine. Roman had been confident that Jake would be the Dom to get Catie to open up, and he'd been right—the result was an engagement.

Of course, the *Sizzle* article—and Lola's fury— had been collateral damage. And, as Roman recalled with a grimace, Jake hadn't been thrilled about being left out of the loop, either.

"You did not have Lola to deal with," Roman finally said. Then something clicked. "What do you mean, 'the same reason?' It's hardly the same situation."

Jake stopped, his hand on the door that led to the Volare performance space, and looked at Roman with something akin to disbelief.

"Incredible," he said, shaking his head. "See if you say the same thing in a couple of months."

Roman glowered. He would let it go. At the moment he had too many other things on his mind—namely, Lola. He was used to being able to easily see how the pieces in any given puzzle would fit together, and for this reason the various situations surrounding the future of Volare didn't worry him. They occupied him, but they did not worry him.

Lola was another matter.

"What is this?" Roman said, gesturing at the

stage. There were a number of people bustling about, doing hurried bits of choreography, blocking out steps, coordinating lighting effects.

Jake grinned. "A burlesque show from L.A. They come highly recommended."

He had really been out of the Volare loop.

"I've been busy," he said.

"Yes, with your wedding."

Jake was one of the few people who knew the origins of the fraud marriage, which made that comment…annoying. "Yes," Roman said, "with the publicity campaign."

"It seems as though Lola has forgiven you for lying to her about Catie."

"We have reached a kind of…working détente."

Jake laughed out loud again, an unusual display of emotion from the normally reserved man. "Is that what you're calling it?"

Roman clenched his jaw and reminded himself, over and over, that this was a good friend, and that he probably deserved some teasing for what he'd put Jake through. Over, and over.

Roman took a deep breath. At least he did not have to worry about the operation of Volare while both he and Lola were concerned with other things — Jake obviously had it under control.

Control. Or lack of it — that was really the issue.

That was what bothered him the most. It was not only unlike him; it was unlike Lola. They were both too responsible to engage in the sorts of risks they were taking; they had stopped communicating like adults, and simply gone after each other like animals. In a D/s relationship, that was suicidal.

Jake clapped his friend on the arm, startling

Roman out of his reverie. It happened more and more now: he'd be thinking about the situation with Lola, and he'd get lost in it. He shook his head, grumbling angrily.

"It's good to see that you're human, Roman," Jake said, only half-joking. "Maybe this is all for the best."

With that, his friend left him to go speak to a woman wearing only creatively placed pasties.

Roman stood motionless, held rigid in a sort of shock.

*Human.*

Why did that reverberate? Why did that make him think of Samantha?

He exploded from his rigid stance, moving with such sudden speed and determination that he turned the heads of several nearby dancers. His nostrils flared, his heart thudded, and his arms coiled as he opened and closed his fists.

He rarely made mistakes, and he was rarely unaware of it when he did, but he couldn't shake the feeling as he strode through Volare on the way to his apartment that he was losing himself to this blind, raging bullish lust. Right now, he had to find a way to reestablish proper boundaries with Lola. He had to find a way to establish control.

He had to find out what the hell was happening to him — to both of them.

~ * ~ * ~

Lola took her time walking back to Roman's — Christ, she thought of it as *Roman's* now instead of Volare — figuring she needed the time to think.

Thinking didn't help.

No matter how many times she went over the facts, it didn't change them.

She rode the private elevator up to Roman's apartment, one thing in particular on her mind: Ben had told her there was an easy way to get Harold Jeels off their backs. Which was great—for Volare. Lola wasn't totally comfortable with the idea of using someone's private BDSM activities against them, but it was nice to know there might be a way to protect themselves if it came to that.

But if Harold Jeels was no longer a problem, and they no longer had to pretend to be married, what would happen to her and Roman? Would they just…stop?

She had no idea—it wasn't like she had any idea what Roman was thinking.

It bothered her when she wasn't with him. It was like everything they once were was subsumed in this physical relationship. Roman had never been an open book, but she'd felt like she'd known him—known him well enough to love him. Now the closer they got physically, the more remote he seemed, and the less she knew how to approach him at all.

She definitely wasn't prepared for him to be sitting at one end of the immense kitchen counter, waiting.

Waiting for her.

Lola froze, stunned all over again by the feral male beauty of the man. He was still, his eyes burning with that intensity she'd come to expect. She'd never figure out how he did it, but his stare held her motionless, like a hunter cornering his prey. He only sat, his back perfectly straight, his muscular frame perfectly outlined by his crisp white shirt, his dark skin almost golden in the warm afternoon light.

Lola licked her lips. She knew he was waiting for her to speak, to ask, to serve. Everything about him exuded dominance.

"Have you eaten?" she asked. "I could cook something."

He didn't answer, merely raised an eyebrow. They'd only eaten take out, sometimes not even together, since she'd "moved in." Her offer to cook him dinner was the first suggestion of domesticity, of...marriage. Of normal people marriage. What the hell had made her do that? She hadn't even thought about it; it had just come out.

Oh God, what was he thinking? Why did she want him again already?

"Roman, maybe we should talk."

He rose suddenly, exhaling in one long, slow breath. He had her pinned with his eyes; she hadn't moved. Hadn't even put down her paper coffee cup.

"Agreed. After."

"After?"

"Come here."

She started walking before she could even think. Her body belonged more to him than it did to her.

Did he know?

Did he like it?

The closer she got to him, the more she felt it: that familiar charge, the thing that started to invade her brain whenever they were close. Her breathing was shallow, her skin warm, her pussy already moist. Whatever he did to her made her more aware of her body than she'd ever been. She felt every motion, every breeze, every casual brush of fabric…

He stood by the end of the brushed stainless steel counter, his eyes dragging her in close. Lola wasn't short, but he towered over her. His sleeves were rolled up, exposing muscular forearms and large hands. His top button was undone, the top of his chest visible.

She reached out to touch him.

He grabbed her hand.

"I did not give you permission to touch me," he said.

Lola snapped to attention. That was… She recognized that. That was formal. That was domination. That was controlled, not the impulsive ferocity of animal Roman.

She almost groaned, fighting against it. She just wanted him *now*.

"Look at me," he ordered.

She did. His jaw was clenched, and a vein throbbed in his forehead. He looked like he was struggling, too.

"This has gone on too long, Lola," he said. "It's too chaotic. Too unstructured. Without boundaries. That is my responsibility. I have been…remiss. I intend to correct that now."

A thrill rippled through her at his words, and at the same time some part of her balked: that would mean distance between them. The only time they were close now was in that wordless space where they had incredible, mindless sex in those uncontrolled, un-scene-like fits.

But oh God, the prospect of a proper scene with Roman. She wanted him all the ways it was possible to have him.

"Yes, sir," she whispered.

He took the coffee cup from her hand and placed it on the counter. For the first time she noticed there was a small velvet bag there.

"I never properly disciplined you for hiding from me at the clerk's office," he said casually, reaching for the bag. "Did you think I'd forgotten?"

There was a small, hard smile on his lips. Lola stiffened.

"No."

"Good."

Roman casually began unbuttoning her blouse without even looking, his deft fingers completing the task with practiced skill.

"Look straight ahead, Lola," he said. She heard a metallic *clink* on the counter. Apparently he'd found what he'd been looking for in that bag, and he wanted it to be a surprise.

He turned his attention back to her, and pulled her blouse completely off. Her bra followed. He paused then, then took a moment to play with her nipples. She felt him smile as they hardened in his hands.

"So perfect," he said. "Do not move."

He bent down, one hand still kneading her breast, his grip getting harder, rougher, and pulled her skirt over one hip, then the other. She was only in her underwear and stockings now. His free hand roamed freely over her body, tracing the curves and planes, teasing her stomach, where she fluttered at his touch. He removed her underwear, careful not to disturb the stockings.

"Step out of them."

She did, trying to control her breathing. She had become spoiled. Holding out for gratification, not touching him, not having him immediately inside her — she was starting to sweat.

He slipped his hand between her shuddering thighs and kissed her stomach. Then he swiped one finger along her slit, coming away wet.

"Good," he said, standing up. He reached for whatever was on the counter — she hadn't looked; she could still obey — and then she felt the sharp bite of clamps on her nipples.

She sucked in her breath.

"These are on a lead, Lola," he said. "Don't fall behind."

And he walked off, a light metal chain trailing behind him.

Lola felt the first tug on her nipples, the clamps biting into her flesh even more, and began tottering after him, unsteady on her heels for the first time in her adult life. The pain was just the sharp kind to drive her pleasure, and the sight of Roman walking imperially ahead of her…

He tugged on the chain again, two sharp pulls, two sensations streaking through her body to her throbbing sex.

"Come on, Lola," he said lightly.

He led her down the stairs to the floor where most of the private rooms were, and into a wing she hadn't been in before. The lighting was more subdued here. Dark, dramatic lighting.

Roman opened the last door on the end, and led her through.

It was a giant playroom.

# *chapter* 15

Roman had led her to a playroom that had already been prepared.

There was a padded spanking bench on one end, and suspension restraints rigged on the other. There was a St. Andrew's Cross on the far wall, and the sidewalls were decorated with various tools, the way a medieval hall would have weapons. In the center was a bed.

Lola felt her eyes widen. She hadn't played with any of this stuff, not as a sub, in so long...

Roman began to wrap the chain around his hand, drawing Lola forward. Her nipples screamed; her sensitivity was increasing. She felt warm and flushed, and she looked down to find a pink blush spreading from her chest outwards. The silver glint of the nipple clamps caught her attention, and the sight of herself, clamped and chained for Roman, heated her.

"Lola," he said sharply. "On the bench."

Lola bit her lip to keep from smiling. This was shaping up to be more 'funishment' than punishment, and she was absolutely, one hundred percent ok with that.

She mounted the spanking bench, mindful of the chain still attached to her nipples, and bent over it. Her breast came just over the edge of the padding, her arms on two armrests extending from the bench, her knees resting in the stirrups. She took a moment to center herself, already feeling like she could slip into subspace; her pulse thundered in her core.

Roman walked around to her front. He lifted her chin and unclipped the chain from the clamps. Then he fastened restraints around both of her wrists. He moved behind her, and she felt the leather restraints close around both of her ankles.

Then the stirrups swiveled on their hinges and spread her legs.

Roman placed one hand on the back of her calf and swept over the length of her body in one long caress.

"This won't be funishment, Lola," he whispered in her ear.

*Oh fuck.* Of course he could read her mind. Of course.

She tried to shift, but the restraints held fast. The clamps brushed against the edge of the bench, and she either whimpered or moaned—she couldn't tell.

The next thing she felt was a leather edge drawing a line down the back of her leg. He was tracing the seam of her stocking with...a riding crop?

She shivered.

"Why did you hide from me, Lola?" he asked.

"I told you," she said, her body clenching and unclenching in anticipation, "I just needed a moment."

The crop snapped on the back of her thighs, just below the curve of her ass. She jolted, the nipple clamps providing a stinging chaser.

"That is a half truth, no?" he said, lazily running the crop up the inside of her thighs.

Her mind raced. What did he want her to say? The truth was that she had been overcome with the sight of *him*. That she had been overwhelmed by what had happened, scared that she couldn't take it, that she'd only get her heart broken again...

"It's true," she lied.

He hit her again, harder, right on the tenderest flesh, and she cried out. Tears pricked her eyes, and she thought, weirdly, about how she hadn't felt actually pain in a scene in so long.

She was remembering why she liked it.

It was starting to drive her higher, higher, up to a place where most of her anxieties fell away...

He hit her again.

And again.

Ten quick strokes, until she was flying.

"Roman," she sobbed.

"Tell me," he said.

"You were too much," she gasped. "I couldn't... I was afraid."

She felt something else now—still leather, but round—tracing patterns on the sensitive skin of her buttocks. Whatever it was trailed down, slowly, until it made gentle circles around her entrance.

"Afraid of what?"

He didn't wait for an answer, but slowly penetrated her with the handle of the crop. She groaned, clenching around it, aching for release.

He pulled it out.

"Afraid of what, Lola?"

"You."

There was a pause. Maybe she imagined it.

"Me? Why?"

She shook her head, desperately thinking of a way to back track.

"No," she said, her words coming between gasps. "Us. I was afraid of us."

She heard him hiss. She thought he'd hit her again—she wanted it, wanted the release of more pain and pleasure. Instead she heard a *click* followed by the buzz of a vibrator, and her vision went white as he pressed it directly against her clit.

She screamed something—but not in words.

He pulled away just as she came close to the edge.

"Roman!" she screamed, rattling her restraints, her nipples burning, "*Please*."

"No."

She screamed in frustration this time. He spanked her with his open hand, harder than she would have thought possible.

She closed her eyes, and when she opened them again he was standing in front of her. She raised her head to try to look at him and wondered why he hadn't asked more questions. Why he hadn't followed up.

Instead he removed the clamps from her nipples. She hung her head as he started to play with her breasts, rolling her painfully engorged nipples between his fingers, driving her more insane. Her whole body was primed for him.

"What frightened you about us, Lola?" he said very softly.

She groaned. She couldn't. She couldn't say it. The words wouldn't form.

"I can't," she said. "I don't know how..."

His fingers squeezed her bruised nipples. She craved more.

He bent down, tucked her damp hair behind her ear, and kissed her harshly. She felt tears begin to fall, and then he was gone, moving behind her again, and she found herself hoping he would beat her red and raw, hoping for the kind of pain that could finally, finally release this pressure of knowing she was probably in love with this man she couldn't have.

She felt cold, thick lube fall between her butt cheeks, and her back arched at the shock. Again she pulled against the restraints, and again she was reminded that she was helpless.

"I advise you to relax," he said, rubbing the lube into the sensitive flesh. She had chills, her mind whipping back and forth, her body spasming randomly.

She felt it. Textured rubber, pressed against the tight ring of her anus. He twisted it against her, drilling into her slowly, surely. She hadn't had anyone near her ass in a long time, and her body fought against it, tensing and relaxing, tensing and relaxing. Finally he slapped her thigh.

"Relax."

Her mind blanked. He pushed the plug in with

a final *pop*, and the pain overwhelmed her, eventually lulling into dull pleasure.

She sighed.

"No, Lola," he whispered, "Your punishment isn't over."

He didn't know that she welcomed more pain, that she craved the release—she'd been walking around scared of the inevitable emotional pain that this situation promised her for so long that she'd learned to ignore it, but that didn't make it easier. When he'd struck her it had begun to release, the physical draining the mental, and now she needed more.

"Yes," she said.

But he didn't hit her. Instead, she felt the tip of his cock push up against her pussy, and she groaned.

That kind of release would work, too.

He pushed in slightly, and pulled out. Pushed in, pulled out. Her clit was throbbing, and the anal plug was just a tease; she wanted to feel full of him completely, to obliterate what remained of her thoughts. She tried to strain toward him, but the restraints held her back. She rattled them again, frustrated.

"To the brink, Lola," he said, and plunged into her fully.

She screamed. His full length and the plug he'd pushed into her—she was stretched, fuller than she'd been in ages. Complete. He pounded into her hard and fast, pushing her right up to the edge—and then he was gone.

She screamed again, this time in anger.

Her fists clenched, her breath came in gasps, and

her back arched as much as it could on its own. In a few minutes, she came back down.

And then he was back.

Fucking her to the brink, over and over, and leaving her there, swollen and hungry and empty.

Until she screamed incoherently. Until she begged.

"Don't hide from me again, Lola," he said, teasing her swollen clit with one finger.

"Fuck you," she gasped. "You hypocrite."

Everything stopped.

She couldn't believe what she'd said. Couldn't breathe for it. But it had been true; she'd known it as the words had come out.

*Oh God, oh God, oh God…*

Leather slapping against leather, one of her ankles freed, then the other, Roman coming around the front and his hands working even quicker there. Her wrists free, nothing holding her in place except that she was afraid to move.

No matter; Roman lifted her easily, slung her over his shoulder, walked to the bed, and threw her down.

He grabbed her legs behind the knees, keeping them spread in the air as he kneeled over her, his erection bobbing, shining with her wetness.

"No hiding, then," he said, looking directly at her.

His eyes were wide, bright pools of black, and for one long moment she felt like she could fall into them—and then he was falling on her, driving inside her, and all conscious thoughts were gone.

He started slow, filling her even deeper than he had before, pushing her legs up next to her head so he could go so deep that he hit the end of her.

She screamed when that happened, too.

"One hundred strokes, Lola," he rasped.

This time, though, he kept a hold of her. He settled his elbows in on either side of her head, fixed his eyes on hers, and fucked them both up and over the edge.

He recovered first.

He always recovered first. It was against nature. Just once, Lola wanted to fuck him senseless. She wanted him to know what it felt like. As it was, she let him clean her off, let him slowly, gently remove the plug, let him rub her whole body down with lavender oil until she felt like that boneless rapture would last forever.

Finally, she let him pick her up, the both of them stark naked while he carried her back to the bedrooms.

His bedroom.

He set her down on his bed, the bed she'd slept in since she'd arrived, the bed he'd never once shared with her. He turned down the smooth, soft sheets and tucked her in.

She realized that, again, he wasn't going to stay.

Her hand shot out from between the sheets and grabbed his.

"I know there's something you're not telling me," she said.

Her voice sounded parched, unused. She hadn't realized what her body had been through. He looked at her, his brow furrowed. Then he kissed her on the forehead and left.

When he came back a few minutes later, he had

a glass of water.

"Drink," he said.

She obeyed.

It didn't make her any less stubborn.

"I told you to stop protecting me," she said.

Roman sat next to her, his bulk giving her warmth, his hands still free to stroke her face.

"I cannot," he said. He was smiling, but sadly. "This is who I am."

Lola started to push herself up on her elbows, pissed off all over again, ready to read him the riot act, when he put his hand on her chest and gently forced her back down.

"Listen," he said.

He brushed her hair away from her face again, traced the line of her jaw, checked to see if she was cold. She'd never seen him like this. Never seen him so…concerned.

"Lola," he said, almost to himself, "I failed to protect a woman I loved."

Her heart stopped. Her breathing stopped. Everything: the world, it stopped turning.

*Did he mean…?*

*No. His wife. His real wife.*

"You mean Samantha?" Lola asked.

Roman didn't seem to notice. He only nodded. "Yes. Samantha."

She was almost about to speak, about to let out all the craziness, all the pent up hopes and frustrations, when finally he spoke:

"I failed to protect her," he said, stroking her cheek, "and she died."

Lola didn't know what to say. She let the silence settle between them, searching Roman's face for a clue. There wasn't one; he kept looking at her, like...like...

"Roman, she had a congenital heart defect," she whispered.

He smiled sadly. "Yes. But stress was an exacerbating factor. No, let me explain," he said, putting a finger to her lips and shaking his head. "I was not careful, not as I should have been. I allowed Samantha to become involved in my businesses. Some were in her name, for taxes or permits or...it does not even matter. I listened to lawyers. She agreed. But it exposed her to liability. So a competitor, he wanted to put pressure on me for a bid, so he sued Samantha. It involved the trust that cared for her parents. I would have taken care of anything and everything, we all knew, but Sam, she was not built for that kind of thing. Sam was a writer, a poet. Did you know that?"

Lola grabbed his hand, wanting to feel it warm, held in hers.

"Yes, Roman. I knew that."

Roman squeezed her hand back. "She was, in a way, a stereotype. Always so fragile, so anxious. Not suited for the life I led, in retrospect. It doesn't matter why or how—I failed. She paid. And I could never take it if something like that ever happened to you," he said.

He never looked away. She couldn't have if she'd tried.

She didn't know what to do. Didn't know what he wanted, what he meant. The only thing she could hear for a long time was the beating of her own heart, the rushing of her own blood.

And then, all at once, she sat up and kissed him.

He was stiff, surprised, caught off-guard. She kept kissing him. His lips, his mouth, his body — eventually they betrayed him, just the way he always managed to get Lola's to betray her.

He fell into the kiss, long and languid, balanced above her, so careful not to crush her. Soon she convinced him not to be so gentle.

Soon he was naked.

Soon she had him inside her again, coaxing them both up, in sync, together, watching him the whole way through.

It was wordless, careless, and powerful.

And later, when Lola woke up, he wasn't there.

# *chapter* 16

The trip to L.A. confirmed it: Roman would not be moving away from Lola, at least not anytime soon.

It had been only two days, two days filled with meetings and tours of the nearly completed construction of soon-to-be Volare LA, a stylish modification of a formerly residential compound in Venice Beach, two days where he might have, at another time in life, been amply distracted by the sort of beauty that was commonplace in L.A.

Two days of wanting Lola so badly he could almost taste her, and not having her.

It had pissed him off.

So much so that he barely heard Chance when he called. Only later, sitting bleary-eyed in the limo after taking the red eye to New York, did he remember the specifics and think, *Shit. Chance doesn't want Lola to know he's coming home.*

*You did not tell Chance that you married his cousin.*

*You did not tell Chance that you are fucking his*

*cousin.*

It didn't seem like the type of conversation to have over the phone. Neither, for that matter, were any of the many conversations he might choose to have with Lola.

He didn't call her.

But he did think. Mostly he thought about her, and not "them" — he thought about her skin, how it had an almost iridescent glow in moonlight, how it always smelled sweet, how it took on a shine when she'd begun to sweat. He thought about the way her body stretched right before she contracted in an orgasm. He thought about the way she tasted.

He thought about how good it had felt to hold her, that last time. He thought about what a fantastically stupid idea it had been to step outside the scene he had so painstakingly created, and he thought about how he had been helpless to do otherwise: she had been there, wanting him, asking of him, and he had been powerless to say no. He might never be able to say no to her.

He wanted her more than he could remember wanting anyone or anything since Samantha.

Samantha.

He made himself a drink in the back of the limo; it was late for him, but early for New York. Normal rules did not apply.

Normal rules did not apply: he could say that about the Lola situation.

He could almost taste her again, every time he licked his lips. It felt as though he'd been waiting ages to feel her, to see her. Two days. He didn't care. He jabbed at the elevator buttons with rising impatience, loosening his tie on the ride up, his cock already twitching to life.

The door opened on the foyer to his apartment and he charged through it with a sudden burst of energy, ready to bury himself inside her.

He knew where she'd be; he'd forfeited the use of his own bed almost immediately when she'd moved in without even thinking about it. He didn't think about it now; it didn't seem important. A motel by the airport would have been as desirable if that's where she'd been sleeping.

He rushed down the stairs, not bothering to keep quiet, although he knew from experience that it didn't matter much in this place—it was large enough that the sheer volume of space dampened sound. Still, he found himself slowing, walking with light, quiet steps as he approached what was once only his bedroom. He'd found himself thinking of it as hers, as crazy as that was; he'd never been totally attached to any room after Sam, so yes, it had become Lola's. Nothing was really his.

Except, as he slowly opened the door to take in the sight of a nude, sleeping Lola, a soft white sheet half covering her beautiful body, he thought: *Yes. Mine.*

He stopped, transfixed by the sight of her.

He had never told anyone about his feelings of responsibility—of guilt—about Samantha's death, about his failure to protect her. He had never even said it aloud to himself; he'd just let it fester at the heart of him.

But now he'd told Lola. He still didn't know why. But he did know this: he felt...lighter. It had confirmed, obviously, everything he felt about his need to protect Lola, even from himself. But now that he felt that she understood, it was easier. He'd always been confident that she knew he didn't involve himself romantically, but now that she had some inkling as to why...

Well, no, not the whole inkling. The fact was that he didn't think it were possible that he could ever love another woman the way he loved Samantha, and that seemed tragically unfair to any woman who might attract his interest.

That, he would never say.

He didn't know how long he stood there, watching Lola's chest rise and fall while the sunlight slowly seeped in. She looked so happy. Blissful. His desire for her never left him, but still he found he couldn't disturb her. What sort of bastard would? Instead he collapsed into an overstuffed armchair and contented himself with watching her sleep—for now.

And, of course, thinking about the things he would do to her when she woke up.

It was hours later when he finally woke up, totally unaware that he'd passed out in that chair. Lola was gone from the bed. He smelled bacon. She'd woken up to find him in that chair, and now she was cooking breakfast.

It wasn't until he left the room, now with a few hours of sleep and his brain functioning at something approaching normal, that he noticed that someone had moved the fully-made bed outside of the door to the bedroom; it took the place of the couch where he had spent so many nights lately.

It took his sleep-deprived brain a few moments

to catch up. *Lola. Making a statement.*

*Brat.*

He had every intention of disciplining her that morning, but he walked into his airy, light-filled kitchen to find Lola sizzling bacon and ham and a Spanish omelet, and for just a moment—just long enough—his stomach superseded his brain.

"Oh, good, sleepyhead is awake," she said, flashing him a grin. "Just in time. We have an appointment."

"What?" he said. His mouth was watering. Lola was cooking in just one of his shirts.

She plated the food and placed it in front of him.

"I left you a voicemail. We're going to look at a special location today at Dagmar's recommendation."

She hadn't buttoned the shirt all the way. He could see the outline of her breasts.

"What?"

"Roman," she said sharply. "A location for the wedding—that huge publicity thing that is happening in just a few weeks. The Cloisters. There was a cancellation; this is a big deal. Be ready to go in thirty minutes."

And she walked off toward the bedroom.

If he hadn't been famished, he would have spanked her right there.

*Later*, he thought, and he devoured his breakfast, feeling strangely content.

~ * ~ * ~

Lola did her best to act normal.

Two. Days.

Three, if you counted mornings.

All that time had passed since the last time they'd had sex. And not just sex—she had to be honest with herself about that; what had followed the highly constructed scene had been anything but formal, or controlled, or safe. It had been all about crossing boundaries, not drawing them. "No hiding," he'd said.

It had felt so raw.

And then, of course, he'd gone and slept in that chair. He hadn't said anything about the bed she'd had delivered and made for him; she had figured that he'd have a sense of humor about it, but then she'd found him passed out in a chair, right across from where she'd been sleeping.

She wished he'd gotten into bed with her. Well, maybe it was better that he hadn't—maybe that would have only made things worse.

She'd spent those two days wishing for things she mostly knew to be impossible, and it hadn't helped. Now, sitting in the back of another hired car with Roman, she did her best to lower her expectations.

Roman cleared his throat. The poor man hadn't gotten much sleep, but he wasn't letting it show. Lola found herself wishing she could have taken better care of him.

"So where is this place that we are going?" he asked, smiling at her.

She couldn't help but smile back. Even sleep deprived, the man was gorgeous.

"The Cloisters," she answered. "It's way uptown. It's a satellite of the Metropolitan Museum of Art for some of the medieval stuff. It's built to look like a castle or an abbey, I think. Dagmar thinks it might be properly dramatic for the press, if they let her have full run of the place, which might not happen."

Roman raised an eyebrow. "An abbey? For nuns?"

"There are no nuns, Roman," she said, smiling. "No one for you to defrock."

He merely looked at her. She shivered.

There was a silent moment that was somehow awkward, and then he took her hand. They spent the rest of the ride in silence, which suited Lola, as she had plenty of freaking out to do in the privacy of her own head.

She had missed him incredibly over the course of the last two days. Granted, it had not just been any two days — it was the two days after what she could only describe as a transformative sexual experience. Well, for her, anyway; she had no way of knowing what it had been for him, because, as always, Roman didn't say.

"I am sorry that I have not been as helpful with the wedding preparations as I should have been," he said as their car turned into one of the many small parking lots nestled in the park surrounding the Cloisters.

"Yeah, how'd your business trip go?" She tried to sound casual. She knew Roman still had some non-Volare concerns, but it always came as surprise to be reminded that Volare was not his whole life, especially because, well, it was her whole life. It made her feel insecure, which she hated.

"Fine." Roman clipped the word as he helped

her out of the car; this was clearly not something he wanted to talk about, which was fine with her. She smiled as she felt his hand at her back, and he stepped to the "street" side of her, even though there was no real street to speak of.

"I am sorry, Lola, that I have left this business to you. I should have been more helpful, dealing with the publicity and the arrangements, but I have had other concerns. I promise I will be more available," he said gravely.

Lola was almost shocked. He seemed genuinely regretful.

"Well, there is this reporter who keeps saying we're supposed to give an interview," Lola said. "You kind of need to be here for that."

"I will schedule it today," he said.

Lola took a deep breath and fought off the queasy feeling in her stomach. They were right outside the entrance, on a stone platform, temporarily alone. She wanted to get this out of the way before they entered such a reverential building.

"One more thing," Lola said. "About that."

Roman turned, and the sun hit him full on. He was breathtaking, his bronzed skin accentuated by his white shirt, a slight smile on his face, bright eyes sparkling.

*Shit.*

"I got some information about Harold Jeels," she said. "Some photographs."

Roman immediately came closer, his expression intense. "Tell me."

"Harold Jeels was into the fetish scene. Is, probably. But there are photos, is the thing."

Roman narrowed his eyes. "That is…what you call insurance. But something like that is dangerous, and…" He seemed to struggle for the right English word, something she hardly ever saw him do. "It is wrong," he finally said. He seemed angry.

"I know," she said. She almost wished she hadn't brought it up. "I don't like having them, either."

"Who sent these to you?"

Now she *really* wished she hadn't brought it up. But what choice did she have?

"Ben," she said, and forced herself to look up at Roman.

## *chapter* 17

Roman stiffened, drawing himself up to his full height, and his expression darkened, something that seemed unaccountably sad to Lola on this beautiful day. She watched him closely, aware of a growing tangle of nervous tension in her chest, trying to divine what was going on in his head.

"You have been in contact with Benjamin Mara?" he said.

"Yes," she said, maybe a little defensively.

"Why?" He barked out it out like an order. Lola felt herself getting angry.

"Why is that any of your business?" she countered.

She started to walk off into the Cloisters, but Roman stopped her — his hand around her arm was enough physical contact to completely scramble her emotions and her thoughts. She wished he didn't have that sort of hold on her; it was incredibly unfair. She was always trying to figure out what

Roman thought—meanwhile, Ben had come right out and told her exactly what he thought *and* felt. And yet Ben had been the one to betray her.

Roman pulled her back to him, right up to his chest, where she could feel his heat. Her body responded, and inwardly she cursed.

"It is my business because you are mine," he said gruffly.

Lola's looked up into his eyes, her breath caught on those last words. He didn't look romantic, or emotional—he looked fiercely jealous.

"We have an agreement," he went on.

Oh, right. The agreement. Physical exclusivity. Of course.

"The agreement pertained to…physical relations," she said bitterly, looking away. "So relax. You don't have to care."

Roman hissed and threaded his hand through her hair, his thumb gently stroking the side of her face.

"Do not tell me what I care about," he said. "Why were you speaking to him?"

Lola wanted to scream with frustration. She should walk away from this right now, tell Roman he had no right to criticize her, that if he wasn't involved with her romantically then it wasn't any of his damn business, but no matter how many times she told herself that, her stupid, treacherous feet just would not move. Her hands wouldn't push him away; her eyes wouldn't look anywhere else. She was his prisoner, and he didn't even know it.

"*Not* that it's any of your business, since we're not, you know…" She couldn't look him in the eye and finish that sentence, so she just jumped ahead. "But I met up with him for coffee—because he asked, and because I wanted to hear what he had to say. He apologized."

Roman grunted. He didn't seem happy, but it wasn't like he could fault the guy for apologizing.

"Did he say he had been drinking again?" Roman asked.

"No," Lola said. "In fact, he said he hadn't. And you know what? As big a jerk as he was, I'm proud of him for that."

If a cloud had passed in front of Roman's face before, now it was a category five hurricane.

"He doesn't deserve for you to be proud of him," Roman said. "He doesn't deserve for you to speak to him. He does not even deserve to look at you."

"Great, Roman, thanks so much for telling me. I never would have known without your help!" Lola was getting really angry now. At least Ben made an attempt to communicate. At least she *knew* how he felt, even if he had been a total douchebag. "Did it ever occur to you that maybe *I* needed to know some things? That maybe it would help *me* to hear them?"

Roman looked stricken, and let her go. She wished he hadn't; she felt weaker without his hands on her, suddenly cold.

"This is so fucked up," she muttered to herself.

"Lola," he said, and it was his tone that got her attention; he never sounded like this, so unsure of himself. He cleared his throat, and now his voice was low and fierce. "Lola, I...I do not like you talking to him. I do not like him. I do not trust him.

And if you gave the word, I would end him."

She felt his hands envelope hers, his fingers meshed with hers, and found herself lost in his eyes again. He'd just said something borderline insane, and yet his eyes were soft. His hands were warm.

What the hell was happening here?

"But I want what is best for you," he said. "Did it help you to speak to him?"

"Yes," she said. "I think so."

He bent down, and his lips brushed her forehead. "Good. I hope you do not have to see him again. I will contact the reporter and make arrangements for an interview. Now let's go, and think of better things."

Bewildered and disoriented, Lola followed him into the museum.

The Cloisters were, of course, beautiful. An elaborate extension of the famed Metropolitan Museum of Art, built, at great expense, to look and feel like a true medieval abbey, it housed one of the world's best collections of medieval artifacts in a way that felt weirdly intimate. You could walk around casually amid stained glass windows, huge, faded tapestries, giant stone rooms with tiny little alcoves. Roman and Lola were some of the first visitors of the day, and had the place largely to themselves. It was easy to get lost in the surroundings and imagine that you were back in the thirteenth century. Lola couldn't help but wonder what a Volare wedding would be like here. It intrigued her to no end to think about what Dagmar would do with a place like this, even if she couldn't imagine that anyone in their right mind would let her throw a wedding here, let alone a Volare wedding.

"Can you believe this place?" Lola said.

Her voice echoed softly off of the broad stone walls, and she looked up at the cathedral ceiling soaring above her.

"Do you like it?" Roman said.

"Yeah," she said. "But I'm trying to picture, like, a wedding. A *Volare* wedding."

Roman was standing on the other side of the room, where he'd been reading the plaque accompanying pages from an illuminated manuscript. Now he looked at her, an unreadable expression on his face.

"I can see you, standing right where you are in the light from that window, in your dress," he said.

The air between them shifted.

Lola laughed, but it sounded forced. She looked down.

"Actually, that's not the dress anymore," she said.

She heard his boots scuff on the stone floors. "What do you mean, 'that's not the dress?'" he demanded.

She should *not* be blushing. She ran a sex club; she wasn't some sort of innocent. She should *not* be blushing at the memory of what he'd done to that dress.

The shop girls had made a show of disapproving, but Lola could tell they were more envious than anything else. Stella had managed to contain herself. Roman had paid for all of it.

"You saw me in it," she said, turning her back

and pretending to inspect an eleventh century sarcophagus. "Before the wedding."

Roman's steps echoed off the stone, building her anticipation step by step. She knew he was close. When he spoke, she closed her eyes.

"I *liked* you in that dress," he said.

He was right behind her.

"I know," she said. Thinking: *The one you ripped off of me?* She hadn't allowed herself to think more deeply than that; as crazy as Lola was about this situation, she knew that this whole area of thought was extra dangerous. Thinking that it meant anything at all that Roman had taken one look at her in her fantasy wedding dress and decided he had to have her right then? She looked at a medieval map hanging on the wall: *Here be dragons.*

*Yeah, no shit.*

"But..." Her reasoning was abandoning her, even as she struggled to say it. "It's bad luck. We don't need any more trouble, right?"

Lola found that she actually meant it. She wasn't normally superstitious, but then again, nothing about this was normal.

"You do not appease lady luck," he said, "You seize her."

She laughed, more out of nervousness than anything else. That was such a Roman thing to say, and at the same time, what the hell did it mean?

"You've seized a lot of luck, huh?" she said, trying to ignore that she could now feel his breath on her neck.

"Yes," he said, nuzzling her.

Lola thought about his past, how it was like one of those giant blank spots on the maps on the walls.

She'd been joking, but if she thought about it for two seconds, she knew that of course he'd seized every opportunity that came his way. The man had come from nothing—he'd been a street kid in Barcelona, his parents dead. She didn't know the details of his steady ascent through the business world, but she knew it hadn't always been pretty.

A man like that—if he wanted her, wouldn't he just take her? If he hadn't already made it clear that he wanted her, for real—forever—wasn't that a pretty good indication that it wasn't going to happen?

"*Carina*, what is wrong?" he said, slipping his hands around her waist.

She felt his broad chest at her back and leaned into it, the warmth she got from him bittersweet under the circumstances.

"I was just thinking that you tend to take what you want," she said, her voice sounding impossibly small, even in this room of echoes. "And that therefore what you want, and what you don't want, isn't exactly a mystery."

He buried his face into her hair, and she heard him inhale as his fingers pressed into her flesh. He squeezed her hips, then quietly slipped his fingers under the edge of her light sweater.

She gasped, but only slightly.

"You think I am so simple," he said.

She laughed, and still managed to sound nervous. "Not simple," she said. "Direct."

"Ah," he said, his hands massaging the muscles that flowed from her hips down to her core. Abruptly he stopped. "Come. There is something I want to show you."

He took her hand and began to lead her forward, around the edge of the sarcophagus. Lola experienced the same sudden dislocation she felt every time she lost physical contact with him, and followed, shaking her head. They reached one of those little velvet ropes, barring their way to a narrow staircase.

"Roman, I think that exhibit is closed," she said.

"Perhaps," he said, easily lifting the heavy post anchoring the rope. "But I take what I want, so it is no problem, no? Come."

Lola wanted to smack him, but she let him pull her up the narrow stone steps, until they reach a small room with stained glass windows, and a giant iron bell in the center.

"What *is* this?" she said, fully expecting Roman to give her some sort of lecture on medieval history.

"I have no idea," he said, and he stripped off her sweater. Lola did a double take. He said, as though he hadn't just removed an item of her clothing, "But it is secluded."

Lola looked down to find Roman had already unbuttoned her shirt. The man had a way with a woman's clothing. It was almost a superpower.

"Wait, what are you doing?" she said, even though it was pretty obvious.

"Taking what I want."

"Roman!" she whispered, trying to re-button buttons as fast as he got to them. "Seriously, this is a museum. A museum we might need really soon."

He stood over her, smiling that devilish smile. He took her in his arms and brought her close, so close she could feel his impressive erection against

190

her belly, and she sighed. He brushed away her hair and kissed her neck.

"You need a history lesson," he said, and moved lower down her neck, towards the spot that always made her weak. "Do you know what *droit de signeur* means?"

"Umm," she said, leaning into his arms. "No. Does it have to do with museums and getting arrested?"

He laughed low and slow, almost musically. She looked down and was only halfway surprised to see that her shirt was open. Roman unhooked her bra, freeing her breasts. The chilled air made her gasp, and he playfully pinched her nipples. She halfheartedly tried to cover up, but he batted away her hands, shaking his finger.

He said, "It describes an old medieval custom. It translates as 'right of the lord.'"

"Roman, seriously," she panted, which she was pretty sure didn't help her case.

"Lola, very seriously," he said, forcing his hand down the front of her skirt. Her eyes flew wide open, and he looked directly into them and grinned. "I am your lord."

"Oh God. Roman…"

"Yes," he said, his hand thrusting between her legs. "This is mine. Right of the lord. *Droit de signeur*."

He smiled to find she wasn't wearing underwear, as he'd strongly suggested. Then he slipped one finger inside her, then another, pushing them deep enough to stroke her g-spot. She nearly collapsed, but he pinned her against the rough stone wall and kept stroking.

"I want what is mine," he said into her ear.

Lola tried to speak, but only a strangled moan came out.

"I'm going to take what is mine right now," he said again. "Because I can. What do you say to that?"

"Oh God," she breathed, and then against all good judgment, she caved: "Yes. *Yes*."

"Yes *what*?"

She almost giggled, and then stopped when she saw the look on his face. That look said she was going to get fucked, hard. Her breath hitched. "Yes, my lord?" she said.

Roman smiled briefly, as though stifling a laugh, and them made his face go stern. "Very good," he said.

He bunched her skirt up around her hips, exposing her sex. He took a moment simply to look at her, long enough that she felt exposed and raw in a way she hadn't felt in years. Something about Roman made her feel new and vulnerable, as though all of her hard-won life experience was rendered null and void by a single touch from this man, and it was totally, completely, stupidly intoxicating. Also infuriating. But all of it—*all of it*—was drowned out by the sudden, heavy feeling that swelled in her core.

"Roman," she groaned, "Please, just do it."

She hadn't even been aware that she was going to say it. Roman paused, one hand holding her left leg around his waist, the other holding her shirt wide open so he had free reign of her breasts, and he fixed her with that *look*.

"You think that is begging?" he said, the only

other sound the sound of his zipper unfurling. "I will make you *beg*."

He locked eyes with her, and she lost sight of all else. Then his hips rose as if they were a tide all unto their own, and he pierced her straight through, his erection buried deep inside her. Lola shrieked as he drove her up against the wall, her blouse and sweater bundling together, dragging against the stone; she folded her arms around his neck and pressed her forehead to his.

He thrust upwards again and again, her whole body jolting with each and every stroke, her shoulders rubbing red against the rough stone and her lips hurting as she pressed them close together, unwilling to scream and hear it echo throughout the sleepy museum.

His fingers dug into the undersides of her thighs as he held her up against the wall, and with each thrust the head of his cock dragged across her g-spot, driving her ever higher. She thrashed against him, the sudden flare in feeling, already so fucking close to the edge, leaving her wild and a little crazy. Roman just held her tighter, pinned her harder, and drove himself in and out with a restraint that drove her insane.

And then he stopped.

"Oh, what the fuck," she cried, and tried to move against him. His grip on her only tightened.

"No," he said, breathing hard. "Beg."

She squirmed in his grip, feeling full to the brim, her mind focused on only one thing: release.

"You're such a—"

"*Beg*."

He hoisted her up higher, and she hit him

around his shoulders, grabbing handfuls of hair.

"Please, Roman," she said, "You jerk, I'm begging you. *Please*."

He actually laughed. "Hmm?"

"Please fuck me," she said. "I need you to fuck me, Roman."

He pulled his head away from hers and met her gaze. "Don't forget it," he said, and buried himself inside her.

## *chapter* 18

"Put this on," Lola said, shoving a dry-cleaning bag in Roman's general direction. He assumed it held a suit.

He barely registered it. Lola was running around in nothing but a towel, a towel that did not quite fit securely across the top, and which kept threatening to fall away entirely. He was rooting for gravity.

Then he remembered he didn't need to root for anything.

Lola scooted by, mumbling something about a dress, and Roman grabbed the errant corner of her towel.

Naked Lola.

"Roman!" Lola said, turning around and not even attempting to cover up. "We have the rehearsal dinner in less than an hour."

"Rehearsal dinner," he mused, walking toward her slowly. "Is that not supposed to follow a wedding rehearsal? And yet we had none. Your customs confuse me," he said.

"It's traditional," she said, her voice losing volume as he approached her naked body. "A rehearsal dinner is traditional."

"Nothing has been traditional so far, has it?" he said.

"It's for Volare," she whispered. He was quite close to her now. "It's for them…to have…fun…"

"And us?" he said, his hands encircling her waist. "Are we to have any fun?"

She lowered her eyes, a submissive gesture he loved to see from her.

"We still have Harold Jeels and the press on our ass," she said. "It's supposed to look real, Roman. It's supposed to look like…"

Roman tightened his grip on her waist but said nothing, knowing what she had left unsaid. "Look real." The phrase bothered him. With members of the public, of the press, who were already starting to lose interest? Easy enough. With Volare? Doable.

With Lola?

Everything had been in somewhat of a holding pattern in the past few days. Then pictures of the two of them arguing outside the Cloisters had surfaced online, Dagmar had declared Volare the only secure venue for the wedding, and Roman had been unable to get in touch with Chance. The wedding was in one week. One. Week.

"I did not say you could move," he said harshly. Lola froze. "Why the one week delay? Why not—"

She huffed impatiently. "Dagmar told you, you just weren't listening. She has to throw them off or something, since they took those pictures of us fighting outside the Cloisters. And she has to organize the vendors. Look, I don't—"

"Don't interrupt me," he said.

Silence.

She was getting better at this.

She was not a sub that all Doms would want. But she was a sub he would want. Did want.

Couldn't bear to leave.

He had received a call about construction in L.A. earlier in the day. Nearly completed. He would have to decide soon whether to stay or to go. He could no longer remember why it had ever seemed possible that he could simply pick up and leave for six months, a year. Maybe longer.

"You are stressed," she said, her voice softer. She was close to him, her white skin luminous in the soft light from the bathroom that had become hers. He had accepted that she would stay in his room, but he slept on that ridiculous mattress in the hall, stubbornly refusing to concede her point and answer the unspoken question. She couldn't have him in her bed all night, even if he couldn't tell her why.

Now she reached up and cupped his cheek, her hands soft and warm. The way she looked at him, her big green eyes gone soft and wide, all her empathy and understanding spilling out, there for him to take—begging him to take it…

It undid him.

"What are you so worried about, Roman?"

He didn't answer. Her eyes on him made him feel…raw. Like she could see the things he tried to hide. Like her gaze strafed away his defenses. He hated it—and he loved it.

Only Samantha had made him feel like that. Samantha had made that feel safe.

Lola felt safe—until he remembered. Until he remembered what he—what this—would inevitably do to her.

She pressed up against him, the warmth of her penetrating his clothes. He could smell her. The peach shampoo she used, the Chanel she always wore, the scent of her sex, always lingering. That light from the bathroom filtered through her red hair, turning it every shade of fire, and settled on her soft face. She had no idea what she did to him.

What she'd always done to him.

"Lola," he said, letting his head fall toward hers.

"You can tell me," she said.

He couldn't. "No, Lola," he said. His voice sounded strangled. "This is only mine."

She laid her head on his chest and wrapped her arms around him, pulling her naked body as tight against him as she could. She felt good to him like that. Felt right.

"Ok," she said, and she pressed her lips to his chest, kissing him through his clothing. "Whatever you need."

*Whatever you need.*

He saw the shadow of a dimple in her cheek and felt her smile more than saw it, heard it in her voice. "Or are you just getting worked up about what I'm going to do at this dinner?" she asked. "It's a Volare event, after all; I'm sure there'll be…distractions…"

She looked up at him with that teasing smile, biting her lip. He saw through her, just as she saw through him, and he knew she was only trying to distract him from whatever was on his mind.

It worked.

"What do you mean, distractions?" he said.

"Oh, you know," she said, pushing off his chest and sauntering towards the bathroom, her perfect, plump ass drawing his eye like a magnet. "I'm sure people will get out of hand. It will be hard to resist. They'll all be watching us. Some will be watching me. That Salvador guy has been—"

He caught up with her just before she reached the bathroom, one hand slipping around her waist where he could press it flat against her belly, the other grabbing her wrist. Slowly he brought her wrist around to the small of her back, and watched her back arch with that slow, supple grace.

Just the feel of her skin against his…

She made him insane.

"No one else watches you," he said.

She laughed. "Roman, it's Volare. It's a sex club. We run it. How could you not—"

He ran his hand down her lower belly to cup her sex. "No."

Her breathing became ragged, but she soldiered on. "It's not like they haven't seen me in scenes before…"

"*No.*"

The idea of Lola and anyone else, even from afar, even if they didn't even touch her—it made him crazy. Ever since he'd allowed himself to touch her, she had become his. His alone.

"No," he said again, and let her wrist go. He slid his hand along the curves of her body, feeling every inch, *wanting* every inch, until he got to her breasts. He indulged himself with her nipples,

CHLOE COX

playing with them, kneading the flesh, holding off just to torment himself a little longer.

He could lose himself like this, caressing her stomach there, kissing her neck here, could lose himself in the feel and pull of Lola, the sounds of Lola's pleasure, the look on her face...

"Get on the bed," he said.

He followed her, shedding his clothes as he went. The look on her face when she saw his erection tested his self-control. He wanted to watch her this time, and wanted her to watch him. Wanted her to know that she was his, and his alone.

"Spread for me," he said.

Oh Jesus God, she was beautiful. It hurt him, somewhere deep in his chest, just to look at her.

He had meant to go slowly, but the closer he came to her the stronger her pull, and as he lowered himself over her he found he couldn't stop himself. He plunged into her, finding her wet and hungry for him. He couldn't go deep enough in her, driving in harder and harder, looking for a way to bury himself totally.

That she screamed out his name helped.

That he felt her inner muscles begin to shudder, begin to suck him in further, helped.

He pushed off, rising above her, not breaking his stroke but needing to see her face: her brow was furrowed, her mouth open, her hands scratching at his shoulders and his face.

"Mine," Lola said.

He fell upon her, biting her neck and leaving his mark as he pumped into her.

Later, after they had cleaned themselves up,

already late for their own rehearsal dinner, as Lola fixed his tie for him, he thought, *What the hell is happening to me?*

# *chapter* 19

Stella Spencer had outdone herself, with a little bit of help from Dagmar. The two women had managed to turn the main room at Volare into what looked like a fantasy movie set interior. Specifically, it looked like the inside of a luxurious tent, complete with samovars, lamps, a few hookahs, and various bits of BDSM equipment strewn here and there among the low tables.

"Stella?" Lola asked. "This almost has a...sheikh theme, you might say."

Stella giggled. She'd already had a glass or two of champagne, and she'd been a lightweight since at least college.

"Maybe," she said.

"What did Bashir say?"

"Um..."

"Never mind, I can guess."

"Actually," Stella said, blushing all the way to her roots, "I kind of doubt that."

Lola laughed, happy for her friend. No matter how stupidly complicated Lola's sex life got, it always made her feel good to think about how Stella had finally gotten what she deserved — a smoking hot sheikh who was completely crazy about her. It made it seem like sometimes things went right in the world.

Lola needed some of that at the moment.

The party — rehearsal dinner, technically, even without a rehearsal, or without any idea how Dagmar was going to pull off a wedding in this same place in a week's time — was in full swing, and Lola was already beginning to miss Roman.

It was ridiculous.

She watched her friends and acquaintances flirt and drink and chase each other around the smoking oil lamps and well-laid tables, and all she could think about was Roman. She couldn't believe she'd said "mine" like that right when he was about to come. He'd said it to her before, all kink-ified, and she'd known he'd meant it in that animal way — only *she* knew how true it really was.

Did he know what she'd meant? How could he if she didn't just come out and say it?

And even though they'd just had sex, she wanted him again. Would it ever stop? Would she ever be able to look at him and retain full brain function at the same time?

She watched him through the shimmer of two smoking braziers as he laughed at some story from Jake, the light dancing off of his bronze skin, and thought: *Nope. Probably not.*

*Look at the man.*

Lola put a hand to her neck and rubbed at the

bite marks that Roman had left there not even a few hours ago. His mark. She loved it. Roman looked across the room and saw, and heat swept through her.

"Oh hey, food's ready," Stella said at her side. Lola jumped—she'd been lost in Roman. Again.

She shook her head and tried to regain some semblance of control while Stella wound through the crowd, clinking her champagne glass and making way for the servers.

"Everyone sit down," she said, trying to take some of the giggle out of her voice as she looked around at the many piles of cushions. "Or you know, recline, or whatever. Dinner's here, is the point!"

Lola smiled as Bashir wrapped his arms around Stella from behind, and Stella squealed. She could only guess at what the sheikh was whispering to his future wife, but it was met with Stella's clear approval.

Not for the first time, Lola found herself envying their intimacy, and she inwardly scolded herself for being so negative.

"What are you thinking?"

Lola whirled around to find Roman studying her intently. Great. Why did he always ask her that question when she couldn't tell him the truth without things getting incredibly weird?

"Nothing I can tell you," she said honestly.

He wrinkled that perfect forehead in concern, and not a little bit of pique. "What could there possibly be that you could not tell me?" he said.

Lola wanted to laugh at his adorable male naïveté, but thought better of it. That would require

204

it's own explanation, after all. Instead, she just smiled up at him and said, "Allow me a little bit of feminine mystique, won't you?"

He reached out and hooked a finger in the fabric of her wrap dress, smiling slightly, but with just a hint of worry. "You have all of that, Lola," he said.

"Hey, everyone! We're about to get into toasts and all that, so…you know, throw back a drink or something, because it's about to get weird."

Bashir laughed and dragged a very tipsy Stella into his lap, while the rest of the room cheered. Everyone was a bit more drunk than Lola had anticipated. Apparently Roman had the same thought, because he whispered something to Jake and the more extreme pieces of equipment began to roll out of the room at the hands of various volunteers.

"Lola, come," Roman said, holding out his hand. She took it, and he pulled her down in his lap. "Bashir had the right idea."

Lola couldn't keep herself from smiling, or from rubbing her hands against his chest, even through that now damnable shirt she'd helped him put on earlier in the evening. She'd loved doing that—she loved helping him get ready, making him breakfast when he'd let her, taking care of him. She knew she should be careful about that, knew it was dangerous to let herself think it meant anything, but…

"I'm tired of being careful," she whispered.

Roman's arms tightened around her.

She hadn't meant for him to hear.

Across the glowing brazier that served as a grill for their group of cushions, Lola saw Jake Jayson

CHLOE COX

begin to stand up. He was there with Catie, the woman who had, nominally, been the source of so much strife between her and Roman—Catie, the woman who had initially infiltrated Volare for the chance to get a big tabloid exclusive. Catie had needed the money to pay for her grandmother's care, and she had, in the end, come around and confessed—mostly because she'd fallen completely in love with Jake—but the whole thing still reminded Lola that there was at least one time when she hadn't been able to trust Roman.

*He said he'd been protecting you.*

She believed him. But was that enough?

*Who are you kidding—enough for what?* It wasn't like Roman was begging her to be his real wife. It wasn't like this was a real relationship.

Lola closed her eyes and tried to compose herself while Jake clinked his glass in that characteristic aristocratic way of his.

"I'm told I need to tell a story about the groom," Jake began. "I've never been a best man before, and I imagine after this I won't have to worry about being one again."

Jake looked over at the two of them, and Lola thought she saw...no, she couldn't be sure. The man was unreadable, as always, but there was a hint of something. Jake was one of the only people who knew that this wedding—or their relationship, or whatever it was—was fake, and yet Lola knew him well. Jake hated deception. Hated lying. Had this thing about integrity.

Lola hadn't thought about what they'd asked him to do until just that moment. And yet, the look he gave them...

"I wasn't sure what kind of story might be appropriate for this setting," Jake was saying. Already there was a smattering of laughter. No one really knew what was appropriate at a Volare wedding. "But I think I have a story that might, in a way, be about the bride and groom. It's about how Volare got started."

The room quieted down, and even Lola perked up. Most people hadn't known that there was a story to Volare's founding beyond the fact that Roman and Chance had wanted a club of their own. Lola had known there was something more to it, but only from the look that Chance had gotten on his face when she'd asked about it — something that had told her not to ask about it again.

Now it appeared that Jake knew. Lola felt Roman tense all around, and turned to look at him. He was rigid, his jaw pulsing. She took his hand in both of hers, and pressed them together.

"Lola wasn't there," Jake said. He was looking at the two of them now. "This was years ago. But I think — in my own humble opinion — that it is part of what made Roman the man for her now. Years ago, in a terrible, pretentious BDSM club that shall not be named, there was a woman who was in trouble. Her safewords were ignored. The Dom involved was popular, the regulars cowed, the place apparently devoid of ethics."

The rest of the room watched Jake in near total silence. Lola watched Roman. What was it about this story that made it so personal?

"Everyone likes to think that, if confronted with such a situation, they would do the right thing," Jake went on. "The truth is that most people do not act. Roman was there, however, as was Chance. They acted. They took action that night, and the next night, and so on, until that club was gone. And they took care of that sub. *Roman* took care of the sub. And then they built a place where that would never happen again."

Jake paused, and Lola saw the ghost of something, something powerful, pass across Roman's face.

*Roman took care of the sub.*

He had protected her. That should be a good memory, a proud memory, but Roman's face…

*Oh my God, it was Samantha. That's how they met.*

Lola fingers dug into Roman's hands with the shock. It was one of those leaps, one of those jumps her mind sometimes made without sufficient evidence, and yet when she looked into Roman's eyes as Jake talked about the nameless sub, she *knew*. She could read him and his grief and the all the years he'd carried it with him right then and there.

Roman had always been Samantha's white knight.

And then, in the end, he felt that he hadn't protected her from the thing he believed killed her.

It was stupid, and irrational, in exactly the way broken hearts are stupid and irrational, and it made Lola's heart break for Roman all over again. And for herself, too, because right then she knew she could never replace a ghost — not so long as Roman carried that around with him.

Everyone else was watching Jake. Lola was watching Roman. She reached up to take his face in her hands, and was honest to God surprised when he turned to her all on his own, his eyes indescribably sad, as though he felt himself failing all over again.

"No," Lola whispered. "Don't grieve. You were always her protector, Roman. Every woman should be so lucky."

And she kissed him so he wouldn't see her tears.

The toasts got bawdier and bawdier, and the drinks kept flowing, and Lola could have kissed every single person who made Roman laugh and forget about his grief. She didn't know why Jake would call that a story about the *current* bride and groom—in fact, she was pretty sure she'd have to find a way to kick his ass as soon as the wedding was over—but she was determined to make Roman forget all about it.

Roman didn't have any family, in the strict sense, but it was clear as the night went on that his friends were his family—Volare had become his family. Which seemed, to Lola, perfectly right. With each story and each toast, she began to see, even more than she already had, how Roman had touched or changed the lives of almost everyone there.

Sneaky guy. He kept making everyone laugh, too. And when there was a lull or attention was directed elsewhere, he'd turn her head back and kiss her.

He knew she'd figured it out. He knew she knew, and he kept thanking her, over and over again.

Lola was just thinking how she could learn to live with the bittersweet realization that Samantha would always be around. That maybe she didn't need all of Roman, if this, right here, being in Roman's arms like this as he seemed to damn near read her mind, as he lightly stroked her skin, as he brushed his lips against her neck, if this was the best she could do?

Maybe she could learn to live with that. Maybe she could be happy with that.

She was thinking about all the ways to make that work when the one person who would never allow her to settle for anything waltzed right back into her life.

"Where's my cousin?"

Chance Dalton strode right into the middle of the room, head whipping around like he couldn't be bothered to wait for an answer. All six-foot-something of the broad-shouldered, military-trained man looked pissed off. Lola, still wrapped in Roman's arms, froze.

She hadn't told Chance anything.

She hadn't been able to *find* Chance to tell him anything. His company just kept saying he was unreachable except for emergencies, and she figured he was off in some warzone somewhere. Besides, "phony engagement to your best friend—don't worry, it's fake—but kind of worry because we *are* having sex and I don't know what that means" didn't seem to rate as an emergency.

Roman didn't stiffen, but she did hear him sigh.

Chance locked on them. Lola wished she could actually burrow into Roman's chest and just let him deal with it.

"I hear there's a fucking wedding?" Chance bellowed. The whole party had gone quiet.

Roman gently disentangled himself from Lola, kissing her cheek as he did so, and rose to face the music. Lola forced herself to look at Chance — and found him smiling.

"My best friend and my cousin," he said, shaking his head. Then he wrapped Roman in a giant bear hug, winking at Lola over his shoulder. "About damn time. Get over here, dummy."

Lola got up amidst the cheers and applause and let her cousin practically break her ribs with his hug, but her eye caught Roman's, and he appeared to be wondering the same thing she was: did Chance know the ceremony was fake?

It still was, right?

# *chapter* 20

It took quite a while for the party to settle down after Chance's surprise arrival—if "settle down" was really the right phrase; the festivities and flirtations had been going on for a while, and by now the place was charged with so much sexual tension it was practically palpable. And Lola was finding that being with Roman in front of Chance was like trying to speak a foreign language. She hadn't realized how accustomed she'd gotten to playing up her sexual role with Roman until she was faced with the prospect of doing it in front of her freaking cousin, which just broke her brain.

It wasn't that Chance was one of those guys who couldn't handle seeing their female relatives with a guy; he knew that Lola ran the sex club he partially owned, after all. Chance was what you call equal opportunity liberated, and he respected Lola as her own person, making her own decisions. If he hadn't, she would have made sure that he learned to.

But seeing her with *Roman*?

Lola couldn't put her finger on why, but that seemed different. And yet she just responded to Roman *that way*. She always had, but since this whole wedding fiasco had started, she'd discarded whatever mental filters she'd had in place with regard to Roman, and now she didn't know how to get them back.

And, to add to it all, if she acted like that in front of Chance, would she be lying to him? She drew the line there. She did not want to lie to her only family.

So she was mostly sitting perfectly still and not speaking at all.

"You're awfully quiet, Lo," Chance said.

"Oh God, who told you?" she blurted out.

Roman laughed, choking on his wine, and Chance grinned.

"A lot on your mind, Lo?"

She smacked him in the arm. "Talk, Dalton. What do you know?"

Chance poured himself another big glass of wine, still grinning. "I called Ford when I got into town to check in on business. He brought me up to speed. This is like a Broadway production you got going on here."

Lola turned to Roman, momentarily reminded of something that had bothered her earlier in the evening. "Roman, where is Ford? I thought we'd see him here."

Roman seemed to think about it before answering. "He's in Los Angeles on some business," he said with finality.

"I have to admit, though, I kinda liked the idea of the two of you together for real," Chance said, smiling. "Would simplify my holidays."

Lola smiled back at him. Chance had apparently inherited the adventure gene from both of his parents — Marcy and Rob were currently in Mali with the Peace Corps. There weren't many traditional Dalton family outings.

Lola watched Roman and Chance joke around, two guys she never would have guessed would end up as best friends, and decided she didn't want to rock the boat just yet. Whatever she and Roman were, well, she could figure it out for herself before she talked to Chance. All in all, this was probably a good thing, right?

She could handle this.

She didn't need a guy to be totally head over heels in love, with eyes only for her, to be happy.

So she was feeling cautiously optimistic as she looked down to check her phone.

It was a text from Ben.

BEN: Did you get my delivery?

Without even thinking about it, she texted back, "*What delivery?*"

BEN: To your apartment.

Lola paused, trying to think of the best way to handle this. A very big part of her did not love the way that Ben pursued a woman he believed to be in a relationship — it just reminded her of Ben's own infidelity. But Ben in general felt like this big open door in her life, something she needed to close, if only because, for some unfathomable reason, the man still had some hold over her.

She replied to his text.

LOLA: I haven't been to my apartment in weeks.
BEN: I should have known. I'm sorry.
LOLA: I don't know what to say.
BEN: Say you'll give me another shot.

Lola blinked. She hadn't meant to give Ben an invitation or to encourage him or to lead him on, but she'd kind of done it anyway. Why? She wasn't someone who did things like that. Yet here she was, sitting here with Roman — the man she unequivocally wanted and who she couldn't say whether or not he wanted her back — while she was texting Ben — the man who had told her that he wanted her all the time, no matter how inappropriate.

Shit.

Lola had to be brutally honest with herself: Ben made her feel better because Ben was willing to say the things Roman wasn't. It wasn't right, it wasn't ok, but it was true.

She picked up her phone with a sigh.

LOLA: Ben, I'm getting married. You can't say things like that.

She waited, tense and hunched over her stupid phone, not totally clear on what she was so upset about. She had just lied to a man who had lied to her to get him to stop—what? Saying nice things to her? Her head was spinning.

Her phone buzzed.

BEN: You're right, I'm sorry. I want to be friends even if that's all we are. I love you.

Lola didn't realize she was breathing heavily until she felt Roman's hand on her arm. She jerked her head up.

"Are you all right?" Roman asked. Lola could see that Chance was now distracted by a new petite sub, and the party around Lola was quickly devolving as people snuck out in pairs or groups.

"I'm fine," she lied. She looked down at her phone.

BEN: I'm always here, if you ever need me.

She quickly locked her phone.

Not even a month ago, Lola had promised herself she'd never need Ben again. It was wrong to gain comfort from this, and yet she did. She was ashamed. Talking to Ben to get some kind of reassurance was just too fucked up, and it wasn't fair—both to her and to Ben.

She obviously did not have as good a grip on this situation as she thought.

"Lola." Roman's voice had become stern, a rough timbre with the suggestion of his Dom voice. Lola reacted to it automatically. Her abs tightened and whole body anticipated his touch.

Just his *voice* could rip her out of her pensive

mood and remind her of where she was — and what he was.

*My Dom.*

"Jesus," she muttered.

Roman smiled, reached his strong arms out, and pulled her back into his lap. She loved it there, just being close to him, his heat enveloping her, his scent all over her, his hands on her body. Things felt right so long as she was in Roman's arms. It was when she had to leave that the problems started.

"Lola," he whispered into her ear, "I have something to ask you."

Lola could have sworn that her heart stopped beating entirely for one long, quiet moment. Then Roman stood up, cradling Lola in his arms, and threaded his way through the party in the direction of his private apartment, and her heart made up for it by beating double time.

*What does he want?*

~ * ~ * ~

Roman had controlled himself ever since Lola had turned and seen the grief he thought he felt privately, all through that rehearsal dinner, all through Chance's sudden arrival.

Now he was done.

He held Lola in his arms, carried her as though she were weightless, felt proud that she threw her arms around his neck and clung to him, and all of it with one thing on his mind: he would show her what this meant to him.

He had never been more surprised at anything

in his life. Lola had taken his face in her hands, looked him right in the eye, and let him know she *knew*. That she didn't know the exact details didn't matter; she was one of only a few people in that room who had any idea what he was feeling in that moment, and she was the *only* one to see without prior knowledge. To see, just on the basis of how she saw him.

And then, even with everything—even though his grief over Samantha was exactly the thing that had stood in the way of prior relationships, even though it was exactly the thing that prevented him and Lola from being *real*—she offered him only comfort. She saw that, and her reaction was to help him. To soothe him.

This woman.

This woman deserved…

He kicked open the door to his apartment, feeling like he was on fire. The woman in his arms deserved far more than he could give her, maybe than any man could give her, but he would give her as much as he could—tonight.

"Roman, are you ok?"

It was the first she'd spoken since he'd picked her up with the single-minded zeal of a barbarian. The truth was: no. He was not "ok." In an ideal world, he would fuck this woman until she forgot her own name, and then again until they both passed out from pleasure, and they would wake up together, happy and content. But he knew that could not happen. He knew from experience that if he did that, he would wake up convinced, for one split second, that it was Samantha that he held in his arms, and then when he realized that it was not, when he remembered that Samantha was dead, the grief would be renewed, and it would poison everything he did have with Lola.

He could not allow that to happen.

He would settle for second best: he would give her orgasm after orgasm, until she lost her mind.

He kicked open the door to his bedroom, a room he hadn't slept in himself in weeks, and threw Lola down on the bed in front of him.

"Lola, before we begin…"

He watched with some satisfaction as her eyes grew wide, and then heavy with lust. She knew exactly what he meant by "begin."

"Before we begin, I would like to be clear: Harold Jeels will most likely no longer be an issue after our interview tomorrow, and after the coverage of the wedding. Our prenuptial agreement still stands. You can dissolve the marriage at any time and take your equity stake in Volare. You will not be bound to me. But I can tell you one thing now: I will still want you."

Lola opened her mouth as though to say something, but no sound came out. Just as well; he was not done.

"I want this. I want you. I will always want you. I want you to be my sub, no matter what you choose to do."

She drew herself up on her knees, her red hair falling over her shoulders, the tops of her garters — *garters* — visible just under the hem of the dress he'd hiked up while carrying her.

Damn it, did she know what she did to him?

"Yes," she said, her voice barely above a whisper.

"Take off those clothes," he said.

~ * ~ * ~

Every time he told her to strip, it sent tiny shivers down her spine and through to her core.

She looked him in the eye while she did it. She wanted this to be good for him. No, scratch that, she wanted to be the *best* for him. He'd just said what she'd been thinking: that they could keep doing this. That whatever it was that they were doing, they could find a way to work it out.

Her heart had soared.

She pulled the tight dress up over her head, leaving only her matching black bra, underwear, and, well, garters and stockings. She'd picked them especially for him, wondering if they'd get to play again after all that had happened earlier.

The look on his face told her she'd made a good decision.

He swallowed. "All of it," he said. "Off."

She was fumbling with her bra when he lost his patience. He pounced on the bed, pushing her down under him, tearing at her clothing. In no time at all she was completely naked, held under him.

He pinned her hands up above her head and bent down to kiss her, long and slow with his roving tongue. Lola felt the last of her reservations, her anxieties, all of it, just begin to drift away, the way they always did when she felt Roman on top of her. This was really all that mattered. This was what she was beginning to live for.

"Lola," he said, rising up to look her in the eye, "I don't know how to say some things. I will show them to you instead. Tonight you will come until think you can no longer take it. And then you will come again."

And he hooked her ankles into restraints she hadn't even known were there.

# *chapter* 21

Lola took a deep breath. She'd been restrained by Roman before. She'd been emotionally leveled by Roman before.

But never both at the same time.

Roman took her hands and placed soft leather cuffs around her wrists, hooking those into the headboard. She was now restrained spread eagle on his bed — her bed? She'd been sleeping in it. He'd slept in the silly bed she'd had made for him, just to get him to say something about it.

*No*, she thought as she tested the restraints. Definitely still Roman's bed.

He was on his knees, still wearing the suit she'd made him wear earlier that night, balanced between her legs. He seemed to be taking in the view.

"So beautiful," he said under his breath. "You don't even know, do you?"

She didn't have time to answer him before he

ducked down for another kiss, his hands taking the opportunity to explore her helpless body. He ran one hand down the side of her face, down her neck, to her breast, and let the other ride up her thigh, so slowly, and stop just inches away...

"Oh God," she said.

He kneeled between her legs and smiled. "Not yet," he said, and shrugged off his suit coat. His tie came next, then his shirt, then his trousers. Roman stripped himself with almost the same skill with which he always stripped her.

The result left her breathless.

In all their encounters, she'd never really looked at him—*really* looked at him—naked. He was beyond magnificent. They'd left the light on in the bathroom, all those hours ago, and it glowed against his skin now, the shadows deepening the ridges and planes of his bronzed body. He was already erect, almost proud, swollen and darker than the rest of him.

"Lola," he said softly, his hands beginning to work their way up her legs. "I want to see."

And he thrust two fingers into her, hard, twisting them as he did. She arched off the bed at the sudden intrusion, bucking against her restraints, and she heard him chuckle softly.

"So sensitive," he said, and she looked down just as his thumb passed over her clit.

"Oh shit, Roman," she cried, her arms pulling at the restraints in reflexive reaction to the lightning suddenly coursing through her. "Please, I need you inside of me."

"Come first," he said, and crooked his fingers inside of her while his thumb began making quick circles around her clit.

She rose up almost too quickly, catching the thread of a light orgasm that only left her hungrier. When she opened her eyes again there he was, smiling like a wolf. He licked his fingers.

"I'm going to have so much more of you," he said, and climbed off the bed.

She wanted to scream in frustration. All she wanted, over and over again, was Roman, any which way she could get him. She was so far gone that she nearly moaned just to see him return, though she couldn't see what he carried.

"Close your eyes," he said. "If you open them, I will only make you wait longer."

She did as she was told, though she felt like, at this point, if it weren't for the restraints she could practically hover off the bed. Roman dipped his fingers into her again and she clenched around him, only to be rewarded with a slight chuckle as he spread her own juices around her clit. She moaned again, lifting her hips off the bed, and then she heard it click on.

The buzz of a vibrator.

She fought to keep her eyes closed.

"Roman—"

He put it directly on her clit. Lola screamed, her body unsure whether to register the sudden influx of sensation as pleasure or pain. Roman took care of that for her by plunging into her, the vibrator still held against her clit. She felt the contractions coming, yet still building at the same time, and her confused body writhed under him as he drove into her again and again.

"Come," he growled, and she felt his lips

around her nipple as she came again—or continued to come?

She was screaming.

She was sure she could hear herself screaming.

Her body was shaking uncontrollably as he slowly pulled out his still erect cock with deliberate wickedness.

"Open," he said.

Lola opened her eyes to see Roman over her. She tried to rise up to kiss him, but found herself inhibited by the restraints. He brushed her cheek, in that way he always did, and smiled beatifically at her.

"Look at me this time," he said.

And then she felt him slowly, slowly enter her to his full length, stretching her in this position. She pulled against her ankle restraints, wanting to wrap her legs around him and pull him even deeper, but he only shook his head and thrust harder.

"First, come," he said.

He held himself over her like that, looking at her so that she felt even more naked than she in fact was—*how does he do that*—and [drove] into her with unrelenting force until he pushed her up and over one more time, looking into her eyes as she came screaming his name.

She was covered in sweat. Her body ached. Aftershocks raced through her with unpredictable fury. She was starting to feel delirious.

It felt...unfair.

"Please..." she managed, rattling her restraints.

"Yes," he said. "Now. This time."

And he released her arms and legs, only to wrap

them around his body.

This time, they came together.

~ * ~ * ~


Roman wasn't dreaming. He just slowly became of aware of consciousness as sleep receded in gentle, lapping waves.

What he became aware of first was a warm, breathing, pulsing body under his. The smell of peaches. A fierce, sudden attachment, wanting to reach out and hold her.

Lola.

But there was something strange about that. No, not strange — nothing felt strange — it felt right.

Something new.

It took him a few moments after that to realize what had happened.

He had fallen asleep with her. On her. They slept together, exhausted, drained, physically depleted. *He had slept*. And he had woken up, knowing it was Lola, not thinking, even for a second, of Samantha, not until he remembered there was something new about the whole experience.

He rolled to his side, pushed himself off the bed, not totally sure that he *wasn't* dreaming.

There she was, her limbs still entangled with his, naked and glowing. More beautiful than he'd ever seen her.

What had he done now?

Slowly at first, then faster, faster, that brief peace that he'd felt upon waking was replaced with the dread certainty that this couldn't be that simple.

Roman had tried over and over again to cure himself of what happened when he tried to move on. And each and every time, without fail, he was wrong, and the result was always the heartbreak of a woman he cared about.

He had learned to be careful. Had guarded those women against himself.

And this time...with *Lola*...he'd slipped.

With Lola.

The only woman he cared for, looked out for, because her heart was his own—he'd slipped, and now...

Now, always supremely in control, Roman Casta had no idea what was happening.

He looked down on Lola's sleeping face and watched her reach for him, watched her frown slightly when he wasn't there. He couldn't bear to make her unhappy even now, when she was unconscious. What would he do when it inevitably came upon him again and he screwed up for real? He had broken many hearts accidentally in the years before he'd learned that his grief over Samantha would always, always make itself known, always insinuate itself between him and the woman in his bed.

But he couldn't bear the idea of breaking Lola's heart.

Not her.

Never her.

He lay back down, pulling her to his chest, and lay awake the rest of the night, thinking about what he              had              to              do.

# *chapter* 22

Lola woke up certain that she was dreaming. Had dreamed. She rolled over to stretch out and whimpered softly. *That* part of the night had definitely not been a dream. She looked on the other side of the bed and saw a Roman-shaped hollow, and thought, *Oh my God, that part wasn't a dream, either.*

It shouldn't be such a strange thing, just sleeping with a man. But it wasn't any man, it was Roman — Roman, who she now, finally, had to admit she was completely in love with, probably always had been in love with, almost certainly would always be in love with — and it was Roman who avoided sleep with a woman like it would kill him.

She *hadn't* dreamed it. She really had woken up in the middle of the night, his arms still wrapped around her, his heart beating strong and steady under her cheek. She'd turned her head, brushed her lips to his chest, and gone back to sleep smiling.

A cold thread of panic wound its way through her: where was he?

Gone?

No: she could hear someone in the kitchen. Clanking pots and pans — good Lord, was he trying to cook? She almost shot out of bed just to catch that sight when she saw the clock.

*10:00 A.M.*

The reporter that Roman had arranged — what was her name? Denise something or other? — she was going to arrive in an hour.

*Shit. SHIT.*

Roman was probably getting ready, probably staging something. She should be up and helping him; instead he let her sleep. She smiled.

She winced when she swung her legs over the bed, still surprisingly sore, but then she smiled even brighter.

It was going to be a good day.

A good year.

Maybe a good life.

She rose from the bed as delicately as she could and headed for the bathroom for a quick shower. The bathroom had a vase full of fresh cut flowers — Roman's service must have been around in the evening, after they'd gone to the dinner. The sight of flowers reminded her of Ben's unknown "delivery," and she felt a twinge of guilt, remembering their texts the previous night.

How could it seem so long ago?

She showered in record time, eschewing her normal long, luxurious hot water extravaganza, only because — and she knew this was a little nuts,

but she felt like she got to be a little nuts today —
she wanted to see Roman. She wanted to go help
before the reporter arrived. She wanted to cook
him breakfast.

*Too late*, she reminded herself. He was probably
trying to cook to impress the reporter. She could
make lunch later and make up for it.

She threw on one of those low-maintenance yet
stylish one-shoulder tops and some skinny jeans,
tousled her wet hair, and went out to find Roman.

She felt damn sexy just being near him.

She found him in the kitchen, a tower of copper
cookware piled on the expansive counter next to
his workspace at the stove; the man was making
crêpes, and had apparently had to rummage
through every expensive, unused piece of cookery
to get to his special crepe-making equipment.

The crepes themselves actually looked amazing.
There were bowls of strawberries, sliced bananas,
apples with cinnamon, chocolate sauce.

It was literally the best breakfast Lola could
have conceived of.

So why wasn't he looking at her?

"Chef Roman," she said, pulling herself up on
one of the kitchen barstools, "You know the
reporter lady is coming by soon?"

Roman looked up from the crêpe he was
making, a shadow of doubt flickering in his eyes.
Then it was gone, replaced by a cool mask of
reservation. He said, "I'm aware, yes."

Maybe she was just imagining it — maybe this
was just the usual post-intimacy craziness people
talked about. Lola had never really fallen victim to
it before, but she figured that if it would happen

with anyone, it would happen with Roman.

She tried again.

"So do you have anything in particular you want to get across to her?" Lola said.

Immediately she hated that she'd said that. Like she was getting all arch and prim and naggy about some stupid interview that absolutely paled in comparison to the importance that was Roman Casta holding her through the night. It wasn't what she really meant. It wasn't even close. So why had she said it? What she really wanted to say was, 'What the hell is wrong with you? Why are you being like this? Wasn't last night special? Didn't it mean something?'

Roman poured another crêpe onto the griddle.

Lola watched Roman's brow furrow in concentration or pain, she couldn't tell which one. Given the simplicity of making a crepe, she didn't think it was probable that the cooking was taking up so much of his brainpower, but the alternative...

"There is something we need to talk about," he said.

He plated a strawberry-chocolate crepe and placed it in front of Lola, but she'd lost her appetite.

"What?" she asked.

She forced herself to look up at him. He looked pained. Like he hadn't slept at all. There were lines on his face where she could never remember seeing them, shadows under his eyes. Even his hair seemed in disarray, falling forward into his face.

He leaned on the other side of the table, his shoulders bunching and his forearms roiling like twisted cables of rope. He stared at her intensely, his eyes boring into her with some message she couldn't interpret.

"I said yesterday that we should continue," he said. "And that is true. But not without some modifications."

"Modifications?" she said weakly.

He winced. "Yes. The exclusivity requirement seems onerous, under the circumstances."

"What circumstances?" she said, almost reflexively. Then she actually processed what he'd said. "The exclusivity requirement? What are you saying?"

He looked her directly in the eye, his own eyes like sharp shards of obsidian. "If this is to go on, you should be free to…see other people, no? You can leave at any time after the ceremony, and the equity in Club Volare will still be yours." The crepe started to burn, and he quickly tended to it. "You deserve happiness, Lola. You should look for it."

Lola held his gaze, but her body, as if of its own accord, went slowly cold.

"I should?" she said. She didn't even recognize her own voice.

She would have wished that, at that moment, he couldn't meet her gaze. But he did. He looked terrible, pained, and tortured, but he did.

"Yes," he said.

It seemed like they stood there for a long time, looking at each other. Like Lola's brain took too long to process the actual words that had come out of his mouth. Like she had all the time in the world to think about every other failed relationship she'd ever had, every other moment where she'd misjudged a man, every other time when she'd felt like she'd left herself out and open, hopeful and yet just waiting to be hurt.

And then the doorbell rang.

Roman dusted the flour off his hands, truly annoyed.

"She is early," he said, and looked back at Lola. "I wanted to have this conversation finished before she arrived."

"Finished?" Lola said. "In what universe do you see that as possible in like, less than an hour?"

Roman frowned. The doorbell rang again. He looked at Lola, and she couldn't believe what she saw in his face: pain.

What the hell? What right did he have to be at all pained? This was *his* doing.

"Please, Lola," he said, "Think about it."

And then he went for the goddamn door.


"So," Denise Nelson said, giving them both an arch look over a mountain of untouched crêpes, "You've covered this slow burn romance pretty well. My readers will love it. Every girl wants to get the guy she falls for when she's young," she said, smiling at Lola.

Lola did her best to smile back. Roman took her hand in his. She still felt cold.

"Now — and I do hope this will be on the record, even though it wasn't in the approved questions," Denise said with a sharp smile, Roman noticeably tensing, " — but I just have to ask you about the second location. Our L.A. office is going crazy with gossip."

"Second location?" Lola heard herself say.

Denise gave her a coy smile. "Don't try that with

me. We've had people out to look at the location in Venice. You know construction workers are just the worst gossips?"

The silence felt heavy. Lola was sure she could hear dust spinning in the air. Roman sighed and ran his free hand over his face, like it could wipe the slate clean.

Finally Lola looked at Roman and cocked her head, like she was only teasing her new husband. "Might as well tell her, hon," she said.

Inside, she was thinking: *Please let this be a mistake. Please don't say you lied to me, too.*

Roman squeezed her hand, squeezed it so hard it almost hurt, but kept his poker face turned towards Denise, the busy journalist.

"That's not really for public consumption," he said, "You understand, we will do a proper announcement when it's ready. Through you, at your magazine. Since you've been so good to us."

Even Lola could hear the implicit threat there. She almost laughed—Roman didn't mess around. A morally crusading state senator like Harold Jeels was one of the few things on the list of things Roman couldn't buy, but he could damn well buy Denise's freaking magazine if he felt like it. But Roman wasn't a bully, and Lola knew he wouldn't take that path.

He was just a fucking heartbreaker.

"Ok!" Denise said, breaking the silence with raised eyebrows. "I think I've got what I need for the text to accompany the wedding layout. We're coordinating with Dagmar, so you don't have to worry about any of that—we'll just want our photographer to get his shots in."

"That's great," Lola said, practically shooting up from her chair when the reporter rose.

And awkward pause followed. Lola moved so quickly it was hard not to notice. Both Roman and Denise looked at her, one warily, the other with obvious curiosity. Normally Lola would never make a scene, but she had suddenly hit her limit. This was too much. She couldn't — *couldn't* — just sit and pretend anymore. She couldn't continue with this charade in the aftermath of the epic mindfuck Roman had just pulled on her.

She should see other people?

She deserved happiness?

He'd been planning another Volare location? On another coast?

He'd lied to her. Or at the very least kept her out of the loop. She could only think of a few reasons he might choose to do that, and every single one of them made her feel even worse. Lola's brain went into overdrive, turning over all the different pieces of information, trying to find a way to fit them together that didn't make Roman a liar. Someone who had used her, presumably. Who didn't give a shit about the one rule she'd made: don't lie to me.

Who didn't care if she went and fucked someone else.

Lola had told herself she was handling it pretty well. Hell, she was proud of the way she hadn't fallen to pieces, the way she'd greeted Denise Whatsherface, the way she'd handled the interview. She thought she'd achieved the exact mix of sexy and sophisticated that Volare was going for, with just enough hint of mystery-type stuff thrown in. She'd laughed coyly at Denise's questions about how she and Roman had met, about how they ran Volare together, about how they managed the secrets of powerful people. She'd even looked at Roman with genuine compassion when Denise had asked about Samantha.

She'd actually thought, *I am superwoman. I can handle anything*.

But now Lola noticed that her hands were starting to shake, no matter what she did, and her throat ran dry, so dry that she coughed, looking around for water. She ran to the kitchen island, all decorum and composure gone, and drained one glass, then another.

"Lola, you all right?"

It was Roman. She could hear him walking toward her. She thought of him touching her, and she was suddenly desperate to be somewhere else, anywhere at all, when her heart finally broke.

She could feel it coming, like an impending storm.

"Lola," Roman said. He was so close. Right behind her. She couldn't even look at him.

"I'm fine," she said, pulling away from him. "Here, Denise, I'll walk you out. I was on my way anyway."

And Lola walked out of that apartment, and out of Volare, without looking back.

# *chapter* 23

Roman knew he had to let her go, but that did not make it easy.

That was an understatement. On the outside he was a rigid, immovable statue, his muscles tense and his fists clenching as he watched Lola leave; on the inside, he raged and thrashed against restraints of his own devising, wanting nothing more but to keep hold of her. To keep her there.

He stood still as she walked out the door, practically vibrating with the desire to hold her back.

After she was gone, he waited for all of that to pass. It didn't.

He waited through long moments while his chest ached, his stomach turned, and his lungs couldn't get enough air. Finally, he collapsed back on the couch, the cushion still warm where she had been sitting, and forced himself to go over all of the reasons why he could not continue this. Why she had to find somebody else. Why he could not keep her forever.

After he'd woken up and realized what had happened, he'd lain awake the rest of the night, turning the situation over in his mind, but always coming back to the same conclusion: he must stop this. He must stop it before it got worse. And nothing had changed. The fact remained that Roman knew he couldn't offer Lola what she deserved, and, if he let this continue, he'd do her irreparable harm. Ever since Samantha, it had been impossible.

He still marveled that, when he'd woken up, he hadn't gone through the usual sick disorientation, thinking for just a moment that Samantha was still alive. He'd really known it was Lola. Reveled in Lola. That was the first time that had happened since Samantha's death. He had not thought it possible. But his immediate reaction had been fear and regret—fear for Lola, regret that he had allowed himself to slip. Roman was more certain than ever that he would inevitably end up hurting any woman unlucky enough to fall in love with him, and Lola was the one woman in the world he could not bear to hurt, and he was allowing it to happen.

He'd been weak, and look what he had done already.

Inexcusable.

So when Chance stormed in in a whirlwind of rage, Roman was actually glad. He looked forward to getting what he deserved.

Chance stopped himself just a few feet from where Roman still sat on the couch, his hands threaded through his hair.

"What the fuck is *wrong* with you?" Chance demanded.

Roman looked up. How long had he been sitting there? The long shadows and orange light indicated that it had been much longer than he'd thought. Hours. She had left hours ago.

"I made a very grave mistake," Roman said.

"Yeah, no shit, asshole. Hey, *look* at me," Chance said, smacking Roman's hand away from his face. "Stand up and tell me what the fuck you think you're doing."

"I'm protecting her," Roman said.

He was sure he had done the right thing.

He was less sure the right thing was supposed to feel like this.

"I said stand up," Chance growled, "and say that to me with a straight face. Do you seriously believe that? Have you gotten that fucking dumb?"

Roman shook himself out of his daze of grief, and stood to his full height, looking directly at Chance. An unlikely best friend, but the best man Roman had ever known. Unfailingly honest, even when the truth was unpleasant, even when it would harm him.

Roman liked that about him.

"I understand if you want to hit me," Roman said.

"You are a fucking moron."

"What else could I do to protect her, Chance? It had already gone too far."

Chance just shook his head. "I take it back. You give morons a bad name. You really think you were protecting her?"

"You know I was."

Chance closed his eyes and pinched the bridge of his nose. Very slowly, he said, "On what planet does Lola need protecting?"

"Everyone needs protection sometimes, Chance. From some things."

"Lola can handle herself, and you know it. She can handle you. This is about you, Roman," Chance said, stepping closer so his face was only inches from Roman's. "This is about you being a coward."

Roman gritted his teeth, welcoming the flash of anger. Being angry was better than what he had been feeling, that was for damn sure.

"Watch what you say, Chance."

Chance just laughed. "You're in love with her, you unbelievable dumbass, and you just fucked it up."

Roman blinked, but Chance didn't let him speak. "I'm not blind, Roman. I haven't seen you like that with anyone since Samantha. Not even with Samantha. You're different now. We all are. Maybe ten years ago Lola wouldn't have been right for you, but now... I've never seen a man so obviously in love with a woman as you are with Lola. And I saw it in one goddamn night."

Roman suddenly felt like he'd aged ten years. Maybe it would be best for Lola if he went to L.A. Maybe that would give her the best chance to move on with her life without having to cope with the stress that their relationship caused.

Even as he thought it, Roman knew he'd never do it. The idea of being separated from her made him feel sick.

He said, "Since Samantha..."

Chance exploded. "Jesus, Roman, *Samantha is dead*. Do you honestly think she'd want this for you? Or do you think she'd want you to be happy?"

Roman snapped his head up, but Chance didn't blink.

"You know I'm right, Roman. But I'll tell you what. Why don't you sit there, you dumb fuck, and you think about it. And if you can honest to God tell yourself that you can go through life without my cousin, that you'll be able to look at her when she's hurting because of what you just did and not do something about it, then you're not the Roman Casta I know. You're just the dude who broke Lola's heart because he was afraid."

Roman shook, his fists balled up tight. He was furious, but not just at Chance.

"Yeah," Chance said, turning away from their standoff. He walked back to the door, pausing just in front of it. "You think about it. And if you come up with the wrong answer, I really am going to have to kick your ass for messing up the lives of two people I care about."

# *chapter* 24

Lola couldn't sleep. Huge surprise.

She'd found herself halfway to Stella and Bashir's place before it had occurred to her that maybe that wasn't the best choice. Stella and Bashir were planning their own wedding, and, truth be told, the last thing Lola wanted to see right then was a happy couple. It would just make her feel like more of a fool.

So she'd returned to her own apartment for the first time in weeks. She didn't know what to expect, exactly, but she was relieved to find no press hanging around. Without a steady stream of gossip about the membership of Club Volare, their attention had moved on to celebrity bed hopping and overdoses, so Lola probably wouldn't have to worry about getting photographed or having people go through her trash until the glossy wedding special came out.

Right. The big, flashy wedding ceremony to

commemorate their sham marriage.

She was still supposed to go through with the wedding.

She *had* to. It was her own fault she'd gotten her heart broken; she had actually known better, she'd just...made a mistake. And even though it looked like Harold Jeels could be neutralized with those photographs that Ben had sent her, that didn't mean Volare wouldn't be a target in the future. Roman's press strategy was still the right one.

Ugh. The Harold Jeels photos—they made her feel awful just knowing she had them in her possession; and, to top it off, they made her think about Ben. He had only sent her those because he was trying to help. He'd gone through the trouble of hunting them down because he'd thought they would protect her.

Or because he thought they could help him win her back. Which was possibly a little twisted, right there.

*You have fantastic taste in men, Lola.*

She wished she could sleep. She'd slept so well in Roman's arms. It had been perfect, or as close to perfect as she thought she was going to get, but then it was as if someone had flipped a switch and Roman had gone from being caring and understanding and tender, in his own macho way, to...whatever the hell that was this morning.

She had been willing to put up with anything. She had been willing to settle for second best, knowing the ghost of Samantha would always be hanging around. And he had thrown that in her face.

What the hell had she been thinking?

243

*Oh man, come on, get angry. Get pissed off.* Anything would be better than this aching hole in her chest. No matter where her thoughts went, she always had to circle around to one thing: he didn't want her.

It was simple as that.

She was crying again in no time, annoyed with herself but unable to stop, when her phone buzzed across the nightstand. She snatched at it, grateful for the interruption, but mostly — pathetically — hoping it would be Roman.

It was Ben.

BEN: How YOU doin'?

Lola laughed in spite of herself, and answered just to have something else to think about, just to give her fingers something else to do. Sitting in her bed crying was not really working out for her.

LOLA: Terrible.
BEN: What happened? Trouble in paradise?
LOLA: Yes.
BEN: Oh shit I'm sorry. Do you need a shoulder to cry on?

Lola hesitated. The truth was that she *did* need a shoulder to cry on, preferably a shoulder who would understand exactly why this latest thing was a such a big deal to her, and that narrowed the field down considerably. It was basically just Roman, which, for obvious reasons, wasn't going to work out; Stella, who was probably happily asleep with Bashir; and Ben. Before she could respond, he texted again.

BEN: I really mean it, just as a friend. Where are you? I'll come to you.

It was pure weakness that made her text back. But then, she'd been worn down for weeks and then dumped. She wasn't feeling particularly strong.

LOLA: My apartment.
BEN: Be there in 20.

~ * ~ * ~

Roman couldn't sleep. He appreciated the irony. Anyway, he certainly deserved it.

So he'd gone for a walk. Manhattan would always be one of his favorite places, especially at night, when the city started to get weird, when the layers of artifice started to come off. Of course, that was when some people put them on. New York was a strange place.

It was a city he got to know with Samantha. Most of the city held memories of her, and of him, learning how to be a good husband, learning how to love someone properly, fully. Good memories.

He found himself drawn to Central Park. Specifically, to that bench right at the bend in the path by Strawberry Fields. It was where he and Samantha had always ended up when they went on walks together. In the summers there was always an ice cream guy nearby, and they'd sit there feasting on Good Humor bars and ice cream sandwiches, just watching people relax, have fun, be happy. It was where they'd had most of their own moments. She'd told him that she loved him on that bench. He'd proposed to her on that bench.

In retrospect, he could have made it more memorable, but he'd been young and dumb. Though, according to Chance, he still was pretty dumb.

Roman sat on the bench. He leaned back. Leaned forward.

It didn't feel right.

Possibly because it was one in the morning. Possibly because he hadn't been there in a while. But that bench had been 'the place' he'd had with Samantha. That bench used to be home, of a sort.

"Shit!"

Roman looked around; there was no one nearby. It had been a woman's voice, and she had been in pain. A moment later, and that was confirmed. "Ow! Shit, shit, shit, this is really bad."

It came from around the bend, just through the new foliage. Roman strode around the path and found a young woman decked out in jogging clothes limping heavily.

"Let me help you," he said, and moved towards her.

He didn't expect the scream. It was one of those things that, again, in retrospect, seemed rather obvious.

He also didn't expect the mace.

"Get away from me!"

"Hey!" Roman said, backing up quickly, well out of range of the mace. "I'm not going to hurt you. But you cannot walk on that ankle — I can see that from here."

"I don't know you," the woman said. She was leaning on a tree now; she really couldn't put any weight on that ankle.

"Do you know many people in the park at one in the morning?" he said. "Jogging alone at this hour is ill-advised."

"Screw you. I couldn't sleep. Seriously, don't come near me, ok?"

"Ok."

Roman put his hands up in mock surrender. "I will stay at this distance, yes? But I will not leave you here, alone, wounded, in the middle of the night. Do not even try to argue that point; you will not win."

"How do I know you're not, you know...?"

"Because I'm staying over here."

She leaned more heavily on the tree, bringing her face into the pale light from a far-off streetlight. She looked to be in her mid-twenties, brunette, probably pretty when she wasn't terrified and nursing a badly sprained ankle. He could see the evidence of adrenaline in her eye movements, her breathing, the way her hand was shaking.

She looked at him angrily and said, "What are we supposed to do? Just sit here until someone comes and finds us?"

Roman pretended to think about it. Adrenaline often warped people's thinking. He tried not to smile. "We could do that, yes. Or we could use a cell phone."

She gave him a fierce look and said, "Stay where I can see you."

Luckily there was an EMT bus stationed nearby,

and in about ten minutes two weary-looking EMTs packed her up, her ankle now swollen up like a balloon. It wasn't until she was safely in the care of the EMTs, being taken in for X-rays, that her manner softened. She called to Roman as she was being loaded into the back of the bus, her eyes wet and her expression contrite.

"Thank you," she said.

"Of course."

"Um…" She seemed to be searching for what to say. An EMT held the door open for her. She called out, "Get home safe!"

The door shut. The bus drove away. Crisis averted.

The words stayed with him. *Get home safe.*

Memories of Samantha no longer felt like home. Places that held the remembered feel of Samantha no longer felt like home.

Home wasn't a feeling he'd had the luxury of growing up, and so once he'd had it, he learned to recognize it. Or thought he had. The last time he could remember feeling at home was the previous night.

Lola felt like home.

He knew where he had to go.

# *chapter* 25

Twenty minutes turned out to be the exact right amount of time for Lola to begin to regret taking Ben up on his offer to come over. It was the middle of the night, and ex-boyfriends usually came over in the middle of the night for exactly one reason, and that was *not* what she wanted. Now she was super stressed on top of feeling sad and hurt and humiliated.

She was just wondering how late was too late to text Ben back and tell him nevermind when her doorbell rang. That alone freaked her out; what the hell had happened to her doorman? But then she remembered that Ollie would recognize Ben, would think he was ok. It wouldn't be the first time Ben had come over kind of late.

Why did she have such a bad feeling about this?

"One second!" she called out, casting around for her bulkiest sweatshirt. She was already rocking the sweatpants—it had been that kind of a night.

She'd say hi, she'd say thanks, and then she'd send him home. She really was kind of exhausted. Nothing tired her out like crying.

"Hey," she said, opening the door. Ben stood there in his black leather jacket, gray hoodie, faded jeans, shadow on his chin. He smiled softly at her, raising an eyebrow rakishly, and lifted a plastic grocery bag full of various ice cream pints.

"I brought supplies."

Lola had to smile. She stayed back, not really sure what kind of greeting to go with. A hug would seem…misleading. Dangerous. Possibly bad news.

But Ben didn't even try for one. In fact, he kind of kept his distance.

Probably nothing else he could have done would have relaxed her more than that.

Lola let him in, thinking, *Maybe we really can be friends.*

It wasn't until he bumped into the doorway on his way to the living room that the bad feeling returned.

"Ben, are you—"

"Tired? Hell yes, it's the middle of the night," he said, giving her his most charming smile. "But you needed me. What can I do for you?"

"Honestly, Ben, nothing. This was probably a bad idea."

"Oh, come on. I meant it when I said I cared about you, Lola," he said. His gestures were too big, his words overly enunciated. The bad feeling in the pit of Lola's stomach got worse. Ben seemed to notice her hesitation. "Come on, just tell me about it. What did Roman do?"

"It's not really that simple."

"'Course it is. You gonna come sit next to me?"

Ben had sat himself down right in the middle of her couch. She'd be squeezed in next to him no matter where she sat down.

"No."

"Come on, Lola, tell me what's wrong."

Lola knew she should be worried, but what she mostly felt was sad. Because while Ben had been an asshole to her, and there was a really good chance that he would be an asshole again in the future, what made it so difficult was that he was also charming, and funny, and sensitive. He had made a sincere effort to be a better man over the past few years, and Lola knew that the biggest part of that effort was his commitment to Alcoholics Anonymous.

And she was also pretty sure that right now he was drunk.

Ben frowned, then pushed himself up off the couch.

"Come on, Lola, you can talk to me. Seriously. It's important to me that we stay close, you know? I care about you."

"You already said that, Ben," she said softly. She didn't even know where to begin.

"That's 'cause I mean it twice as much. Come on, what did he do?"

Ben took a step toward Lola and she backed away, keeping the distance between them the same. She watched him process what her movement meant in real time. His face fell.

"Lola, come on."

"I want you to leave."

"Lola, what the *fuck*?" he said, exhaling with

frustration. Ben screwed his face up like he was about to cry, hung his head, and took a deep breath. When he came back up, he looked more angry than upset. "I mean, come *the fuck* on, right? Roman? Fucking *Roman?* I could have told you that was gonna happen."

"Ben, I said I want you to leave."

He ignored her and smiled bitterly. "He doesn't want you anymore, right? It turned out you were just like all the rest of them?"

Lola flinched. That was the worst thing about Ben: all that charm, all that charisma. He could use those traits to hurt just as easily as to help. It hurt all the more because he was right: that was exactly what she'd been feeling. She'd been trying to tell herself it wasn't true all night, that she was just really hurt, but hearing Ben say it, even though he was mad, and even though he was drunk, made it seem…real.

She didn't have an answer for him. He took another step closer. Her already small apartment was starting to seem even smaller.

"You always had a thing for him, *always*, way before I ever fucked up," Ben said, working himself up into a righteous, drunken rage. "You had your inside jokes and your fucking looks you would give each other. How long did you want him? Did you have something going on while we were together? Did you? Were you fucking him and just gave me a hard time for fucking up because I got caught?"

Lola felt the wall at her back. Every time Ben asked one of those angry rhetorical questions he stepped closer, as though that would somehow make him right. With a strange detachment, Lola wondered how long he'd been storing all this stuff up. Was it just bad luck that she had happened to get him here on the night he relapsed? Or would it have happened anyway? She couldn't believe how rational she was being until she looked down and saw that she was gripping the bag full of ice cream so hard that her fingers had started to poke through the plastic.

"Ben, you're kind of scaring me."

"Oh, that's such bullshit, Lola," he scoffed. "Total bullshit."

"I asked you to leave. I still want you to leave."

"Lola, we have to work this out."

Ben was close enough that she could smell his mouthwash. She realized that that was why he'd kept his distance at the front door. The thought that he'd put that much thought into this scared her even more.

"You're drunk, Ben," she whispered. "Please leave."

"Lola, no," he said, lowering his voice, trying to make it soft. "You just don't remember how good we were together."

Ben grabbed her arm as she turned away, forcibly pulling her back, and tried to kiss her. A few thoughts went through Lola's head all at once: he'd ignored her every request for him to leave and he'd just put his hands on her, so it was a good bet that he wasn't going to be respecting any other boundaries; he was scary drunk; and he was angry.

She kneed him in the balls.

Then she smacked him in the nose with the bag of ice cream.

And she bolted to her bathroom, the only room in her apartment that had a working lock.

It wasn't until Ben started pounding on the bathroom door that she realized she'd forgotten her phone on the nightstand.

~ * ~ * ~

Roman was so focused on getting to Lola that at first he didn't think much about the fact that her doorman was literally sleeping on the job. He had walked right into the lobby and right past the doorman's desk to the bank of elevators. It wasn't until afterwards that he thought much about it at all.

He checked his watch on the ride up, and only then did he wonder if Lola might be asleep. He was an idiot. It was the middle of the night; he couldn't barge in on her like this. He'd wait, like a civilized person, and let her get her sleep. There was no chance he would sleep until he'd spoken to her, though.

The door opened on Lola's floor, and Roman pressed the lobby button, shaking his head. It was normal to want to tell the woman you loved how you felt as soon as you figured it out yourself, but he'd be damned if he was a jerk about it. The doors were already closing when he heard the noise.

A banging noise. Someone shouting.

Someone shouting, "Lola!"

Roman caught the closing elevator doors and forced them open, his eyes roaming wildly, not expecting to find anything, but looking all the same. Hunting. Weirdly, he thought of that woman in the park; thought about how adrenaline distorts things. He had tunnel vision as he raced down the hall to Lola's door, and he could hear his pulse pounding in his ears — and a man shouting.

Lola's front door was unlocked.

His brain had just enough time to process what he'd heard before he burst into Lola's bedroom, which, all in all, might have made him more forceful than was strictly necessary, because he recognized that voice.

Ben.

Ben shouting, sounding drunk, angry, and mean, trying to break down a door.

Where was Lola?

Nowhere. She was nowhere. Ben was pounding on the bathroom door.

Only for a second longer. Then Roman grabbed the stupid hood that protruded from his jacket and dragged him away. Threw him on the floor across the room. Ben got up, shaking his head, and Roman punched him back down.

He stayed down.

"Lola!" Roman shouted. Insanely, he threw off her bedspread, as though she might be hiding under the covers. "Lola!"

"Roman?"

She was in the bathroom. Of course. Clearly. The adrenaline started to fade and Roman took stock. Ben was groaning on the floor, a hand to his bloody mouth, trying to get up. Lola was in the bathroom. Scared.

"It's me, Lola," he said, never taking his eyes off of Ben. His chest heaved as he drew in great gasps of air.

"You've got to be fucking kidding me," Ben said. "You're the knight in shining armor now? You? The fucking dickhead who treated her like shit?"

Roman was stunned with rage. Almost knocked back on his heels. Ben was up on one knee, rising to his feet, still talking.

"Such fucking bullshit. You treat her like all those other subs that you just use up and toss out, like she's fucking *nothing*, and you're the hero? I fucking love her, Roman. I didnt't string her along for years and then just start fucking her when it was convenient. I didn't dupe her into a fake goddamn marriage because it was politically convenient." Ben looked at Roman's face and laughed. "Oh yeah, there's all kinds of gossip, you piece of shit."

Each statement hit Roman like a punch to the gut. It wasn't the way Ben said them; it was the kernel of truth in each and every one, twisted around to suit Ben's interpretation of the world, but a kernel of truth nonetheless.

He had hurt Lola so much worse than he'd thought.

Roman forced that thought from his mind and grabbed Ben, hauling him up against the wall with one arm pinned painfully behind his back. His focus had to be on making Lola safe. That, right now, he could handle.

"If you move, or try to escape, or even say anything to her that I don't like, I will break your arm, do you understand?" Roman said. "I will *enjoy* breaking your arm."

"Roman, what's going on?"

"I've got him under control, Lola. It's safe to come out if you want. If you don't want to, I can make sure we both leave first."

He heard the door creak open and turned his head. Lola was standing in the bathroom doorway, looking gorgeously angry, even in baggy sweatpants.

"No," she said. "Stay. I don't know what I want."

"Lola—" Ben tried to say. Roman found himself putting more weight on his arm.

He said, "Please don't make me behave in ways I will regret, Benjamin."

Lola was pacing, her eyes darting about, just like the girl in the park. Lola had been trapped in there, and Ben was obviously angry, and Roman could smell the liquor on him. She had been truly terrified. Right then, all Roman wanted to do was take care of her.

"Do you want to file a police complaint?" Roman asked, careful to keep his voice calm. He wanted to do whatever she needed him to do in order to help her feel in control of this situation.

"Maybe. I don't know." Lola had started biting her nails. He couldn't remember ever seeing her bite her nails. Suddenly she turned to Roman, and he saw that she was on the verge of tears. "Ok, no, I've changed my mind. Get him the hell out of here. I just want him gone."

"Done," Roman said. He turned back to Ben and saw that he had been crying, too, and was now about to speak. He leaned forward, close to Ben's ear. "Think very carefully before you speak. If what you have to say makes this even one iota worse for

Lola, I can promise you that you will regret it. Not right now. But soon."

Ben swallowed. Satisfied, Roman kept hold of Ben's wrist with one hand, and with the other seized the hood, giving him an excellent hold. He pulled Ben off of the wall and began to walk him out of the room.

"Wait," Lola said. "Ben, give me your phone. Now."

Roman didn't feel like giving Ben any slack. He let him struggle for the phone with his free hand.

"What's the name of your sponsor, asshole?" Lola said, looking at the phone.

"What?" Ben said.

Roman gave his arm a little twist. "What did I say not one minute ago?"

"It's under Cheesesteak," Ben said. His voice broke, like the severity of the situation was just dawning on him. "I'm not supposed to give out names. Dude loves cheesesteaks."

Lola shook her head and scrolled, then lifted it to her ear.

"I'm calling about Benjamin Mara," she finally said into the phone. "I'm an ex of his. He showed up at my apartment tonight, drunk, and tried to assault me."

Roman closed his eyes and willed himself not to break the arm of a helpless man.

Lola was still talking into the phone. "I think. I don't know. It is safe to say, at the moment, that he has relapsed. And I want you to give him a message when you see him sober, ok? Tell him if I ever see him again, I'm going straight to the cops. I may go to the cops now. I don't know—I don't really want to make any decisions right now. Can you come get him? Great. And yeah, call me to warn me."

She gave her address and then hung up the phone, giving Ben the most withering look Roman had ever seen.

"Ben? Listen to me. Roman's going to take you downstairs. 'Cheesesteak' is going to meet you. If you fail to meet him, he is going to call me back, and I am going to call the police. If you ever contact me again, I am calling the police. If I even hear your voice again, I am calling the police. Do you understand?" Lola was starting to sound like Lola again, but Roman knew she wasn't recovered. She went on, "Tell me you understand, Ben."

Ben was crying openly now, and slurring his words. He said, "I understand."

"Please take him downstairs, Roman."

Roman went about his task grimly. He didn't want to leave Lola alone, and he didn't want to leave Ben unchaperoned, lest he get stupid ideas about making apologies. As they were about to open the front door, Lola called out to him from the bedroom.

"Roman?" she said.

He turned, and the sight of her, looking for the first time vulnerable, open, looking to him for something, left him gasping for breath.

"Yes?" he said.

He watched as whatever light he had seen flare there, however briefly, faded.

"Never mind. Thank you for...this," she said, and disappeared back into the bedroom.

## *chapter* 26

Lola got Roman's text not ten minutes later.

ROMAN: Mr. Cheesesteak has arrived, and Ben is safely in his custody.

She couldn't help but smile—who else would give a guy called "Cheesesteak" the honorific "Mister"? But then she hesitated. What could she say? "Thank you" didn't seem quite adequate, or even entirely accurate. She was still a confused jumble of feelings, as far as Roman was concerned, and now, on top of that, she was a mess from this Ben incident. Before she could respond, he texted again.

ROMAN: Will you speak to me? Please. I want to see that you're all right

That, she could deal with. She didn't know why.

Maybe nonverbal communication would be easier. She said yes.

And immediately after she'd agreed she realized that she wanted to see how Roman would react to the things Ben had said. She'd heard them, of course; it was a flimsy freaking bathroom door. Actually, she was sure that half the floor had heard them. Ben had been drunk and loud. Everything he'd said had been hard for Lola to hear about herself, but in a perverse way she was glad that Ben had said them, because she didn't know if she'd ever have said any of them herself. But now they were out in the open. And they had to be dealt with.

She went to the front door and unlocked it. She was waiting there for him when he came back up.

He looked like hell.

Roman was normally so effortlessly stylish. Now, his jet black hair was tousled; his suit — a casual suit, obviously, even in the middle of the night — was rumpled. But it was more than that. His expression was dark, and his complexion pale, as pale as he could be.

Lola opened the door for him, not sure what to say, now that he was actually here. He took care of that. Wordlessly he walked right up to her and wrapped his arms around her.

"Lola, I am so sorry," he said, stroking her hair. He pulled back and Lola was stunned to see that his eyes were completely bloodshot. "Did he hurt you?"

"No," she said, slightly bewildered. Roman seemed more freaked out than she was. "He didn't get to me. He just scared the crap out of me."

"'Just,'" Roman said, spitting out the word. "I could kill him."

"Roman…"

"Yes?"

"You have to let me go. I can't breathe."

Roman released her, backing away as though he were unsure of his place. She'd never seen him like this. In fact, she was pretty sure no one had ever seen him like this. Roman Casta, the Master, unsure of himself?

"Lola," he said, running a hand through his hair. "I am at your disposal. I want you to feel safe. I will do whatever I have to do to make that happen."

Lola tried not to show that she was stung by those cold words—"at your disposal," like all that mattered was that he felt kind of guilty—because she knew her reaction was unfair, and probably a little emotional, and definitely colored by all the other crap that had happened. She didn't realize just how much her trust in Roman had been damaged, didn't know how emotionally drained she was, until right then. Just the effort of hiding that one last extra drop of hurt…

Silently, she walked back into her bedroom and sat down on her bed. She heard Roman come in behind her.

"Lola, what's wrong?"

"I don't know. I'm just so tired all of a sudden, Roman. This…whatever this is…" she said, waving her hand around at the air between them, "it's just killing me. And then this bullshit with Ben…"

Roman came and knelt beside her bed. He took her hands in his and kissed them.

Ok, now she was worried. "Roman, what is wrong with you?"

"Nothing, not anymore," he said. "Lola, I came here to tell you something important. But you are exhausted, and I do not want to ask anything more of you tonight if you do not feel up to it."

Lola hated to admit it, but he was right. As usual. Her body was already pulling her toward the bed, telling her to sleep, and it was getting hard to resist.

Roman squeezed her hands and said, "But please know that one of the things I need to do is apologize." He looked up at her, his eyes, those dark, shining eyes, begging her. "I have behaved despicably. Stupidly. Very, very stupidly, for cowardly reasons. And I have hurt you, and for that I will probably never forgive myself."

That word—"cowardly"—it looked like it had actually hurt him to say it. Lola smiled at him gently and tried to get a word in edgewise. "Roman, you don't—"

He stood up. "*No.*"

*There* was Roman freaking Casta. Even when exhausted, scared, hurt, and vulnerable, that tone sent a shiver down her spine. That voice shouldn't be legal. He should have to register that voice.

"I know what my obligations are. I will explain in time," he said, standing over her, still holding her hands in just one of his. The other smoothed down her hair, gently petting her. "But now you have to rest. How can I make you feel safe enough to sleep?"

Lola wasn't sure she wanted to forgive him— and, worse, she wasn't sure that, even if she wanted to, she could make herself trust him again—but when he said that, one, perfect thing became clear.

"Stay," she said.

"Always," he said.

Something in Lola twinged at that word, "always," but she was too tired to examine it. She let him pull back the covers and tuck her in, taking ridiculous care to make sure she was perfectly comfortable. He even fluffed her pillows. But when he bent down to kiss her forehead and put his hand next to her pillow, Lola surprised herself by taking his hand.

And then she pulled him down to the bed next to her. Roman didn't say anything; he just wrapped her in his arms and held her until she fell asleep.

When Lola woke up, Roman wasn't there. But about three million post-it notes were.

One on the nightstand. One on what had been, briefly, his side of the bed. One on the blankets. She could see from the bed that there was one on the bathroom door. She squinted her bleary eyes and read the one on her nightstand.

*I haven't left. I'm making you a better breakfast than the last one. -Roman*

*Hmm.*

That had the unfortunate effect of reminding her of what had happened the last time she had gotten excited about Roman making her breakfast. Had that really been only yesterday? It felt like a million years ago. It felt like another dimension.

By the time Lola was done in the bathroom, she had thoroughly replayed all the worst moments from the day before like a particularly grotesque highlight reel of the most hurtful moments of her life. She was right back to having a broken heart. The truth was that she did believe all those things that Ben had said, and she had believed those things even before Ben had said them. Or maybe it was more accurate to say that she had feared them. Whatever the case, they now loomed in front of her, real and true and inviolate.

Roman wasn't in love with her. Roman would never be in love with her.

Roman wanted her to see other people for her own good.

Roman had lied to her, all over again, about a second Volare location in LA. Roman had been planning to move to freaking Los Angeles, and he hadn't told her.

The worst-case scenario: Roman had known that she was in love with him, and he'd done all those things anyway.

Actually, maybe that wasn't the worst-case scenario. If that were actually, incredibly true, then Roman wasn't the man she'd thought he was, and she could see a way to getting over him. Maybe.

She hesitated at the bedroom door, watching him make—was that French toast? Oh God, it smelled heavenly. So he had at least one more surprise up his sleeve. Lola knew that part of her was eager to build up an impregnable case against Roman because that would make it easier to run from him. From everything. From the whole messy situation. But if she were being reasonable, she'd have to admit that the man she'd known for ten years hadn't just morphed into a total complete bastard overnight.

This had to be complicated. Of course it did.

She was still just so tired.

"You're awake," Roman said, smiling, and offered her a plate of French toast.

Lola tried to smile back. Now she was the one who was completely unsure of her footing. Really she had no idea what was going on, and the anxiety was starting to build. Roman had fucked with her head far too much, and holding her through a very scary night didn't fix it. She couldn't let herself depend on a guy who might dump her at any moment.

She stared at the delicious, golden brown French toast.

"No, thanks," she said.

Which was insane. She was starving.

"Is something wrong with it?" Roman asked. "I'll make you something else. We can order out. What would you like?"

"No! I don't… Oh shit, Roman, I can't do this," Lola said, knowing she sounded crazy. She threw her hands up in the air anyway. "I can't eat your French toast!"

Roman paused. Then he put down the plate and turned off the burner. "This is not about French toast, is it?"

"Yes," she said sadly. "Or no. Whatever." She thought for a moment, then darted in, grabbed the plate, and retreated to the couch. She decided to ignore Roman's smile.

"Lola, give me a chance to say what I came here

to say," he said. "It might help."

"Oh no, it's not going to help," she said, viciously tearing a bite out of the most obnoxiously good French toast she'd ever had. "It's going to confuse me. You're going to say something amazing, and it's going to make me think that the impossible is possible, and then somewhere down the line I'll be right back here. Only it will be worse."

There was a silence. Long enough that eventually Lola braved a glance at Roman. He was watching her, the sleeves of his wrinkled shirt rolled up, his collar open, his hair a mess. She knew she shouldn't do it, she knew it was a losing proposition, but she met his eyes. The sadness she saw there made her forget everything she'd just said.

"You have every right to expect that," he said quietly. "I have made many, many errors in judgment, most of them born of arrogance. Some from…cowardice, of a kind."

He still couldn't say that word without looking like he'd sucked on a lemon. Lola knew it was anathema to him, to every single one of his values, and part of her *really* wanted to hear what made him think he'd been a coward.

Roman came toward her and knelt in front of her, the way he'd done the previous night. She groaned. She was supposed to make reasonable decisions with Roman Casta kneeling in front of her?

None of this was fair.

"You don't know the kind of power you have over me," she whispered. "It's not fair."

"I do," he said, fiercely. "I do not expect you to believe me yet, but holy mother of God, Lola, I do. You hold that power over me. No, *listen* to me, please," he pleaded.

Lola had closed her eyes. For him, she opened them, even though she knew she shouldn't.

She'd never seen him look like that. Stricken. Desperate. Urgent.

His voice was ragged and raw. He said, "I came here to apologize for what Chance called my colossal fuck-up, and to explain why I made such a mistake. Why I…chose to hurt you, in the name of protecting you. I'm going to tell you, but I do not expect you to believe me, not yet. Today I'm going to tell you, and then I'm going to spend the week showing you."

"The week before our wedding?" she asked, smiling so she wouldn't cry.

"If you still want to have one," he said.

*Wait. What? What the hell does that mean?*

"Oh my God, Roman, just tell me already," she said. She was already wiping away a tear, and the knots in her stomach weren't even proper knots anymore—they had become full-on nests of anxiety.

He kissed her hands and looked back up into her eyes. This time, he was smiling. "I can't help but be happy, Lola. I'm in love with you. I don't know for how long, but I think for a very long time. You are my home."

Roman leaned forward and kissed her. He was gentle, and tender, until he wasn't, and the hunger in his kiss brought back every moment of physical pleasure he'd brought her so far. She was melting into a puddle as he pulled away.

"I won't ask anything of you now," he said. "I intend to earn what I want from you. I've called Stella, and she is already on her way here to help you for the day. Someone will be here whenever you want. And you will hear from me soon."

He leaned forward again and kissed both of her cheeks and her forehead, murmuring, "I love you, Lola."

She watched in a kind of half-stupor as he gathered his things. She didn't snap out of it until he turned to give her one last, lustful look, and she saw her Dom. Her heart lurched in her chest, and she remembered why she was so nervous.

"Wait, Roman," she said. "You said you have to earn what you want. What is it that you want from me?"

He                grinned.                "Forever."

# *chapter* 27

Stella was no help at all.

Lola said, "Tell me what he's planning, Stella Spencer, or I swear to God…"

Stella ducked a pillow. "I can't! No, I'm not being cute, I actually can't. Bashir won't tell me," she said, darkly.

Lola remembered that this was apparently a big rule violation for Bashir. Given Bashir's training in reading minute facial expressions and the powers of perception that it often gave him, Stella had instituted a reciprocity rule: she wouldn't wear a creepy Kabuki face mask all day long if Bashir promised to be totally open with her in return.

But Bashir was definitely involved in something. Plans were afoot.

"Huh," Lola said.

"Yeah, exactly. Hold your fire," Stella said, tossing the pillow back. Stella had decided that Lola shouldn't leave her bed all day, in honor of whatever the hell was going on. Instead Stella was providing meals, non-Ben tainted ice cream, and movies. They'd just finished *Clueless* and were about to move on to something, as Lola had suggested, with less of a romantic theme. She did not need to start crying again.

"Do you want to talk about it yet?" Stella asked.

"I don't know," Lola said. "I don't know that there's anything to even talk about. I mean, I know how I feel now, I'm not in denial anymore. I'm in love with him. Great. And he might even love me, in his way, but is that even enough?"

"What do you mean?"

Lola looked down at her nails. Bitten to the quick, which: gross. "Well, could you do it? If Bashir had been married before, and she'd died…"

Stella said softly, "I don't know, kiddo."

"Yeah. Me neither. Relationships are hard enough with two people. I feel terrible even saying this, but I'd thought I'd just be willing to, like, settle for being second best—"

"You shouldn't settle for anything," Stella interjected. Lola smiled. Stella's loyalty was touching, but that didn't mean it was realistic.

"Yeah, I know," Lola said. "It's complicated. Plus, all the other stuff, with the lying, and the trust…it's just a whole mess, Stella."

Stella picked up an errant take out menu and pretended to read it. In an overly nonchalant tone of voice that fooled exactly no one, she said, "So are you still gonna do the big publicity wedding thing? That we've been planning?"

"You just want a Volare wedding," Lola teased.

"Not true!" Stella said. "Ok, not *only* true. I

won't lie, though, it's been a *lot* more fun to run the show as a maid of honor. Like an awesome practice run, but with more kink."

"So glad to be of service. And you promised not to tease me about what I still say did *not* happen at the bridal shop."

"Hey, answer the question."

Lola capitulated. "Of course of I'm still going to do it. I'm not going to let Volare down, no matter what, and that Harold Jeels creep is still going to hate us next week, so Roman's plan still makes sense."

But then Lola's heart sunk as Stella's eyes got progressively wider. Finally, Lola snapped: "Oh my God, out with it. What?"

"You really haven't, like, seen the news? Been online?"

"Stella, I swear to God. Tell me."

Stella scrounged around in the various pillows until she found Lola's laptop. She flipped it open and madly mashed at the keys before silently turning it so Lola could see.

It was the website for the *Tattle*, and its feature story was a set of grainy, kinky, only half-blurred out photos of State Senator Harold Jeels in fetish wear, mid-scene. The exact same photos that Ben had sent to Lola. The photos that she had shown to Roman, and that neither of them had ever wanted to show to anyone else—outing someone for their consensual kinks was not something either of them wanted to be involved with.

"How did this happen?" Lola asked.

"It was Ben who sent them to you, right?"

"How did you know that?"

"Roman called me when he saw. He wanted to make sure no one had involved you, and he thought you might still be sleeping. He was right, by the way."

Lola covered her mouth. This made her indescribably sad. "Ben did this? Why?"

"Looks like. Maybe as an incredibly misguided way to get back in your good graces? He hasn't called you?"

"No, but I think Roman might have scared the crap out of him." Lola stared despondently at the screen. They would have beaten whatever Harold Jeels threw at them. There was no need for this. Whatever hang ups the guy had—and there were clearly quite a few—nation-wide exposure was not going to help. "Well, I guess he won't be coming after us for a little while."

Stella slowly closed the lap top, and gave Lola a patented Meaningful Look. "Listen. I only interrupted your official day of rest to show you this so you wouldn't think you were obligated to go through with a sham wedding that would break your heart a little bit more with every freaking step down the aisle. Seriously. As your friend. You don't have to do this."

"Then why did you ask if I was going to?" Lola said.

"I was wondering if maybe you wanted to, you know, actually marry Roman," Stella said. She was impervious to all pillow missiles after that.


"Chance, what are we doing here?" Lola asked.

It was Day 2 after Roman had promised to "earn

forever" from her. She still didn't really know what that meant, but she'd allowed her cousin to lead her through half of Manhattan blindfolded. Now he'd taken off the blindfold to reveal that they were, not in some super cool hotspot, not in a fancy restaurant, but in an otherwise empty boardroom. With a sheet covering the table.

"Is this a heist?" Lola asked. "Seriously, is this the beginning to one of the Die Hard movies?"

"Oh man, wouldn't that be cool?" Chance said. "Don't tempt me, I have the relevant training."

"I will personally kick your ass if you attempt a heist, hot shot military security mercenary dude or no. Whatever your job is."

Chance gave an exaggerated shiver. "Fair enough. You fight mean."

"Chance, what's under the sheet?"

"Not yet. First, I need you to promise me something."

Chance turned to her with his most solemn face, and took both her hands in his. *Oh shit*, she thought. *Not something else terrible*.

"Lola, I need you to promise me that when Roman asks you about this, you'll tell him that I did the song."

There was a silence.

Chance gave her a concerned frown and squeezed her hands.

"Wait, what?" Lola finally asked.

Now Chance grimaced. "Roman made me promise that I would deliver this news in song. Like, a singing telegram. I think he did it just to get me back for calling him a dumbass, which, for the record, he was totally being a dumbass."

"No argument here."

"Well, you know Roman, right? He got me to agree to help before he told me exactly *how* I'd be helping. Then he laughed."

Lola started to laugh. "There's a song?"

"Lola," Chance said, looking worried. "*Please*."

"Ok, fine. But don't forget what I did for you."

Chance beamed, gave her a peck on the cheek, then a brief noogie, and turned around to whip the sheet off the table.

Underneath was one of those beautiful architectural models that looked like a work of art in its own right. It was a compound of several buildings in a sort of zen modernist style, set amidst a well-designed garden, flush with water elements and...palm trees?

"What is that?" Lola asked.

"That," Chance said. "Is Volare LA."

Lola felt herself stiffen, but fought against it. *Keep an open mind, Theroux. He was going to make Chance sing.*

"Go on," she said, still somewhat suspicious.

"Ok, so, here's my version, because I'm not reading this freaking song," Chance said, handing her a sealed envelope. He was still looking at the model of Volare LA. "He had this in the works, and the original plan was that he was going to go out there and set it up, right? But he couldn't do it because he didn't want to leave you in New York. Likewise, he wasn't psyched about the idea of you moving to LA without him, either. So...in a very un-Roman, wussy move—"

"Watch it, Chance Dalton."

Chance stopped and saluted her.

"With an overly developed sense of concern, he decided not to tell you until he'd worked out some sort of alternative. He was still a wuss about it."

Lola narrowed her eyes. She knew her cousin. "And?"

"And," Chance said grudgingly, "he says it's yours if you want it. If that's the choice you make. But, Lola, come on."

"Come on what?"

No way she was moving to LA, but torturing Chance into telling her what the hell he was so antsy about was more than worth the subterfuge.

"Dude!" he said, smiling like a little boy, "*I* want it!"

Lola felt her jaw hit the floor. "You quit the merc job? Or…whatever it was?"

"Yup. Done with that. Moving on. And this is fucking *perfect*. Unless you want it. Basically Roman's gonna move heaven and earth to give you whatever the hell you want, so I'm asking you, as your cousin, don't take the LA club. I've heard the women out there are beautiful, and I'd like to see for myself."

Chance gave her his most winsome grin. She knew what went unsaid: he was probably done with his former job for a reason. He'd seen a lot of violence and death, stuff he'd never talk about, and if anyone deserved a young retirement running a sex club to the stars, it was Chance.

Lola smiled, linking her arm with his while they both looked over the architectural model. It really was stunning.

"Chance," she said. "You're a partner. Couldn't you take the LA club if you wanted it?"

"You'd think, huh?" he said, smiling back at her. "Wait 'till you see tomorrow's surprise."

"What—"

"All further questions will be answered in noogie form, Theroux. Come and check out this place."

Lola let him to play with the model on the table. She still had the sealed envelope. She was meant to read the contents, right? She should definitely open it.

Inside she found only a note:

*I know Chance will not sing, no matter what he has told me. I hope you extracted a high price for your silence.*

*I did not tell you about this out of weakness and cowardice, Lola, even if I could not admit it to myself. I'm sorry. It represented one of the myriad ways I could lose you. That is all.*

*It's yours if you want it. I hope you will stay.*

*I love you.*

*-Roman*

Two days later Lola was going out to get coffee—in her sweatpants—when a limo pulled up beside her as she walked up Broadway.

She wasn't even surprised when the window rolled down.

"Bashir, how you doing?" she said.

"Very well, Lola," Bashir said. "Get in."

Lola sighed. She knew by now there was no point in arguing. She got in the limo.

"So he dragged you into this, too, huh?" she

said.

"On the contrary, it is my pleasure," the Sheikh said in that lofty Cambridge accent. He was smiling. Why was everybody smiling every time they sprung one of these things on her?

"Are you going to tell me where we're going?"

"No."

"Of course. Can we at least stop for coffee?"

Bashir actually laughed out loud. "You are more likely to need a drink."

Lola looked down. Nope, still wearing sweatpants.

Only a few incredibly tense minutes later, they pulled up to a building that Lola did indeed recognize.

"This is Ford's corporate office," she said accusingly.

"Yes."

"You made me think I was going to some kind of…red carpet thing."

"Come," Bashir said, getting out of the limo and extending his hand. He appeared to be enjoying this, nearly as much as Chance had. Lola was momentarily nonplussed at the idea of Bashir singing.

"Well, it's kinda fun to walk through a law office in sweatpants," she conceded.

And it was, in a terrible sort of way. Lola made a mental note to send flowers or donuts or a mountain of highly caffeinated espresso beans to this office as soon as she left. All those over-worked associates eyed her comfy sweatpants with just a little too much weariness in their eyes.

Bashir led her to Ford's office, which she had

expected. And Ford was there, also as expected.

Lola couldn't, however, decipher the vaguely pained expression on Ford's movie-star face.

"Ok, you two, out with it," she said.

"I believe you have the floor, Bashir." Ford really did look distressed. He kept looking down at a stack of papers on his desk.

"Lola," Bashir said, commanding her attention. "You know about my skills in reading facial expressions?"

*Uh oh.*

"Yes," she said, warily. "You can read people like a freaking psychic. Don't look shocked, Stella told me all about it."

Bashir looked vaguely put out, like she'd stolen his thunder.

"Bashir, come on. Of course she told me. You're welcome for setting you two up, by the way."

"And I will be forever in your debt," he said with that well-bred formality. "Roman has asked me to return the favor in part by telling you what I saw when I first joined Volare."

Lola was going to just lose her mind if one more person paused before telling her the big important information they were supposed to tell her. "Which was…?" she said.

"You have been in love with each other since I've known you," Bashir said simply. "You may know that about yourself; that is not my concern at the moment. But you must believe me, Lola, that to the best of my abilities, it has been painfully obvious to me that Roman has been in love with you since I first met him. It was written on his face every time he looked at you."

Lola looked from Bashir to Ford, and back to Bashir. She was, she supposed, in some kind of shock. To their credit, both men waited patiently for her mouth to link back up with her brain.

"Why the hell didn't you say something?" she finally managed to get out.

"What would you have done?" Bashir asked gently.

Lola got his point. She would have laughed him off, freaked out, and run for the hills.

"Roman wasn't ready either," Bashir went on. He seemed fairly unconcerned. "I tell you this now so that you know that, at the very least, he is telling you the truth. He says that you can trust him."

Lola was trying very hard to choke back tears. She had promised herself that she wasn't going to cry anymore; she'd already used up her crying quota for possibly the next decade.

The thought of Roman being in love with her, all this time that she'd been in love with him, was testing her vow.

She turned on Ford. She had not forgotten that he must have known about the LA expansion the whole time. He hadn't been obligated to inform her, since she wasn't a partner, but that didn't mean it didn't rankle. "And what's your role in all this, Mr. Co-Conspirator?"

Ford sighed. "This," he said, pointing at the stack of papers in front of him. "And this," he said again, brandishing another of those envelopes.

Lola took the envelope, but hesitated when she heard Ford clear his throat.

"I'm supposed to explain what this is," he said. "Please understand, this just pains me, as a lawyer.

The pre-nup I helped craft for you two was just a thing of beauty, honestly. And this...this undoes it all," he sighed again. "Lola, sign where indicated, and you'll own every single one of Roman's assets. You don't have to stay married to him. You don't even have to see him again if you don't want to. He's just giving it all to you."

Lola tried to swallow, and found her mouth was dry. She went and took a drink of water from Ford's bar, then changed her mind and made herself a vodka.

Then she coughed for thirty seconds straight.

"Ok, maybe too early for vodka," she said. "Seriously, though, this is ridiculous."

Both men shrugged. They seemed entirely too smug about the whole thing.

"What if I don't sign?" she demanded. "What happens then?"

"I imagine Roman's taxes get extremely complicated," Bashir laughed.

Ford stood, and Lola collapsed in the offered seat. "I just...I mean...what?" she said.

Ford finally smiled. "It is worth it, though, for the look on your face. Open the envelope and read the card. Maybe he explains this lunacy in there."

Shaking, Lola ripped away the envelope and fumbled with the card. There, in Roman's aggressive hand, was another short note.

*You already hold my heart in your hands. The rest is nothing.*

*I love you.*

*-Roman*

"What does it say?" Ford asked.

But Lola was crying too hard to answer.

Three nerve-wracking days passed. Three days in which Lola looked for surprises around every corner, in which she had all the time in the world to wonder about what Roman had planned next, and, worse, about what her reaction would be. She felt like a total jerk for still having reservations after everything he'd already done, but the truth was, he hadn't addressed her single biggest worry: that he only truly had room in his heart for Samantha.

Honestly, she still wasn't sure it mattered if that were the case. It wouldn't change how she felt about him, that was for sure—she'd assumed all along that he'd always carry a torch for Samantha. But she did want to know what she was getting into. She wanted to make sure he wouldn't wake up in a month, or a year, or ten years, and hate her for not being Samantha. Or if that was a risk…she just felt she had to know.

Lola was a wreck by the time her erstwhile doorman called up on that third day.

"A Mr. Roman Casta here to see you," he said.

"Oh shit, seriously?"

"…Yes?"

"Oh God. Oh God." She looked down—sweatpants *again*? Seriously? She was never wearing sweatpants ever again. Ever. She was going to burn all of her sweatpants. She sighed. "Ok, send him up."

She raced into her bedroom and tore through her closet, finally having to face facts: the only clean items were her favorite jeans—which were not so bad, really—and another one of those off-the-shoulder tops that she'd bought in a brief off-the-shoulder frenzy a few months back. Well, at least Roman liked them. She threw her clothes on just in time for the knock on the door; just as well she didn't have time for the mirror.

*Theroux, what are you so nervous about? He's winning you over, remember?*

Then she opened the door, and saw Roman for the first time in nearly a week.

Her mouth stopped working.

She leaned on the door for support.

She felt hot all over again.

He was dressed down, for the first time that she could remember, in jeans that were slung low on his hips and a white t-shirt that did nothing to hide the physique underneath. He held a motorcycle jacket in his hands, and his coal black hair was attractively mussed, like he'd been running his hands through it.

And his *eyes*.

Oh God, his eyes. They simmered. Smoldered. Held her in place.

"If you keep looking at me like that, I'll never get a chance to say what you deserve to hear," he finally said. Neither of them had moved.

Lola thought really, really hard about whether she could force herself to stop looking at him like that.

"Lola," he warned, "This is important. Control yourself."

And he had the cheek to grab her around the waist, kiss her, and give her ass a good squeeze.

He let out a long, slow breath. "I've been waiting for that for a long time," he said.

"Roman..." she breathed. She was ready to jump him in the hallway.

"Not now," he said, smacking her on the ass again. "I have something to show you first."

"If you want to go anywhere other than inside," she said, deadly serious, "you need to stop touching my ass."

She should have known better.

"Oh, Lola," he said with an evil grin, "You have forgotten which of us is the dominant?"

In the blink of an eye he'd pushed her back into the apartment and up against the wall in her tiny entryway. She moaned, already flying just by being so close to him, just by being able to smell him, and then he pushed his hand down the front of her jeans.

He found her already wet.

And then he stopped.

"Lola," he said, his fingers so, so close, "I want you to think about how many blows you've just earned on the spanking bench. Don't forget what we are in the bedroom. Keep that in mind when you think about what I have to say today, yes?"

"Oh God," she said. "Roman..."

He took her face in his free hand and looked her in the eyes just before he kissed her again. This time it was longer, slower. Languorous.

Loving.

"Lola, please," he said. "Please let me show this to you. Then you make your decision, yes?"

"Ok," she said. "But if you want me thinking clearly, you really can't keep touching me."

Roman smiled. "I understand that completely," he said. "Believe me."

He led her on what must have looked like to an outside observer a perfectly pleasant springtime walk to Central Park. To Lola, it was like a suspense sequence in an action film.

*Oh God, what comes next?*

*Is it now?*

*Now?*

By the time they'd turned towards Strawberry Fields she had decided that, if nothing else, she was definitely *not* suited for a career in espionage.

Suddenly, Roman came to a stop. They were in front of a bench. Just an ordinary bench. Nearby there were some kids playing ultimate frisbee, a couple playing hooky from work, lying on a blanket and ignoring the world around them. The whole place was full of sun-dappled joy, and then there was this bench, just another oasis of privacy and calm in the heart of the city.

"What am I looking at?" she asked gently.

"This is where Samantha told me she loved me," Roman said. "It's where we used to come on our walks. It is where I proposed. I have a lot of history with this bench," he said, smiling wryly.

Lola tried to figure out how to feel. Her first instinct was that this was all wrong. She didn't want to be a footnote to his life with Samantha. She *wasn't* Samantha. At the very least...

Roman seemed to notice her discomfort. He bent down and tilted her chin toward him.

"No, Lola, no," he said. "That is the point I wanted to make. It is my *history*. My past. Not my future."

"Roman…"

"I brought you here to help me say goodbye," he said. "Listen, *carina*. Samantha was perfect for the man I was then. I was perfect for her. She died, and it changed me. In some ways for the better, in some ways…"

Lola laughed, wiping away a tear. "Ok, yeah, I get that."

"She was home to me then. Then she died, and I had no home. You were the first light I saw. The only one, in all those years. I have been very, very stupid, and very, very stubborn, but you are home to me *now*. Can you understand that I did not think any one man would be so lucky as to have *two* soul mates?"

Lola looked up at him sharply and he laughed, drawing her close. "You would never expect me to use that phrase, 'soul mates', no?"

"No," she said, mimicking his accent.

"I feel guilty, it's true. So many people in the world live difficult lives, that this…that *you*," he said, his voice breaking, "You are like an embarrassment of riches to me."

They had been drawing closer to each other the whole time, and now Lola couldn't hold back anymore. She put her arms around Roman's waist, and, just slightly vengefully, her hands in his back pockets.

"Roman, I can't take it anymore," she said. "Are you going to ask me?"

His eyebrows went up. "I planned a different event, so you'd have your own place, your own—"

"I swear, Roman, if you make me wait any

longer, I'm going to lose my mind," she said. "Besides, it's kind of...she's part of who you are, too, Roman. She shouldn't be gone completely."

Lola thought she saw those dark eyes shimmer a bit, but then Roman bent down to brush his lips against her forehead. He murmured something that she couldn't hear, and then pressed his forehead to hers.

"Will you marry me, Lola?" he said. "Truly?"

She gave up on her 'no tears' policy and let them stream freely as she kissed him, lightly and tenderly and passionately, and hopefully forever.

When they caught their breath, Lola flashed a mischievous grin.

"I dunno," she said. "How much money do you have?"

She wished she had a photo of Roman's face. Lola took advantage of his stunned silence to grab the signatory pages from Ford's stack of papers out of her back pocket and stuff them, crumpled and useless, into Roman's pocket.

"I don't want this, you nut," she said. "I don't even know what to do with it. Just freaking marry me, ok?"

Even the blissful college couple on the blanket looked up when they heard Lola's shriek, only to see a tall, broad shouldered man carrying a very happy looking red-haired woman out of the park and over his shoulder.

# *epilogue*

Roman couldn't tell if the wedding was, so far, really this insane, or if he was merely in some sort of altered state of excitement, waiting for Lola.

A tiny, intense little blonde woman named Dagmar had ordered him, in severe tones, to relax. And it was just as well Dagmar had insisted, for security reasons, that they hold the ceremony at Volare itself — Roman couldn't imagine everyone would be quite so 'relaxed' anywhere else.

Apparently Lola had decreed that no one was to be stressed out or unhappy at this wedding, and all of the guests had eagerly taken her up on that particular offer. Stella was off somewhere, preparing Lola, Chance was flirting with every single woman he could find, Ford was enamored with a beautiful blonde Roman recognized from the theater, and Dagmar was running a series of photoshoots involving bridesmaids and Volare's best BDSM equipment like a sexy military campaign.

Ava, Jackson's own wife-to-be, and Catie were both happily taking part. Jake and Jackson were watching them, perhaps even more happily.

It was almost a carnival sort of atmosphere, and the only thing it was missing, the only thing that mattered, was Lola.

"Where *is* she?" Roman exclaimed.

Bashir laughed. "I don't think it will be long. I noticed Chance has disappeared, so that is, I would think, a good indication that things are moving along. How many roles is he playing?"

"All of them, I think," Roman said. He had asked Chance to be his best man, and Lola had insisted that Chance give her way. By mutual agreement, and since they were, already, legally married, they informed Chance that he would also be officiating. Roman suspected that this was Lola's attempt to keep her cousin out of trouble. He doubted it would be particularly effective, but he thought it was sweet that she tried.

Damn it. All he wanted was Lola.

"Are you nervous?" Bashir asked.

Roman looked at him. It struck him as such a ridiculous question at first that he didn't immediately realize *why* he considered it ridiculous. As he thought about it a broad smile spread across his face: he wasn't anything even approaching nervous. He just wanted to get started being a husband to his wife.

"No," he said, still beaming.

Just then all the lights in Volare's main room dimmed to almost complete darkness. Maybe moments before the most anxious among them would have started to freak out, two points of light

289

illuminated the floor in the center of the room. Then another two, and another, and another, until there was a slowly moving path leading out to Volare's own large terrace.

Ava and Catie had, somewhere in the last few minutes, gathered themselves together. The two of them led the entire wedding party out onto a terrace that had been, to Dagmar's credit, completely transformed. It was almost entirely covered by a roof trellis, wrapped in vines and all sorts of plant life Roman would never be able to identify. There were flowers of all shapes and sizes interwoven with small lights. He thought he smelled honeysuckle.

Still, none of it was Lola.

"Roman," someone stage-whispered. He followed the rest of the lighted path and saw Stella, Lola's maid of honor, gesturing with her head. "Over here."

Roman tried to figure out what was going on with him. He wasn't drunk. He hadn't had anything to drink. And yet, he was almost light-headed with joy. By the time he made his way to the small clearing under an arch and took his place near Stella, the rest of the guests had taken their seats.

"Where is she?" he whispered to Stella.

"Hush," she said, and gestured for him to look back the way he had come.

The guests had gone reverently silent when the lights had gone off, and now string quartet had started playing. Where had that come from?

It didn't matter. A moment later he saw her.

Roman would never have the words to describe

her, in any language. She appeared, and, as had happened before, everything else simply fell away. He watched her float down their makeshift aisle, her curves wrapped in yet another dress that begged to be removed. He supposed that dress was very beautiful, but he doubted it would remain so once he was done with it, and in any event he would, eventually, have to take someone else's word for it. He simply couldn't take his eyes of Lola's face.

No veil. Nothing separating him from her but the space between them, space that Roman saw closing for the last time. Her clear green eyes held him all the way.

The ceremony itself: a blur. Everything a blur. Roman knew he spoke the right words at the right time because things moved along, but he didn't hear anything besides the sounds of her breathing, didn't see anything besides her face. He remembered the look on her face when she saw the rings he had bought for them: platinum bands with emerald for him, red diamonds for her. He wanted something to remind him of those eyes always.

He would remember that she mouthed the words to him: *I love you*.

He would remember that he cried in public for the first time when he said the words back.

He would remember that, a moment later, while Chance was saying something to entertain the crowd, something that couldn't penetrate their own little world, she gave him an entirely different kind of look. And then she bit her bottom lip.

After that he was just a man with one, all consuming need: to get his wife alone and out of that dress.

Eventually the words ended. Eventually there was applause. Eventually he got to kiss his wife, and it took everything he had to stop at that.

"I need you *right now*," he said.

Lola smiled wickedly and looked down the path that would eventually lead to an exit and his—their—apartment, now crowded with well-wishers.

"There's quite a gauntlet," she said. "Think you'll make it?"

He heard a low rumble come from his chest. He didn't ever mean to do it, Lola just seemed to bring the beast in him out to the forefront.

He didn't particularly mind.

"The question is whether that dress will make it," he growled at her.

He caught the satisfying hitch in Lola's breath as he put his arm around her and began guiding her, at a pretty good clip, down the path.

The first obstacle was Stella.

"Roman," Stella hissed. "Roman! You guys, I know this is, like, the worst timing ever, but good deeds, right? Good deeds?"

She was holding her cell phone out with such a plaintive expression on her face that Roman knew she must have extended herself for someone or something. Probably someone needy, and something worthwhile. Stella was the kind of person who couldn't bear to think of anyone feeling badly.

How could he not stop?

"Who is it?" he said, taking the cell phone.

"Don't be mad."

Roman felt Lola's eyes on him. If he looked at

her he'd forget all about Stella's good cause. He closed his eyes instead.

"Who is it, Stella?"

"It's Harold Jeels," she said, very quickly. "I know, I *know*, and I totally agree, but he's obviously got problems and he's having a really hard time right now and it's just so obvious that he could use help, and he's been trying to contact you to apologize, and…"

Roman put the phone to his ear. "Senator Jeels?"

"Mr. Casta. Please, let me just say…I don't really know what to say. I don't have an excuse. I am sorry if I caused you any difficulty."

The man sounded drained, as though he was ready to give up. Roman sighed.

"Senator Jeels, apology accepted. Do you have any contacts in the scene up in your part of the state? Anyone you can turn to for support at all?"

There was a pause. "No."

"I'll get you some. Apologize to them the way you apologized to me, and they will be welcoming. It's good to be yourself, Senator Jeels. It will be a lot less lonely."

Roman knew what it sounded like when a man was suppressing tears, and he did the right thing and pretended not to notice.

"Stella will take care of you," he said, more gently, and gave the phone back to Stella.

He didn't wait to hear what she said. He scooped up Lola and forged ahead.

"That was very kind of you, Roman," Lola said to him.

"Oh, God, Lola, I hear you *speak* and I nearly lose control," he said.

He doubled his pace.

The next obstacle was Ford.

"Hey, Roman, I know it's not a great time, but I was wondering..." Ford paused to look at the blonde actress he'd been talking to for the entire evening. "I was wondering if I should go out to L.A. to help with the new location?"

"Yes, fine, that's perfect, go do it," Roman said through gritted teeth.

Lola laughed. He would remember that.

"Roman!"

He groaned. It was Dagmar, the wedding planner. She had Denise Nelson and a man with a giant camera with her.

"*What?*" he roared.

"A photo?" she asked.

Nobody had ever seen Dagmar cowed before. It mattered little; the photographer was happy to get a photo of the groom picking the bride up and running towards the exit like he was returning a field goal.

Roman rushed through Volare and towards his—their—apartment with only the sound of Lola's peals of laughter in his ears, the smell of her in his nose, the heat of her in his whole body. He thought he'd go mad when he finally got her alone, but what happened instead was that he was mesmerized. He set her down like the precious person she was, suddenly so very conscious of what she'd given him, and in so much awe of it.

He kissed her. He had no idea how long it lasted. Time belonged to people who didn't have forever.

Lola took the dress off for him, slowly,

languorously, letting him savor it. She was still the most beautiful woman in the world. No matter what happened, no matter how many children she gave him, no matter how old they grew together, she would always be the most beautiful woman in the world.

He almost wanted to cry again when he realized she was *his*.

Instead, he dropped to his knees so he could kiss every inch, every swell, every curve of her naked flesh. By the time he was up to her face again she was panting heavily, her breasts rising and fall, her stomach muscles taut and her hips moving. He kissed her cheeks, her forehead, her closed eyes, and her lips, and then he said, "Mine."

"Mine," she answered back. "Yours."

They breathed together once more, and then Lola broke first. She clawed at his zipper, freed his pulsing cock, and said, "Oh, God, Roman—"

She didn't finish. He lifted her high into the air, she wrapped her legs around him, and he lowered her down while he drove his hips up, plunging his length into her in one, shocking thrust.

Together they thought: *home*.

# *A note from the author...*

Hi! Thank you so much for reading *Marrying the Master*. I hope you enjoyed Roman and Lola's story, and that it brought you a bit of happiness. If you liked it, I hope you'll share it with friends you think might like it, too.

And I'd love to hear your thoughts on *Marrying the Master*! You can connect with me on Facebook or email me at chloecoxwrites@gmail.com, or leave a review on Amazon or on Goodreads. I sincerely appreciate every review — I think they help other readers out, and I learn something with every review, too.

'Till the next book!

Chloe

23709095R00178

Made in the USA
Lexington, KY
24 June 2013